4/1/08

Get **more** out of libraries

Please return or renew this item by the last date shown.
You can renew online at www.hants.gov.uk/library
Or by phoning 0845 603 5631

AF Denison

Hampshire
County Council

Janelle Denison Tori Carrington Leslie Kelly

WEDDING FEVER

*First published in Great Britain 2006
by Harlequin Mills & Boon Limited, Eton House,
18-24 Paradise Road, Richmond, Surrey TW9 1SR*

WEDDING FEVER © by Harlequin Books S.A. 2005
(Original title *That's Amore!*)

The publisher acknowledges the copyright holders of the
individual works as follows:

Meet the Parents © Janelle Denison 2005
I Do, Don't I? © Lori and Tony Karayianni 2005
There Goes the Groom © Leslie Kelly 2005

ISBN 0 263 85031 5

108-0406

*Printed and bound in Spain
by Litografia Rosés S.A., Barcelona*

CONTENTS

Dear Reader,

Having spent eight years of my childhood growing up on the island of Maui in Hawaii, it was great fun to revisit the past and help my characters plan for their future together on such a beautiful island paradise.

Meet the Parents is a story surrounded by Hawaiian customs and traditions. But mostly, it's a story about acceptance and how love really can conquer all. I hope you enjoy reading about Leila and Jason's rocky road to marriage, and cheer for their happily-ever-after. For more information about past and upcoming books, you can visit my website at www.janelledenison.com.

Aloha,

Janelle Denison

* * *

To Leslie Kelly and Tori Carrington; it was a pleasure working with you on this project!
To Don, for eighteen wonderful years of marriage.
Aloha Au Ia' oe. I love you.

Meet the Parents

JANELLE DENISON

PROLOGUE

WEDDINGS, DAISY O'REILLY decided one painfully sunny spring morning, should be outlawed.

From the white dress that cost more than some cars, to the black tux that made most grooms look like waiters, the entire wedding ritual made the Inquisition look painless. Weepy brides and horny bridesmaids, tight shoes and schmaltzy music, all-too-phony smiles and all-too-breakable vows…the whole thing was a bottomless pit in which to dump money. And dreams.

Unfortunately, Daisy was deep inside that bottomless pit. Along with her cousin, she ran an Internet-based business supplying imprinted wedding favors to dewy brides and their clueless grooms. And the cash being tossed down the marriage pit was landing on her with regularity these days, so she supposed she ought to stop cursing the industry that kept her fed, clothed and sheltered.

Maybe she would. Next month. When she hadn't been dumped quite so recently.

"Has he called yet?"

Looking up, she spied her cousin, Trudy, her partner at domeafavor.com, standing in the doorway of the crowded mailroom. "Who?"

Trudy rolled her eyes. "Oh, puh-lease, you know who I'm talking about. Dan the dork who turned you from the smiling, sunny, happy flower after which you're named into this brooding, romance-hating femi-Nazi."

Daisy grunted, then continued packing up the carton full of Hawaiian candy leis they were about to ship off to an engaged couple. She wondered if Hawaiian brides wore them instead of veils…and hula skirts instead of gowns. Sure would be cheaper. Not to mention more comfortable. "You're imagining things."

Tossing her purse on the cluttered desk, Trudy walked over to help. She grabbed the tape while Daisy put the packing slip inside the box. "So he hasn't called. Well, good riddance."

"Yeah. Lucky me," Daisy muttered.

Obviously hearing the tiny hint of hurt Daisy hadn't managed to keep out of her voice, her cousin frowned. "It's not *you*. When are you going to realize you have no luck with men because you keep picking losers?"

"Well, gee, thanks ever so much for making me feel better," she said. She folded the box closed, then held it while Trudy taped it up.

When they were finished, her cousin put the tape

dispenser down, took her hand and squeezed it. "Honey, you're so pretty and smart, and yet you keep going out with jerks, or players who have no intention of getting serious. It's like you want to fail, so you intentionally pick men destined to break your heart."

Daisy's mouth dropped open as her cousin delved a little too deeply into her psyche. There were times, late at night when Daisy was alone, when she would try to come up with reasons for any great guy to fall in love with her. The list was invariably a short one. So each time, she'd say yes to the next Dan the dork or Carl the clueless, figuring there wasn't anything special enough about her to attract—and hold on to—a really great guy.

How the heck Trudy had figured that out, she had no idea. Because, honestly, Daisy had never before even acknowledged it about herself.

"You know I'm right," Trudy said as she finished loading up yet another carton for yet another happy couple somewhere out in engaged America.

This particular carton was filled with tiny metal charms. The little things looked like eyeballs and were, in fact, called evil eyes. Why anyone would want anything with the word "evil" in it at their wedding was beyond Daisy's comprehension. If she ever got married, she figured the closest she'd come would be "evil mother-in-law."

But even the little eyes were better than the final

package of wedding favors they quickly got to work on. Those little candy-covered almonds might as well be called colored rocks. The one time Daisy had tried one, she'd lost a filling.

"So, what are the chances that I can talk you into going out with a nice guy, for a change?" Trudy asked as they finished taping up the third carton.

Daisy reached for the stack of mailing labels that had just finished spewing out of the printer on her desk. "About as good as the chances that I'm actually going to *meet* a nice guy for a change. I'm not entirely sure they exist. Because the only men I meet carry mirrors to check their hair and rulers to measure their…"

"Ahem."

Daisy whirled around, hearing a low, masculine throat-clearing that she seriously doubted had come from her cousin.

It hadn't. A guy with light brown hair, twinkling brown eyes and a familiar brown uniform stood in the doorway. Oh, great. A new package delivery guy. An adorably cute one.

She closed her eyes and swore mentally. Wondering just how much he'd overheard and wondering if her face had reached candy apple red yet, or was still in the cotton candy pink stage, she managed to mutter, "Uh, hi."

"Hi," he replied, looking amused. Then he added, "For the record, I have never carried a mirror in my

life. And my measuring tape is strictly for the packages I pick up."

Bursting into laughter, Trudy said, "Well, I've got
something to do." She sauntered out of the mailroom, leaving Daisy alone with the laughing stranger.

Something to do? Yeah. Right. She had to sit out
in the front office and giggle over how stupid Daisy
had just made herself look in front of this incredibly
cute guy.

"I'm Neil," he finally said.

Neil the…Neanderthal? Neil the…not-so-bad?

Stop it, she reminded herself. *One heartbreak a
month is enough for anyone.*

"Believe it or not," he added, "I have, on occasion,
been called a nice guy. A nice, hard-working, *unattached* guy."

Man, he had dimples. Genuine, lose-yourself-in-
them dimples. Then the unattached part sunk in and her
heart skipped a beat. Because there'd been no denying
the way he'd said the word—almost in invitation.

"So should I just turn around and leave now and
let you pretend nice guys are like leprechauns—non-
existent? Or do you want to tell me your name?"

"I'm busy," she said, trying to keep her tone businesslike and her eyes averted. Because if she looked
at him again, she'd probably start to notice the very
nice way his brown hair curled a little behind his ears.
Or the way his eyes crinkled when he smiled. Or the
great butt in those silly brown shorts.

"Okay, busy," he said, sounding a little disappointed, though not offended. "What do you have for me?"

What did she have? A raging case of pathetic-woman-itis. And the longer he stood here, filling up the air with all his man-stuff, the worse off she'd be. She cleared her throat, forcing her attention to her work. "Three packages."

"They all ready?"

She nodded, then realized they weren't. Not entirely. She still held the pre-printed labels in her hand. Squatting down, she quickly slapped one on each package. "Now they are," she said. "So, uh, feel free to, you know, go."

The smile never faded from Neil-the-nearly-perfect's face as he wheeled his hand-cart over, stacked the boxes on it, and pushed them toward the door. Just before exiting, he said, "Maybe next time, when you're not so busy, you'll actually tell me your name." Suddenly looking more serious—tender almost—he added, "I think I'd very much like to hear you say it."

Then he walked out of the room, leaving her standing there alone, wide-eyed and a little dazed.

"It's Daisy," she whispered, knowing he was well out of earshot.

Though his smile and great looks were the first things she'd noticed, for some reason, now that he was gone, she couldn't get her mind off that gentle, almost romantic way he'd said he wanted to hear her name. As if he hadn't just been flirting. As if he wanted a chance to prove he was the kind of nice guy she'd proclaimed didn't exist.

If only she hadn't been so defensive, so embarrassed about what he'd overheard, she might actually have allowed herself a chance to talk to a down-to-earth man who'd been nothing but nice to her. Neil the nice.

Stupid. She'd been stupid and distracted, rushing around like an idiot to get him to hurry up and leave, when now, not too much later, she wished he'd stayed a little longer.

"Oh, God," she whispered, as something suddenly dawned on her. She *had* been rushed. Distracted. Downright careless.

Throwing her head back, Daisy groaned. Because she had slapped those mailing labels on the cartons without giving any of them a second glance. And for the life of her, she couldn't remember which box was which.

So she had absolutely no idea if three engaged couples somewhere out there in America were going to get what they were expecting for their weddings.

Or not.

CHAPTER ONE

"UH-OH, IT LOOKS like we're going to get lei'd again."

Jason Crofton chuckled at his best friend's ongoing joke about the Hawaiian tradition they'd endured numerous times since arriving in Maui to enjoy their week-long vacation. After spending the past two years building their Internet design company, Website Imaging, into a successful venture, they'd both agreed they needed time off to play and enjoy the fruits of their labors. And a casual, laid-back trip to Hawaii had appealed to them both.

In the two days that he and Nick had been on Maui they'd gone on a hike along the Haleakala Crater and had taken a tour to Hana to view the legendary waterfalls and lush foliage. The evenings they'd spent carousing local bars and generally living up to the wild reputations they'd acquired when they were in college together. Tonight, though, their hotel was hosting a Luau, and since it was part of the package deal, they figured it would be a fun way to start off their evening before they moved on to more lively pursuits later.

"Would you like to get lei'd first?" Jason asked, and motioned for his friend to proceed him in the line of guests waiting to get into the Hawaiian themed party.

"No, I was first to get lei'd at breakfast this morning, remember?" Nick joked, and slapped Jason on the back to push him forward. "You go on ahead."

The next available greeter stepped up to Jason and slipped a fragrant wreath of flowers around his neck. She was wearing an off-the-shoulder blouse in a colorful floral print that showed off her smooth, brown skin. A grass skirt was tied around her slender waist, and a garland of plumerias crowned her head.

"Mahalo nui loa na ho'olaule'a me la kaua," she recited with a soft, welcoming smile. "Thank you for celebrating with us. I'm Leila, and I'll be part of your entertainment tonight."

Jason grinned at the lovely Hawaiian woman, drawn in by her soft, husky voice. "Hello, Leila. It's a pleasure to meet you."

Her gaze met his, and in that moment, as he stared down at the young woman with beautiful, exotic features, long dark hair, and deep, soulful brown eyes, Jason felt jolted by a startling, instantaneous awareness that stole the breath from his lungs. It was a reaction he'd never had with any other woman before, and it caught him completely off guard.

In her eyes he saw the same immediate attraction flare to life before she demurely glanced away and moved on to greet the next guest, leaving him inexplicably stunned by the quick, but very arousing encounter.

As Jason made his way to his seat, his heart was beating hard and fast in his chest, and his palms were damp. It was a phenomenal, telling reaction he wasn't about to dismiss or ignore.

For the rest of the evening, as Nick flirted with the female guests and waitresses, Jason couldn't take his eyes off Leila as she performed up on stage with the other hula dancers. He was gratified to see that her attention was drawn to him, as well. He was the one she chose to take up on stage and dance with, giving him the chance to enjoy a close-up view of the way her hips rolled and swayed to the rhythm of the music.

The seductive way she moved her lithe body charmed him, and the come-hither look in her eyes teased and tempted every one of his male instincts. The chemistry between them only grew hotter, and by the end of the night he was in awe of her natural beauty, captivated by her subtle sensuality, and completely fascinated by the gradual way she let a more playful, flirtatious side to her personality emerge with him.

He wanted her like no other woman he'd ever met, and the pull was strong and undeniable. Inescapable. Inevitable.

After the luau and show ended, Nick headed out to a nightclub with a woman he'd been carrying on a conversation with during dinner. Jason opted to

stay behind and wait for Leila to exit the small building where the entertainers had disappeared into after
the show.

A half an hour later she came out by herself and
headed down the walkway leading to the hotel's em-
ployee parking lot. Her steps slowed when she caught
sight of him leaning against the thick trunk of a palm
tree, and she approached him with a smile that held
equal doses of surprise and pleasure.

She'd changed from her Hula costume into a pale
blue T-shirt that molded to her small breasts, faded,
hip-hugging jeans, and casual flip-flops. Her long
lustrous hair gleamed from the Tiki torches lining the
walkway, as did her dark brown eyes.

"Hi," he said, feeling like a schoolboy with his
first crush, which was something he hadn't experienced since, well, high school.

"Hi, yourself," she said in a sassy tone, which he
found extremely beguiling. "Did you enjoy the show?"

"Very much." Especially the sensual way she'd
danced for him, and with him. "I had a great time."

A few more of the entertainers exited the building,
along with two burly-looking Hawaiian guys. The
duo stopped and stared at where Leila was talking to
him.

"Hey, *kaikaina,* everything okay?" one of them
called out, his deep, gruff voice shattering the quiet
night.

"I'm fine, Paulo." She waved away their concern and cringed in embarrassment at Jason. "Sorry about that."

"*Kaikaina?*" Jason attempted to repeat the foreign word, curious to know what it meant. And hoping like hell he wasn't poaching on someone else's girlfriend.

"Little sister," she explained. "Those two are my older brothers, Paulo and Mani."

"Ahhh." He snuck another quick look over her shoulder, recognizing the two men as part of the Luau's musical entertainment. One played the drums, and the other a ukulele. Neither one had worn such ominous expressions up on stage.

The brothers were still standing guard in the distance, arms crossed over their muscular chests as they scrutinized him in a way that was nothing like the island hospitality he'd experienced thus far. "Uh, they're *big* guys."

She laughed in amusement. "They like to act tough, but they're just being protective. I'm the baby of the family and they take their job of watching over me very seriously." She shot them an annoyed glance, then grumbled beneath her breath, "*Too* seriously sometimes."

Jason couldn't blame them. If he had a sister, or any siblings at all, he'd probably feel the same way. But at the moment, her brothers were putting a major crimp in his plans to get to know Leila better.

He inclined his head toward the path that led down

toward the beach. "Do you think we could go somewhere a little more private and talk?"

She hesitated a second, then he caught a daring, rebellious spark in her gaze that told him that she wanted to be alone with him, too, her bodyguards be damned. "Sure. I'd like that."

She led him to a gazebo just on the edge of the property, right before the sandy beach began. The area was lit by more torches, and her brothers didn't follow along, much to his relief. They were alone, except for the sound of the waves crashing on the shore and the breeze rustling through the coconut tree fronds overhead. He found the whole ambiance peaceful, relaxing, and so different from his hectic, fast-paced life back in California.

"Have you always lived here on Maui?" he asked as he leaned a hip on the wooden railing framing the gazebo.

"Yes. I was born and raised here. As were my parents and grandparents." The pride in her voice was unmistakable.

"Ever been to California?" he asked.

"The Mainland?" She shook her head, causing all that glorious, silky hair to shimmer over her shoulders and down her back. "No, I've only traveled to the other surrounding Hawaiian islands. Is California where you live?"

He slipped his hands into the front pockets of his khaki's, and grinned. "Yep. Born and raised."

She strolled over to a hibiscus bush growing beside the gazebo and fingered the petal of one of the bright-pink flowers. "So, is that where your family is from, too?"

"Actually, my parents were originally from Ohio. They moved to California after they got married, before I was born. They both passed away in a car accident when I was eighteen."

Her eyes widened and a small gasp escaped her. "I'm so sorry to hear that."

"Thanks." Her compassion was genuine, and he appreciated the heartfelt sentiment. "I miss them a lot. It was really hard at first since I'm an only child and the rest of my relatives still live in Ohio."

But the life-altering experience had forced him to grow up fast. Instead of moving back to Ohio to live with relatives, he'd made the decision to remain in California, alone and on his own. He'd worked hard to put himself through college and had built a successful and profitable company with Nick—all by sheer perseverance. Now, he had a good life, and he was grateful for everything he'd learned along the way.

But now that his business was thriving, he was coming to realize that he wanted *more*. Instead of a multitude of short-lived relationships, he wanted one special woman to share his life with. He wanted the kind of deep, abiding love his parents had shared. He wanted a wife to come home to every night, and at least three kids to bring love and laughter into his life on a daily basis.

He'd dated his share of women over the years, but

none had ever inspired thoughts of forever. Maybe the timing hadn't been right. Maybe he hadn't met the right woman yet. Maybe he just hadn't been ready to settle down. Until recently.

There could have been a dozen different reasons why he'd remained single and a bachelor, but at the age of twenty-eight, he knew without a doubt that with the right woman, he was ready to take that leap of faith and put his heart on the line.

He and Leila spent the next hour talking about what he did for a living, as well as her job as an entertainer, too. He learned that she'd been hula dancing since she'd been old enough to walk, and that her upbringing had been steeped in Hawaiian culture. She came across as a good girl, a daughter intent on pleasing her parents and carrying on those customs and traditions. But he also caught glimpses of a woman who was struggling to become her own person outside of those expectations without disappointing her family.

Their conversation was interesting and revealing, and he was amazed at the way she opened up to him. It was as if they'd known one another for years instead of a few short hours, and he didn't want their time together to end.

He came up beside her, plucked one of the hibiscus from the bush, and tucked the pretty flower behind her ear. The bright pink color suited her and matched the blush sweeping across her cheekbones.

She touched the blossom he'd given her and laughed in amusement. "Do you know the meaning behind the hibiscus flower?"

"I can't say that I do." But he was sure he was about to find out.

An engaging smile curved her lips. "It's been said that the hibiscus gives off a vibrant energy, and when a man gives a woman a hibiscus, it's a statement to other men of his virility, as well as an open declaration that the woman who wears the flower belongs to him."

"I have to say, I like that symbolism." He gave her a bad-boy grin and waggled his brows, making her laugh again. Then he grew serious and traced a finger along her jaw in a tender caress that made her shiver beneath his touch. "Leila…I'd like to see you again."

Regret filled her gaze, and she swallowed hard. "I really had a great time tonight with you, but I don't think that's such a good idea."

"Why not?"

Her hands gripped the edge of the railing on either side of her hips, as if she needed that anchor to keep from touching him in return. "Well, the obvious reasons are that you're a tourist and I'm a native. The two don't usually mix."

"Leila…" He inhaled a deep breath, let it out, and decided to be as honest as he could with her. "There's something about you that I've never felt with another woman."

"Nice pick-up line," she said in an attempt to lighten the suddenly serious mood that had settled between them.

"I swear it's not." He couldn't even begin to explain what he was feeling. He just knew that she was unlike any of those other women he'd dated. She was wholesome and real and genuine, her beauty more than just skin-deep. She also had a quiet strength about her that he admired.

She bit her full bottom lip, a hint of reservation in her gaze. "You don't even know me," she whispered, though he got the distinct impression she wished those circumstances were different.

"I want to, though." It was crazy, this attraction of theirs, as well as his fascination with her. But he didn't want to walk away from her. Refused to let her go just yet.

Intent on convincing her just how much he wanted to know her, he closed the distance between them, slid an arm around her waist, and drew her up against the front of his body. She came into his embrace willingly, all soft curves and fragrant skin, a natural, sensual fit against him.

He nearly groaned at how perfect she felt in his arms—an intriguing combination of lush, irresistible sensuality and beguiling innocence. He lowered his head toward hers, giving her a moment to protest his kiss. Much to his relief, she issued no objection. Indeed, her lips were already parting in anticipation and her lashes were closing ever-so-slowly.

She sighed as his mouth touched hers in a soft, seeking exploration. Moaned when the tip of his tongue wet her bottom lip. Coaxing. Tasting. Teasing.

Leila's arms crept up around his neck. Taking his cue from her, he slid a hand under her fall of silky hair, gripping her gently by the nape as he settled his lips more aggressively over hers. The kiss deepened, grew hungry, hotter, and more erotic with each slick slide of their lips, as well as the heat she was generating as she moved her hips against his.

Her response to him was honest and real. The passion between them was instantaneous and intense, the gut-deep longing consuming him just as powerful. Everything about her felt inexplicably right, like he'd finally found that emotional link that had been missing in his life.

And that knowledge both scared and thrilled him.

With an effort, he pulled away from her, just enough to break their kiss. They were both having trouble breathing, and she stared up at him with wide eyes filled with awe and wonder. Her lips were kiss-swollen, her face flushed, and her gaze was hazy with desire. She looked shocked and stunned, in a very good way.

She lightly touched her fingers to her damp mouth. "Oh, *wow,* that was…"

"Pretty damned incredible," he finished for her,

then pressed his advantage while she was still caught up in the foggy after-affects of that mind-blowing kiss. "Spend the rest of the week with me, Leila. I want to get to know you better, and I could use a personal tour guide of the island whenever you're available to spend the time with me."

She shook her head incredulously, and the slow smile turning up the corners of her lips erupted into laughter. "I should say no, because there are a dozen different reasons why getting involved with you isn't a good idea—"

Fearing a rejection, he quickly cut her off. "Don't make me kiss you again and give you a dozen different reasons why you need to give me a chance," he threatened in a low, teasing tone.

She pressed her fingers over his lips to keep him quiet. "I wasn't done yet. I can't even begin to explain or understand what's between us, but I like you, Jason Crofton. More than is probably wise." Her chin lifted a notch, and he watched a rebellious light spark in her eyes, showing him another glimpse of that reckless streak running beneath her good-girl facade. "And because I'm tired of always doing what's right, or what my family feels is appropriate, I'm going to do this for *me*. I would *love* to spend the rest of the week with you."

He kissed her again, sealing the deal.

By the end of his week-long vacation spent with Leila, Jason was a goner—hopelessly, helplessly in love with the Hawaiian beauty. Their affair was wild and crazy and impetuous unlike the cautious, practical relationships Jason had experienced in the past. But that's exactly why he embraced the feelings teeming within him, because he'd been careful for too long.

She admitted to falling hard and fast, too, and in a few short days he'd learned all he needed to know that Leila Malekala was the woman he'd been waiting for all his life. She was wholesome, nurturing, and openly caring, not to mention sexy and bold, with an adventurous spirit that continually intrigued him. She was his equal, and complemented him in so many ways.

She was everything that had been missing from his life since his parents' death nearly ten years ago. And Jason didn't need any more time with her to know that they were meant to be together—despite her Hawaiian heritage that set them apart, as well as the generations of traditions and customs she was expected to live up to. Not to mention her family's objections to her involvement with a *haole,* a white boy and foreigner to them, when they had such high hopes of her reuniting with her childhood sweetheart, Kalani Pakolu, and doing the *right thing* in marrying the island native.

Those were obstacles Jason hoped they'd overcome together, as well as him winning over her family's support with his relationship with Leila.

On the morning of the last day of his vacation in Maui, Jason presented Leila with a gold bracelet he'd had specially made for her, which consisted of a chain of hibiscus flowers adorned with a diamond in the center of each blossom. The significance of what the bracelet implied wasn't lost on Leila. He was claiming her, and making a clear statement that she belonged to him. Now and forever.

As he secured the piece of jewelry around her wrist, Jason asked Leila to marry him and be his wife. With tears of joy in her eyes, she said, *"Yes."*

Unfortunately, trying to convince her family that they were meant to be together wasn't as easy.

CHAPTER TWO

Seven months later

LEILA GLANCED anxiously at the clock on the wall, willing the time to pass more quickly. Another half an hour and she'd once again be reunited with Jason after three long, agonizing weeks apart. After seven months of him commuting back and forth between California and Maui to balance his company's business with their long-distance relationship, and her occasional visits to the Mainland to be with him, their frequent separations were about to become a thing of the past.

With a deep, impatient sigh, Leila continued to pace the cozy living room in the small cottage behind her parents' house, which they'd insisted she move into when she'd made the decision to find a place of her own a year ago. Living within walking distance of her mother and father wasn't what she'd had in mind when she'd decided she needed independence and freedom from familial pressures, but she'd resigned herself to taking one small step at a time toward becoming her own person.

Never would she have guessed just months later she'd meet the man of her dreams and her entire life would change course altogether. And now, in three more days, she was getting married to Jason Crofton, and they'd finally be husband and wife.

The excitement of that thought was eclipsed by other more distressing issues that had cropped up in Jason's absence. With him away settling business matters before taking time off for their marriage and honeymoon, she'd been left to deal with the last of the wedding plans, as well as trying to convince her parents that just because she'd decided to move to California to be with Jason after they married, it didn't mean she was forsaking her family or her Hawaiian roots.

Her parents didn't quite see things that way, and had no qualms telling her so. She was the first of the Malekala clan to ever move away from the Hawaiian islands, and her mother assured her that her ancestors were undoubtedly rolling over in their graves that she was turning her back on her culture and heritage. All for a *haole*.

It didn't seem to matter that she loved Jason and he was the one she was meant to spend her life with—*not* Kalani Palolu, the man they'd hoped would become her husband and their son-in-law. Even after a seven-month engagement to Jason, her parents were still holding out hope that she'd come to her senses and realize she'd made a big mistake, that she'd recognize, just as they did, that her future was with Kalani, here in Maui.

It wasn't so much that they disliked Jason as a person. No, their biggest issue stemmed from the fact that he wasn't a native. One of their own. As a man they respected him, along with his ethics and morals and how far he'd come without his parents in his life. They liked him just fine as her *friend,* but not as a husband for their only daughter. Especially when he was responsible for whisking their baby girl away to another state.

It had been an ongoing argument with her mother over the past few weeks, with Leila standing her ground and defending her feelings for Jason, even while knowing what this union might cost her in the end. They had to come to some kind of compromise and understanding over the situation, and soon, especially now that there was more than just her marriage at stake.

Leila placed a hand over her still flat stomach and smiled despite all the stress and upheaval she'd endured lately—including the frequent bouts of nausea she'd been experiencing for the past week and a half, which struck at the most inopportune times. Luckily, her family just thought she had a touch of the flu. She hadn't said anything to correct their assumption.

Jason deserved to hear the news that she was expecting his baby first, and she refused to tell him something so important during a long-distance telephone conversation. Seeing that pink strip darken on the home pregnancy test she'd taken two weeks ago had been an unexpected surprise, yes, but not an un-welcome one since they'd both discussed wanting children. They just hadn't planned on starting a fam-ily so soon, and she really had no idea how Jason would take the news of his impending fatherhood.

Or how her mother and father would feel about be-coming grandparents.

Another tide of emotion swept over her, and she bit her bottom lip to keep it tamped inside. God, this last separation from Jason had been the most diffi-cult, and she couldn't wait for him to get there. She desperately needed to *see* him, touch him in the flesh, and hear his low, sexy voice in person. She needed to look into his eyes and know that despite a surprise neither one of them had anticipated, that everything was going to be okay.

As if her thoughts had conjured him, she heard a car turn into the driveway, drive past her parents' main house, and come to a stop right outside the cot-tage. She glanced out the window and saw Jason get-ting out of the black convertible Camaro he'd rented at the airport to use for the rest of the week. He grabbed a duffle bag from the passenger seat and headed toward her place in that confident, long-leg-ged stride of his. God, he filled out a pair of jeans like they'd been made specifically for him—soft and faded, but snug in all the right places. Same for his pale blue T-shirt that showcased his broad shoulders, trim torso, and lean hips.

All the chaos of the past few weeks faded away, and there was only Jason filling her vision, tall and gorgeous and so breath-takingly sexy—with his striking blue eyes, tousled sandy-blond hair, and a disarming smile that made her pulse pound hard and fast in her chest.

Giddy with excitement, and with her heart bursting with sheer anticipation, she rushed to the refrigerator and grabbed the plumeria lei she'd made for Jason to welcome him home Hawaiian-style. As soon as he came through the door and saw her, he dropped his duffle to the floor and met her halfway across the living room.

Unable to curb her happiness, she squealed in delight and literally jumped into his arms, nearly knocking him over in her enthusiasm. Her arms went around his neck, and her slender legs, bared by her summer dress, wrapped around his waist as she hugged him tight.

He stumbled back a few steps but managed to catch his footing, as well as secure his hands beneath her bottom as an added anchor. He chuckled at her eager greeting, then groaned as she unceremoniously pressed her lips to his and planted a hot, deep, and downright lusty kiss on him.

Minutes later, when she finally let them both up for air, she unwound her legs from his waist and slowly slid her body down the long, hard length of his until her bare feet touched the hardwood floor.

She looked up into his handsome face, seeing him grinning like a besotted fool.

"I take it you missed me, huh?" he asked, his eyes dark with the same desire and need thrumming through her.

"You have no idea." The garland of flowers she'd made for him were still draped over her arm, a bit squashed from their embrace, and she slipped the wreath around his neck. *"Aloha, Kuuipo,"* she whispered softly, affectionately, welcoming him home as her *sweetheart*. This time for good.

He fingered the petals of one of the fragrant plumerias and waggled his brows lasciviously at her. "God, you have no idea how much I've looked forward to getting lei'd by you."

She shook her head and laughed at his playful comment, which felt so good after the weeks of family-filled anxiety, drama, and tension she'd endured without him.

Pushing all that from her mind, she caressed her hands down his chest and offered him one of her slow, seductive looks she knew he couldn't resist. "How would you like to get laid for real?"

A sinful smile curved his lips. "Oh, yeah. You give great phone sex, baby," he said huskily, reminding her of the hot, erotic fantasies they'd shared over the wires during their time apart. "But it just doesn't compare to the real thing."

And right now, she needed the real thing, too.

Needed to reaffirm their love and their reason for being together before her family, and reality, interfered in their idyllic moment. Taking his hand, she led him down the short hallway to her bedroom. Once there, she reclined back on the fluffy pillows, and he joined her on the bed. He settled in next to her side, half covering her with his body, and wedged a strong, muscular thigh between hers.

He wasted no time in getting down to the sweet, decadent business of kissing her—slow, deep, bone-melting kisses that made her hot and restless and aching to feel that incredible mouth of his elsewhere. Which she knew he'd get around to, eventually.

Ahhh, this is exactly what she craved, she thought with a silent, blissful sigh—to feel cherished and special and loved, which Jason did so exceptionally well. This is exactly what they both needed—time alone, just the two of them, without any worries or concerns except for the pleasure they were about to give one another.

His deft fingers went to work unfastening the buttons down the front of her dress, then pushed the sides apart. Between lush, provocative kisses he unsnapped the front hook of her bra, and she moaned her gratitude as he filled his warm palm with her breast and kneaded the full mound of flesh with his fingers. When he dragged his thumb across a taut, sensitive nipple, then lightly pinched the tip, she sucked in a breath and let out a whimper that caught even her by surprise.

Seemingly startled by her reaction, he lifted his head, frowning slightly as his gaze took in her breasts—possibly half a size larger than the last time he'd seen them—and watched the finger he skimmed across the swollen, engorged nipple. She wondered if he could see the changes her pregnancy was already wreaking on her body. Wondered how he'd react to the news when she told him.

"These past three weeks without you have been the longest of my life," he murmured, his adoration for her plain on his face, reassuring her as if knowing exactly what she needed to hear from him. "I've missed you so much, and I can't wait to marry you and make you mine for good."

Overwhelmed by his words and the past few weeks without him, a huge lump of emotion lodged in her throat. To her horror, tears filled her eyes, which she knew was partially due to her topsy-turvy hormones, but they came rushing forth just the same before she could stop them.

"Hey," he said softly, brushing his fingers along her smooth cheek, his gentle touch a calming affect on her frazzled nerves. "Is everything okay?"

She swallowed hard and managed a smile. "It's been a crazy three weeks, but I'm fine now that you're here. I promise."

Before he could question her further, she knotted her hands in his soft, thick hair and pulled his mouth back down to hers, letting all the built-up passion and desire within her spill forth in a deep, carnal kiss. And that's all it took to redirect his attention to more important matters...like making love to her. There would be time enough later to talk about her family problems, wedding plans, and the fact that he was going to be a daddy in seven and a half months.

The scent of plumerias from the lei he still wore surrounded them, drugging her senses. The soft, velvety petals drifted across her breasts as he moved more fully over her, settling between her spread thighs. Desperate to get him naked so she could touch his hot, bare skin, she pulled his shirt from the waistband of his jeans, yanked it over his head, and skimmed her palms over his solid chest. He groaned as her fingers drifted down to the waistband of his jeans and fumbled with the button fly, even as his hand slipped beneath the hem of her dress and lightly stroked that sensitive, arousing spot at the back of her knee that never failed to make her melt for him.

Just that easily, liquid heat flowed from the depths of her core, and her soft moan of impatient need vibrated against the soft, warm lips devouring hers. He grasped the back of her thigh and draped it over his hip, entwining their half-clothed bodies so intimately that when he pressed his erection against her in a slow, sinuous rhythm, she arched into him and nearly came right then and there.

Lost in the haze of passion, and stunned by her instantaneous response to him, she barely registered the loud clap of the cottage's screen door closing shut, but there was no mistaking her mother's voice calling out her name.

"Leila?"

Realization hit like a dose of cold water. Leila stiffened beneath Jason in complete and utter shock, and it took him a moment longer to realize that someone else was in the house. Before he had the chance to move or react, she was shoving him off her in a panic. He landed on the other side of the bed with an "oomph," and she sat up and quickly began buttoning up the front of her dress to get herself decently covered again.

"Leila?" her mother said again, her terse voice drifting down the hall from the kitchen.

Leila winced. "We'll be right there," she replied before her mother decided to come looking for her.

Beside her, Jason dragged both hands down his face and cursed beneath his breath, his disappointment and frustration obviously as strong as her own. Knowing how her mother had gotten into the annoying habit of entering the cottage at any time without knocking, Leila should have locked the door. But dammit, her mother would have seen the rental car out front. She should have known her daughter would want a bit of private time with Jason after being apart for three weeks.

Then again, it wouldn't surprise her if her mother had deliberately dropped by to make sure there was no fooling around going on.

Finding Jason's T-shirt, she tossed it at him. "Hurry and get dressed," she whispered urgently.

He slipped the shirt over his head, made an adjustment to the front of his pants, then followed her out to the front room to greet her mother. When they walked into the kitchen, Leila bit back a groan of dismay. Jason looked like a disreputable rogue. In his haste to get dressed he'd put his shirt on inside out, the flowers on the lei around his neck were crushed and falling apart, and his thick hair was a disheveled mess. Much like her own, no doubt.

And her mother's sharp, assessing eyes didn't miss a thing. "*Aloha,* Jason."

Her mother's tone was pleasant and welcoming, despite the reservations she had about their impending marriage.

Jason closed the distance between them and placed a kiss on her cheek, as he always did. When Leila had once asked him why he was always so incredibly affectionate with her mother when she didn't return the sentiment, he'd told her that no matter what her mother thought of him, he genuinely liked Nyla Malekala and knew she had a good heart beneath the layer of reluctance she harbored in accepting him as a son-in-law. He was also certain that one day her mother would warm up to him, and maybe even hug and kiss him back.

That was a day Leila wanted to see for herself, as well.

"Hello, Nyla," he said with a smile. "It's nice to see you."

Her mother narrowed her brown eyes and scrutinized the inside-out shirt and his tousled hair. "Maybe a bit too soon though, eh?" she said, her meaning unmistakably clear. "It seems to me there was some *hana 'mai* going on back there in the bedroom."

Fooling around. Leila sucked in a breath, unable to believe her mother would say something so outrageously bold. "Mother…" she said in a low, warning tone. She was a grown woman, and what she did with Jason was her own business and not something she cared to discuss with her mother.

Nyla waved to the container on the kitchen counter. "I brought you some chicken soup since you haven't been feeling well. But it appears you're feeling just fine now that Jason is here."

Leila rolled her eyes at her mother's very parental tone. Honestly, the worst part of her nausea seemed to hit the hardest in the mornings, but with her family believing she had a flu bug, she kept to the pretense. "I *am* feeling better, now that Jason is back."

Jason turned to her, his gaze searching her face, which she was certain was still nice and flushed from their encounter. Hardly the pale, drawn look of a person who'd been feeling ill.

Apparently not caring that her mother was in the room, he reached out and tenderly brushed the backs of his fingers along her warm cheek, then tipped her chin up for him to better inspect her features.

His brows furrowed in concern. "You've been sick?"

"You didn't know?" her mother cut in, her tone infused with disbelief.

Jason didn't even glance Nyla's way, his gaze focused and intent on Leila. "No, I didn't know," he said to her. "Why didn't you tell me?" He sounded hurt that she hadn't confided in him.

She offered him a placating smile. "Because you had so much going on back in California, I didn't want you to worry about me."

"Don't you think that's for me to decide?" he asked gently.

Leila's heart melted. That was one of the many things she loved about Jason. He was so incredibly caring, and he wasn't afraid to openly express those feelings. And because of those traits, she knew he was going to be such a wonderful, loving father to their child.

"Well, seeing that Leila is obviously feeling much better," Nyla said, cutting into the private moment between them. "We'll be having a family dinner at the house in half an hour, and I expect you both to be there."

Nyla's gaze shifted to Jason, and her lips pursed. "And maybe you'd like to run a comb through your hair and turn your shirt right-side out before you arrive, or else you'll have some explaining to do to Leila's father," she added pointedly.

Jason glanced down at his shirt and grimaced in realization. Then he looked back at Nyla with a boyish grin. "Yes, ma'am, I'll be sure to do that."

CHAPTER THREE

FAMILY DINNERS with the Malekalas used to be an intimidating affair for Jason. Now, seven months after officially meeting everyone, he enjoyed all the different personalities and the lively interaction between family members—not to mention the awesome, authentic, home-cooked Hawaiian food he was quickly growing accustomed to.

Sitting across the dinner table from him and Leila were her two burly brothers, both of whom he'd quickly befriended once they were assured that his intentions towards their baby sister were completely honorable. They were good guys who only had Leila's best interest at heart—despite the fact that he wasn't of Hawaiian descent. Jason felt as though he had at least two allies on his side with Mani and Paulo, even if the duo enjoyed giving him a hard time and made him the butt of many jokes.

To his right was Leila's *kupunawahine,* her Nana, a sweet, older lady who lived in the house with Leila's parents. She'd been distant and wary of him

at first because of Nyla's vocal objections, but over
the passing months he'd managed to sway her with
his charm and the fact that he genuinely enjoyed
talking with her. He'd spend hours listening to the
stories she'd tell about Leila's ancestors, and Hawaii-
ian folklore and legends, all of which he'd found incredibly fascinating. It seemed Kalani never had any
interest in Nana's stories, and that had only worked
to Jason's benefit in winning over the older woman.

At the head of the table sat Leila's father, Keneke,
who'd openly disapproved of him in the beginning
of his whirlwind engagement to Leila, but appeared
to be gradually coming around in accepting him as
his daughter's soon-to-be husband. Keneke offered
him a begrudging respect and seemed resigned to the
union, probably because Jason had shown no signs
of letting her family drive him away.

Then there was Nyla, a very beautiful woman who
shared Leila's lustrous, long brown hair and deep
brown eyes. The two had similar features and there
was no mistaking they were mother and daughter.
But where Leila was sweet, vivacious and trusting,
her mother was far more guarded. Nyla was by far
the toughest family member to crack, but Jason was
determined to do so before Saturday. He had to, for
Leila's sake as much as his own.

As he took a bite of the most flavorful sweet and
sour pork he'd ever tasted, he cast a quick glance at
Leila sitting beside him. Despite her mother's claim

that she'd been feeling unwell for the past week, Leila showed no signs of being sick—other than the fact that she was absently pushing food around on her plate to make it appear that she'd eaten more than she really had. Still, her complexion was infused with color, and she'd been cheerful and full of smiles since he'd arrived that afternoon.

"So, how was business back in California?" Leila's father asked, redirecting Jason's thoughts back to the here and now. As a businessman himself, Jason had learned that Keneke understood and respected the dedication and drive it took to make a company grow and prosper.

"Things are good," he replied as he served himself a second helping of sweet potatoes. "I wrapped up all the contracts I had open, which frees me up for the next two weeks for the wedding and to help Leila get her belongings packed up and shipped to California."

"And when do you plan on taking Leila back to the Mainland with you?" Nyla chimed in, her tone not nearly as pleasant as her husband's.

Everyone's gaze fell upon Jason with too much interest, making him feel like the villain in a bad movie. "After our honeymoon."

Nyla pursed her lips, and that familiar resentment sparked in her gaze. "She's never lived away from home before."

From Hawaii. "I know," he said quietly, and fought the twinge of frustration rising to the surface.

Nyla was especially good at handing out guilt trips whenever the opportunity arose.

Beside him, Leila sat her fork down on her plate with a decisive click. "Mother, this is my choice, too," she said, and placed a hand on Jason's arm in a show of support, which he appreciated. "I want to be with Jason, wherever that may be."

"Mark my words, we'll never get to see you," Nyla argued defensively. "Once you move, you'll be too busy with your own lives to visit on a regular basis."

Leila sighed at the never-ending debate. She didn't respond, probably because she knew there was nothing she could say that would satisfy her mother.

As everyone at the table grew silent and concentrated on finishing their meal, Jason sought to break up the tension that had settled over the dinner table. "Sooo, how are the wedding preparations coming along?"

"The bachelor party is all set up," Mani said, as if celebrating the last of Jason's days as a single guy was the most important part of getting married. "Tomorrow night you're all ours, Bro."

"Ohhh, yeah," Paulo added with a sly grin.

Jason couldn't help but wonder what the duo had planned for him, and suspected it was going to be a wild, raucous night. He didn't really want a bachelor party, but Leila's brothers had insisted, and he didn't have the heart to refuse what they perceived as the ultimate male tradition.

"I can't wait," he muttered.

Paulo and Mani just laughed.

Leila glanced from Jason, to her brothers sitting across the table, giving them a pointed look. "On a more important note, you boys and dad have an appointment to get fitted for your tuxes tomorrow afternoon, *before* the fun begins."

"We'll be there," Paulo promised, obviously taking his duties as a groomsman very seriously.

"How many guests have R.S.V.P.'d so far?" Jason asked. They'd opted for a small, intimate wedding, with just close friends and family in attendance, instead of a huge affair.

"About fifty, which is pretty close to everyone we invited." Finished with her dinner, Leila put her fork and napkin on her plate. "The luau menu has been confirmed with the caterer, along with the wedding cake. The flowers for the ceremony and gazebo are ordered, but Nana insists on making our Hawaiian wedding leis."

He smiled warmly at the older woman. "Thank you, Nana. That means a lot to us."

She nodded. "It's a Malekala custom, and my gift to the both of you. I will make the Maile lei for you to wear," she said to him.

He tipped his head curiously. "What's a Maile lei?"

Before Nana had a chance to answer, Mani piped in. "It's sort of equivalent to having a noose around your neck that signals the end of your bachelor days."

Paulo nodded in agreement and added to the explanation. "Hawaiian custom has it, that as the bride walks down the aisle toward where you're standing, the noose, or in this case, the Maile lei, gets tighter and tighter around your neck. If she makes it all the way to you without you passing out, then your marriage was meant to be."

With a dead-pan expression, Mani finished the tale. "However, if you pass out before she gets there, that's it, Bro," he said with a sad shake of his head. "It means you're not man enough to marry your bride, and there's no second chances."

Jason stared at Leila's brothers in horror. He knew the Hawaiians had some strange and different customs, but this one was just plain bizarre. And scarey. "Uh, maybe we should skip the Maile leis," he suggested, resisting the urge to tug at the collar of his shirt.

Mani leaned forward and grinned. "Feeling the pressure already, huh?"

Jason glanced at Leila, who was looking at him with wide, guileless eyes. "How important is this Maile lei to you?" he asked her.

"*Very.* And I have all the confidence in the world that you won't pass out before I make it to your side." She shot her brothers a look that said the gig was up.

Mani and Paulo burst out laughing, and that's when Jason knew that the joke was on him.

"Man, you are so gullible," Mani said, hooting with laughter. "It's just so much fun pulling your leg."

Obviously, the rest of the family had enjoyed the charade, as well. Keneke had a smirk on his face, and Nyla seemed to be holding back a grin, but laughter glimmered in her eyes. Even his own fiancée appeared amused at his expense.

Jason was just damn grateful that the story wasn't true.

Nana patted his arm consolingly. "Now that the boys have had their fun with you, I'll tell you what a Maile lei really is. It is a traditional wedding lei, which was used by our Hawaiian ancestors during the marriage ceremony to bind the hands of the bride and groom to symbolize their sacred union."

Relief poured through Jason. "I like *that* custom." And he especially liked that Nana had come to accept his marriage to Leila as the sacred union it was. He held out the same hope for Nyla.

"So, there hasn't been any normal wedding glitches?" he asked Leila, surprised that everything had gone so smoothly.

"Well, just a minor one. Those candy leis I ordered as our wedding favors aren't here yet. When I called the Internet company, domeafavor.com, they said that they were running a bit behind but assured me that the wedding favors would be imprinted and here before Saturday."

"Good enough." He kissed her cheek and smiled

at her. "I appreciate you getting everything done and finalized while I was away. You've done an amazing job putting the wedding together."

She returned his smile, though she suddenly looked very tired and weary. And emotionally exhausted. "I was happy to do it."

Jason truly believed Leila's statement, but it was apparent that the stress of the past few weeks without him had taken its toll on her. Dealing with her mother's resistance while trying to plan a wedding and reception was tough enough, not to mention catching the flu on top of everything else.

Fortunately, in another few days it would be over and their lives together would finally begin. Hopefully, with her parents' blessing.

AFTER DINNER Jason headed outside with Mani and Paulo while Leila stayed behind to help her mother clear the table and do the dishes. Unfortunately, her mother was giving her the silent treatment after the exchange between them at the dinner table about her moving to the Mainland with Jason.

Leila put away a container of leftover sweet and sour pork in the refrigerator and released a long, low breath that did nothing to ease the tension coiling within her. It was important to her that her mother came to accept her choices, especially now that there was more at stake than just her relationship with Jason. Now there was a baby involved, a grandchild, and Leila desperately wanted her child to grow up in a loving environment, free of the resentments her mother currently harbored.

With that in mind, she turned toward her mother and addressed the issue at hand. "Mom, I really wish you'd stop punishing me for wanting to marry Jason."

Standing at the sink where she was washing the dishes, Nyla stiffened at what she obviously perceived as an accusation. "I just don't want you to make a mistake you'll regret later."

That was an impossible notion, Leila knew. With all her heart and soul, there was no doubt in her mind that she was meant to be with Jason.

Grabbing a terry towel, she began drying the clean plates her mother put on the dish rack and gave their conversation an unexpected twist. "Was marrying Dad a mistake for you?"

"Of course not," her mother said with a disapproving frown. "But that's different."

Leila was well aware of the *differences* her mother was referring to, and strongly disagreed. "It's no different, Mom. Jason might not be a native, but he's a kind, caring, hard-working man who'll take good care of me and our family. He has many of the great qualities Dad does, and most importantly, I love him."

That declaration didn't seem to sway her mother in the least. "You've changed since you've met Jason. You're no longer the proper, modest girl you once were."

Leila grit her teeth. Yes, her mother had raised her to be sweet and demure when it came to men, dating, and relationships because that's what her own mother had taught her. And for years Leila had been that mild-mannered, accommodating woman, until things had turned serious between herself and Kalani and she'd realized how unbalanced their relationship was. She'd been too passive and too eager to please, and knew she'd end up being a submissive wife if she'd married him—eventually feeling stifled and very unhappy.

Thank God she'd come to her senses, because marrying Kalani would have been that huge mistake she would have grown to regret—and resent.

After their break-up, she'd embraced her independence and freedom. She was now a confident, self-reliant woman—personality traits her mother had a difficult time adapting to, even now. Leila had also vowed that the next man she became seriously involved with would accept her as his equal, and she'd found that, and so much more, with Jason. Not only were they best friends and lovers, they were partners in every sense of the word.

"I *have* changed," Leila admitted as she put away the last of the clean and dried dishes. "For the better."

Her mother didn't reply, which was an answer in itself.

Drawing in a deep, fortifying breath, Leila met her mother's gaze and absently placed her hand over her still flat stomach. For the baby's sake, she had to get through to her mother somehow, to soften her up and make her realize she needed to compromise a bit, or she'd end up alienating not only Jason, but Leila as well.

"In three days I'll be Jason's wife, and the best wedding gift you can give both of us is accepting Jason as part of our family. I love Jason, and nothing is going to change that fact. So please try to be happy for me and support my decision."

That said, she left the kitchen in search of her fiancé. It was time to tell him about the baby.

As soon as Leila stepped out of the house, Jason couldn't miss her distressed expression. Obviously, things hadn't gone well with her mother, which wasn't a huge shock anymore.

Excusing himself from the conversation he was having with her brothers, he met up with Leila on the porch. One look into her soulful brown eyes and he knew they needed time alone.

"What do you say we go take a walk, just the two of us?" he suggested.

A grateful smile touched her lips. "I'd like that."

Grasping her hand in his, he led her toward the path that gradually gave way to the sandy beach just beyond Leila's family home. The sun had already set for the evening, and silvery moonlight guided their way as they walked quietly along the shore for a few minutes with their bare toes sinking into the damp sand. Catching sight of an area shadowed by large palm trees that would afford them some privacy, he headed in that direction.

Once they reached a secluded spot, Jason backed Leila up against the large trunk of the tree and dipped his head to nuzzle her neck, inhaling her sweet, womanly scent. His hands came to rest on her waist, and he pulled her hips snug against his. He was already hard with wanting her.

A delicate shiver coursed through her, and a soft sigh escaped her lips. "Jason…I need to talk to you."

"Ummm, talking is so over-rated," he said as he trailed warm, damp kisses along her jaw to the corner of her mouth. "Didn't you see that at dinner tonight?"

"Yes." Her voice was a soft, breathy whisper, and she turned her head so their lips met and touched in a gentle caress. "But there's something I need to tell you."

"In a little bit," he promised, not wanting talk of her mother to spoil their time together. Framing her face in his hands, he looked deeply into her eyes. "Right now, the only thing you need to tell me is that you love me as much as I love you."

Her eyes shimmered with emotion as she gazed up at him with pure adoration. "I do love you. More than I ever thought possible."

A slow, lazy smile curved his mouth. "Good, because you've made me a very happy man. Now hush and let me make you a very happy woman," he said as he unfastened the buttons securing the front of her dress, unhooked her bra once again, and filled his palm with her soft, lush breast. Slowly, he brushed her taut nipple with his thumb.

Her eyes closed on a barely restrained moan, and her head rolled back against the tree. "Jason…"

"Shhh," he whispered against her ear, refusing to let anything spoil this moment, or the pleasure he wanted to give her. "I want you to relax. No thinking about anything but you and me and how good I'm gonna make you feel."

Lowering his head, he kissed her soft and slow, until he felt her knees go weak and her body go slack. He pushed his hand beneath the hem of her dress, dragging the material upward as he skimmed his palm along her inner thigh, and gently urged her legs farther apart. Then, he slipped his fingers beneath the elastic band of her panties and touched her intimately.

She was all softness and wet warmth, and wonderfully aroused. He filled her with one finger, then two, and delved his thumb between her slick folds. He groaned deep in his throat, his erection straining painfully against the fly of his jeans at the thought of his shaft being enveloped in all that creamy, irresistible decadence.

She gasped, clutched at his shoulders, and pulled her mouth from his. "Oh, Lord, Jason. What are you doing?"

He gave her a lopsided grin, finding and stroking

her clit in a slow, knowing rhythm. "I thought that would be obvious. I'm going to finish what we started this afternoon, before we got interrupted. We're all alone, and I want this just as much as you do. Let me make you come."

The tease of his fingers, and the promise of pleasure was all it took for her to surrender complete control over her body to him.

"Yes," she whispered.

He'd been dying to taste her plump breasts earlier, and he did so now. He ran his tongue over her engorged nipple, then opened his mouth wide and suckled as much of her as he could. Amazingly, at the same moment he felt the beginnings of her orgasm clench at his deeply buried fingers. She'd always been responsive physically, but this was the quickest she'd ever climaxed, and he was stunned and quite pleased with himself. Then again, they'd been tempting and seducing one another over the phone for the past three weeks, and that had been foreplay in itself.

She shuddered and whimpered as her climax hit hard and fast, then the tremors gradually ebbed, leaving her panting and trying to catch her breath.

He stared down at her, waiting for her to recover. He'd never seen her look as beautiful as she did at that moment, with her face replete with passion, and her bare skin all aglow with moonlight and desire. Her lashes drifted back open, revealing the dazed and shocked look in her eyes.

He chuckled as he pulled his hand out from beneath her dress. "I guess you really needed that."

"I…umm, yes, I suppose I did." She gave her head a perplexed shake. "My body feels so ultra-sensitive."

"That's definitely a good thing, sweetheart," he said with a grin. "What do you say we go for a second round, with me deep inside of you?"

She laughed huskily and nodded enthusiastically. "Oh, yeah, let's."

He wanted her so badly, and he was going to take her right then and there, up against the tree. He was so eager to finally make love to her that he knew it wouldn't take him long to find his own release. Leila's hands were tunneling beneath his shirt and his fingers dropped to the zippered fly of his jeans when their tryst came to an abrupt halt—for the second time that day.

"Yo, Jason!" Paulo called out from somewhere behind them, down by the beach. "You ready to head back to the apartment?"

Jason jerked back from Leila, the sound of her brother's voice putting an immediate damper on his ardor. "Dammit," he muttered irritably beneath his breath.

Leila was far more persistent. "Tell him to go on without you."

"I can't." He straightened his shirt and sighed, his frustration obvious. As was his resignation over the situation. "Mani left to meet up with some friends for the evening and took their car, and I promised Paulo a ride home since that's where I'm staying for the next few days, too."

"Jason?" Paulo again.

"Yeah, yeah, I'll take you home," Jason said, loud enough for Leila's brother to hear. "Just give me a few minutes."

"Sure thing." Paulo sounded *way* too cheerful. "I'll be waiting for you up at the house."

Jason pressed his forehead to Leila's and looked into her eyes. He was glad to see that she no longer appeared stressed or upset. At least he'd accomplished his initial goal of taking her mind off of other matters for a little while. Hopefully, she'd remain relaxed and calm for the rest of the evening, until they met up again in the morning.

"I swear, your family has the worst timing," he grumbled good-naturedly. "I'm betting your mother sent Paulo out here just to make sure there's no *hana 'mai* going on between us."

"You're probably right." She laughed, though the sound was strained. "I'm sorry that you got cut short."

"Hey, you're worth waiting for," he reassured her, rubbing his nose against hers.

When they arrived back at the house less than ten minutes later, Jason walked Leila to her place and gave her a good-bye kiss that was a poor substitute for the throbbing ache in his groin. Then, he drove

Paulo back to his apartment where Jason settled in on the couch for the evening. After traveling for a good part of the day, he was actually quite exhausted.

It wasn't until Jason woke up the following morning that he realized he'd never given Leila the chance to tell him whatever had been bothering her—before he'd set out to divert her attention with more satisfying pursuits.

Rolling out of bed feeling more refreshed after a night's sleep, he showered and got dressed, intending to remedy that mistake when he saw Leila this morning.

CHAPTER FOUR

LEILA WOKE to the rich, overwhelming smells of coffee and bacon, and her belly immediately turned over with a familiar swell of queasiness. She groaned, burrowed her face deeper into her pillow, and waited for the sick feeling in her stomach to subside.

"Wake up, sleepyhead."

Jason's low, masculine voice and cheerful tone did little to calm her morning bout of nausea. Forcing her eyes to open, she glanced at the clock on her nightstand, then to Jason, who stood by the side of her bed holding a wooden breakfast tray, looking sexier than a man had a right to. Especially when she was feeling so crummy.

"It's eight in the morning," she said in a raspy voice. "What are you doing here so early?"

A disarming grin appeared on his lips. "I realized we never got the chance to talk last night, so I thought I'd surprise you with breakfast and we can talk now, before we both head off to our separate appointments for the day."

Trying to ignore the start of a headache, she mentally reviewed their schedules. It was Thursday, and it was going to be a full day for both of them. She had her final fitting for her wedding dress and other errands to take care of, and he was going to the tuxedo shop with the guys. Then this evening, he'd be at his bachelor party until late into the night, no doubt.

Oh, yes, they definitely needed to talk this morning.

Pushing her pillows against the headboard, she sat up in bed, determined to have this important discussion with Jason before they were interrupted again. But as soon as Jason set the tray over her lap and she got one strong whiff of the meal he'd made for her, her tummy threatened to rebel in a very ungracious manner.

A pitiful moan escaped her, and she pushed the tray away.

Jason caught it before everything spilled onto the mattress. "Honey, you're suddenly pale and you don't look so good." Concern creased his brows as he gently touched her forehead. "Are you okay?"

Tears filled her eyes, her hormones and the stress of the past three weeks finally getting the best of her. "No, I'm not okay," she said in a soft, trembling voice. "It's morning sickness."

His frown deepened. "You mean you're getting a relapse of the flu?" he asked in confusion.

He was such a typical guy. She would have laughed at how obtuse he was at the moment, but her nausea had risen up to her throat. "No, I mean I'm *pregnant.*"

And with that abrupt announcement, she scrambled off the bed, bolted for the bathroom, and promptly threw up.

PREGNANT. The word resonated in Jason's head as he paced out in the kitchen where he was waiting for Leila to finish in the bathroom and join him. Dealing with a sick woman wasn't his forte, let alone a sick, *pregnant* woman. After he'd knocked on the closed door and made sure she didn't need anything, he decided he was better off getting out of her way until the nausea passed.

They were going to have a baby. His mind spun with the knowledge. Undoubtedly he was shocked and stunned by Leila's news, and not at all sure what to make of the situation—or the source of Leila's tears. Was she upset? Did she not want the baby? He had no idea how she felt about this unexpected surprise, but he intended to find out—and reassure her that this changed nothing between them.

He heard her come out of the bathroom and a moment later she shuffled into the kitchen wearing a tank top and sweat pants. Her top hugged her curves, and that's when he *really* noticed her breasts, which looked fuller than he remembered. Already, subtle changes were transforming her body, and he wondered if those changes were part of the reason why she'd come undone so quickly with him last night.

She'd brushed her hair and washed her face, and the color was back in her cheeks. But she still looked weary and now unsure, and when he opened his arms to her, she didn't hesitate to accept his comforting embrace. She snuggled into his chest, and he felt a shuddering breath course through her.

"I'm sorry," she whispered against his neck.

His heart ached for her, along with that vulnerable catch he heard in her voice. Tucking a finger beneath her chin, he lifted her face up to his, trying to gauge where that apology was coming from. "For getting sick, or being pregnant?"

"A bit of both, I suppose." Her shoulders lifted in a delicate, uncertain shrug. "This wasn't exactly a planned pregnancy."

"Sweetheart, you have absolutely nothing to apologize for." He gave her a teasing grin. "I was going to marry you anyway."

She laughed and slipped from his arms. She took a can of Sprite from the refrigerator and grabbed a box of saltine crackers from the cupboard. "Thank you for making me breakfast. That was so sweet of you, but these days I can't get much down first thing in the morning, and certain smells really set me off."

Since she wasn't going to eat her breakfast, and he didn't want it to go to waste, he picked up a piece of bacon and popped it into his mouth. "So, it's like this every morning?"

"Most." She nibbled on a cracker. "Some days are

worse than others, and luckily it passes after a few hours."

"Ahhh," he said in understanding. "This is *the flu.*"

She nodded. "Or so everyone else thinks." She poured Sprite into a glass, and took a small drink.

"How long have you known?"

"I found out right after you left. I missed a period and took one of those home pregnancy tests and the positive sign turned a bright shade of pink. Then I started getting sick in the mornings."

He rubbed at the back of his neck. "Leila, why didn't you tell me before now?"

"Because I didn't want you to worry about me or be distracted while you were trying to tie things up business-wise in California. Besides, this wasn't something I wanted to tell you over the phone."

His mouth quirked with a grin as he remembered what had transpired back in her bedroom half an hour ago. "Well, I do have to say the way you told me is quite memorable."

She ducked her head sheepishly. "At least I made it to the bathroom in time instead of getting sick on your shoes."

He was glad to see her joking with him, but he was still worried about her. "Are you okay with all this?"

"Me?" Her tone rang with incredulity and her eyes widened in startled surprise. "I'm more concerned about *you* being okay with this unexpected pregnancy."

"I know we weren't planning on starting a family so soon. And I'll admit I'm still a little shocked over the news," he added, and tenderly brushed the back of his fingers along her soft cheek. "But I've always wanted a family of my own, and with you, and I figure we just got an early start on things."

She bit her bottom lip, her eyes filling with dread. "I have to tell my parents."

He didn't see that as a problem. "I'm making an honest woman out of you," he teased playfully. "Besides, how can they not be happy about a grandchild?"

She dragged her fingers through her hair and away from her face. "My mother is already having a tough time with us getting married and moving to California. I can only imagine how she's going to react when she learns she's going to have a grandchild so soon, but she won't be able to see the baby on a regular basis."

"We'll come and visit often."

"And I honestly hope those visits will be enough," she said, her voice catching.

He was certain her out-of-whack hormones were causing her to blow things out of proportion—especially her parents' possible reaction to her pregnancy. Still, he did his best to reassure her. "It'll work out, Leila. I promise."

He pulled her back into his arms and hugged her tight, hoping like hell her parents didn't make a mockery of his promise.

LEILA HAD PEGGED her parents' reaction too damned accurately. Hours later Jason was still feeling the sting of Nyla's quiet resentment, along with the disappointment he'd seen in Keneke's eyes. What should have been a joyful announcement had turned into an emotionally draining event. He had no doubt Leila's parents viewed him as the bad guy in this entire scenario—the man who was taking not only their daughter away from them, but their grandchild, as well.

Watching his bachelor party unfold from the sidelines, Jason finished off the last of the beer in his bottle and moved farther away from the action taking place. The stripper Paulo and Mani had hired for the evening's entertainment was currently peeling off layers of her hula dancer outfit and had the group of guys enthralled with her enticing performance. So far, Jason had managed to avoid being the center of attention, and he preferred to keep things that way, especially when his mind was on Leila and how she was fairing after that afternoon's debacle with her parents.

She'd been visibly upset afterward. While he'd wanted to stay with her, she'd insisted he go to his bachelor party and have a good time because there wasn't much they could do about her parents' reaction.

Jason felt differently. There had to be some way to make the situation more bearable, even if it meant there were certain things he had to give up. Leila was the one who mattered the most to him. And ultimately, he couldn't bear to see her suffer any more when it came to her family.

Because he'd lost his mother and father at such a young age, family, and being a part of one, was extremely important to Jason, and he hated that he'd caused so much dissension in Leila's home. In two short days the Malekalas were going to be his family as well, which meant making amends any way he could.

After spending the afternoon trying to figure out a way to make everyone happy, he'd come up with a possible solution. But it entailed talking to his friend and business partner, Nick, first, and making sure he wouldn't be compromising the success of their Internet business in any way. And since Nick wasn't arriving in Maui until tomorrow, there wasn't a whole lot Jason could do until then.

Loud, raucous cheers pulled him from his thoughts, and he glanced toward the sound just in time to see the stripper, now down to a skimpy bikini top and G-string, plop herself into Paulo's lap and shimmy her hips provocatively.

Grateful that he wasn't the one in the spotlight, Jason shook his head and laughed...until he saw Leila's old boyfriend, Kalani, heading toward him. Paulo and Mani had invited their male friends to the bachelor party, most of whom Jason had met over the passing months, Kalani included. But other than a brief hello, his fiancée's ex was the one guy Jason usually kept his distance from.

Kalani was a good-looking Hawaiian with dark hair and eyes, a native who reminded him too much of why Leila's parents thought Jason was second best for their daughter. This was the man they'd wanted Leila to marry, and instead she'd chosen him.

"Looks like you could use another beer," Kalani said, and offered Jason a fresh, cold bottle of the brew.

Was he that transparent? A smile quirked the corner of Jason's mouth as he accepted the other man's friendly overture. "Thanks."

"No problem." Kalani took a long drink from his own bottle, and regarded Jason thoughtfully. "You really have it bad for her, don't you?" he said after a few quiet moments had passed between them.

Uncertain where Kalani was heading with his question, Jason played it cool. "What do you mean?"

Kalani pointed the tip of his beer bottle toward the stripper, who'd moved on to another admiring male in the group. "Most men would be living it up at their bachelor party and be more than happy to be the center of that woman's attention. But you're content to watch from a distance. It doesn't look like you're enjoying your last few nights of freedom all that much."

Jason shrugged. "That woman just doesn't do anything for me."

"Like I said, you really have it bad for Leila." Kalani laughed.

There was no sense denying the obvious, so Jason didn't even try. "I guess I do."

Kalani took another long swallow of his beer, then his expression turned more serious and direct. "I have to admit that I'm disappointed that things didn't work out between Leila and myself, but I can see that she's really happy with you. I guess it's the way things were supposed to work out."

Coming from Kalani, that show of support was huge, and Jason didn't know what to say in return. All he really knew of Leila and Kalani's relationship was that Leila had been the one to break things off. Jason didn't know the reasons behind his fiancée's decision to end the relationship, but he suddenly found himself curious.

Kalani patted him on the back in male comradery. "Leila's a great girl, so take good care of her."

"I plan to," Jason replied without a second thought.

"See that you do, or else you'll have Paulo and Mani to answer to." Kalani's tone was light and teasing.

Unable to help himself, Jason grinned wryly. "Yeah, and I get the feeling they'd break my knee-caps if I ever did anything to hurt their baby sister."

Kalani's brisk nod confirmed that thought. "Knee-caps and a few other body parts, I'm sure."

Jason chuckled, liking the other man's humor. He could also see why Leila's mom and dad liked Kalani so much. He was a genuinely nice guy who, luckily for Jason, held no grudges.

"Congratulations, man," Kalani said solemnly, and held his hand out. "I'm happy for you both."

"Thanks," Jason said, shaking Kalani's hand in a firm grip. "I'm a lucky man."

"That you are," Kalani agreed, and clicked his bottle to Jason's in a silent toast. "Now, if you'll excuse me, I'm going to enjoy the rest of the evening's entertainment."

Jason grinned. "Have fun."

CHAPTER FIVE

JASON ARRIVED at Leila's the following morning after running some last-minute errands and making arrangements for their wedding night together. He wanted tomorrow night to be special and memorable. And with luck and Nick's support, he'd be able to give Leila the greatest gift of all. What he had planned was unexpected and certainly a last-minute ordeal, but he felt confident that he'd made the *right* decision.

Feeling upbeat and optimistic about their future together, Jason entered Leila's cottage only to find her sitting on the living room couch with her face buried in her hands. There was a big opened box on the coffee table in front of her, and while his first thought was that she wasn't feeling well and her morning sickness had lingered, he didn't think that was the case at the moment.

Concern swept over him and he started toward her. "Leila, what's wrong?"

She lowered her hands, giving him a glimpse of just how upset she was. Her eyes were moist, as if she'd been crying, and the frustration in her gaze spoke for itself. "You aren't going to believe what happened."

He sat beside her on the couch, certain nothing could be so bad that they couldn't figure out a way to work through the problem. "Try me."

"Domeafavor.com, the online place where I ordered our wedding favors, sent me someone else's stuff instead of our Hawaiian candy leis that are imprinted with our names and wedding date!"

Ahh, now there was a big tragedy, Jason thought in silent amusement. And he supposed to a bride-to-be, a mix-up like this was a huge catastrophe. But considering everything else they'd been through the past few days, this mistake was small potatoes in comparison.

"Did you call the company and let them know about the mix-up?" he asked calmly.

She nodded. "Yes, and they were extremely apologetic about the situation. Apparently, our wedding favors were sent to another couple by mistake, an Efi and Nick Constantinos in Detroit, Michigan." Her voice began to rise as she grew more and more distraught. "The woman told me that we weren't the only ones who received someone else's stuff, instead of their own. And of course she apologized profusely and assured me I'd be credited for our order and could keep these favors. But that doesn't do me much good when they're all imprinted with another couple's name."

Tears welled in her eyes and she shook her head.

"What a mess this is!" she choked out. "You know this is all my mother needs to see to believe it's a sign from the Hawaiian Gods that we shouldn't get married."

"Honey, your mother would use any excuse she can find to convince us not to get married," he teased lightly, even though there was too much truth to his words. "I don't care whose name is on those wedding favors, or what they are, it's not going to change *my* mind about making you my wife. And that's all that matters."

She gave a great big shuddering sigh. "You're right."

"Of course I am," he said, knowing a good amount of her reaction was due to her hormones wreaking havoc on her emotions. "So, since the company told you to keep the items, why don't we go ahead and use them and make the best of a very funny situation?"

She lifted a delicate brow, a hint of her playful side emerging. "You find this amusing?"

"In the scheme of things lately, yeah, I do." He ran the tip of his finger down the slope of her nose. "Just think how the other couple is going to feel about getting our Hawaiian candy leis."

She laughed in agreement, the sound soft and sweet.

He motioned toward the box on the coffee table. "Let's see what we've got to work with."

Scooting forward, Leila pulled out two different items—a cigar and a small gold box—and handed them both to Jason. "Cigars and a box of pastel candy. Hardly a Hawaiian wedding tradition," she said wryly.

He grinned, glad to see her humor resurfacing. He cast a quick glance at the words imprinted on the favors, and came to the conclusion that these particular items had been meant for an *Italian* wedding.

"Salute!"
Luke and Maria Santori
May 21, 2005

"Well, the cigars are obviously for the male guests," he said, twirling one between his fingers. "And I believe these are bombonieres for the women."

"Bombonieres?" she repeated, her expression creased in confusion. "What is that?"

"It's a box of candies." He shook the favor so she could hear the rattling sound the hard candied almonds inside made. "A bomboniere is a traditional Italian wedding favor."

She appeared both intrigued and surprised at his knowledge. "How do *you* know so much about Italian wedding traditions?"

"Nick is Italian, and they had these kind of favors at his sister and cousin's weddings," he explained. Then he met her gaze. He had another piece of interesting information about the favors he wanted to share with her. "Know what else is an Italian custom relating to the bombonieres?"

"No. What?"

"Well, it's said that the number of candied almonds that are in this box indicates how many children the couple will have."

Her eyes widened and sparked with curiosity. "Really?"

"Yep." He rattled the box of candies again and waggled his brows at her. "Shall we see what Fate has in store for us?"

She placed her hand on her belly and grinned at him. "Sure, though we're already ahead of the game by one."

He opened the gold box, counted the pastel almonds, then let her do the same.

When she was done, she gasped in shock. "*Five?* We're going to have *five* kids?"

He chuckled. "I'd be *very* happy with five children."

"Oh, Lord!" She dropped back against the couch. "Let's get through this one first, and then we'll talk."

"Fair enough." He put the cigar and candies back into the bigger box, figuring they had plenty of time to discuss *their* family affairs later. "By the way, Kalani gave me his blessing to marry you."

Her head rolled against the back of the sofa, a frown etching her features. "He did?"

"Yep." He reclined against the couch next to her. "I thought it was quite nice of him, actually."

"When did you see Kalani?" she asked, a cautious note to her voice.

"Your brothers invited him to my bachelor party last night."

"Figures," Leila muttered, rolling her eyes at her brothers' lack of social decorum. Didn't Paulo and Mani realize it was in bad taste to invite an ex-boyfriend to her current fiancé's bachelor party? Obviously not.

"I'm sorry about that," she said, truly apologetic that Jason had to deal with Kalani. "He shouldn't have been there."

"It didn't bother me at all." He smoothed her hair away from her face. "He's a nice guy."

"Yes, he is," she agreed, and even she heard the hesitancy in her tone, which Jason promptly called her on.

"Sounds like there might be a 'but' in there since things didn't work out between the two of you."

She sighed, pondering the best way to explain her relationship with Kalani. "He *is* a nice guy, but he wasn't the right guy for me."

"I already know that, since *I'm* the right guy for you."

She laughed, his claim on her warming her deep inside.

He reached for her hand and laced their fingers together, connecting them not only physically, but emotionally as well. "Why did you break up with Kalani, especially when your family liked him so much?"

"Because my family wouldn't have had to *live* with him, and I would have." Leila turned more fully toward Jason and curled her legs beneath her on the sofa. "Just like my brothers, Kalani comes from a very traditional family, where the men are raised to be the providers and the head of the household, and the women are demure and accommodating."

Absently, Jason twirled the gold plumeria band around her ring finger. "That night at the luau when I first met you, you were demure and shy. Those were the qualities that initially drew me to you."

"You know what they say about old habits dying hard. That's how *I* was raised, to be subdued around men. When I first met you, I was just breaking out of that reserved shell of mine and testing my new-found personality."

"Well, you blossomed into a beautiful, independent, sensual woman." He lifted her hand and placed a warm kiss in her palm.

"I like who I've become," she stated empathically. She only wished her mother would come to understand and accept the changes she'd made in the past year. "When I was with Kalani I realized that our relationship was totally unbalanced. Marrying him would have been a huge mistake. In time I would have felt stifled, and probably would have grown to resent him. But with you, I'm my own person, and we've always been on equal ground."

He reclined against the corner of the couch and

pulled her with him so she was lying against his side. "Little did you know it was my intention to keep you barefoot and pregnant all along." His tone was low and teasing.

She laughed and punched him lightly in the belly for that chauvinistic remark, earning an exaggerated *"oomph"* from him for her efforts. "Seriously, Jason, you've always accepted me for who I am, without any expectations. That's why I fell in love with you."

He considered that for a moment. "Is that the *only* reason?"

She drew lazy patterns across his T-shirt-covered chest with her finger, circling his nipples before skimming her way down to his flat belly. "Well, your sexy smile and hot body caught my attention, too," she said huskily. "And that first kiss you gave me in the gazebo…no one had ever kissed me like that before. You stole my breath, and I just knew you were going to steal my heart, too."

His fingers slid into her hair, cupped the back of her head, and drew her down for a kiss that was just as slow and sweet and drugging as that first time. Her lashes fluttered shut as he nibbled at her bottom lip, coaxing them to part so he could sweep his tongue inside her mouth and take her deeply, thoroughly.

His wicked, wonderful mouth continued to seduce hers, making her blood run hot and sluggish in her veins. Her breasts tingled, grew heavy, and her nipples tightened with almost painful intensity. And between her thighs, a steady, throbbing sensation began.

Feeling restless and needy, she shifted closer, moving her body up and over the heat and strength of his. She pressed him deeper into the sofa cushions and straddled one of his hard, muscular thighs with her own, welcoming the pressure and friction against her aching feminine mound.

But it wasn't enough. She needed *more,* and she broke their kiss to tell him so. "I want you inside me." And judging by the rock-hard erection nudging her hip, he was more than ready to accommodate her request.

He stared up at her, his eyes a smoky shade of blue, his sandy-blond hair tousled around his head. "No morning sickness to deal with today?"

"It passed as soon as I got up this morning, thank God, and I'm finding that being pregnant is making me, well, *horny,*" she said with a shameless, tempting grin. "Just kissing you is getting me turned on."

A strangled groan vibrated deep in his throat. "Which explains your quick orgasm the other night."

"Ummm. My body is definitely more sensitive. My breasts, my sex…" she murmured in his ear as her hand found the thick length straining against the zipper of his jeans and stroked him. "And, I still owe you for the other night."

He caught her wrist before she could unzip his

jeans and pulled her hand away, his expression filled with pained regret. "As much as I'd like to, we can't."

"Why not?" Before he could answer, she added, "I'll be sure to lock the front door this time so there won't be any interruptions."

"I have to go pick up Nick at the airport." He glanced at his watch. "His flight is arriving in about half an hour."

"How about a quickie, then?" she suggested, and gyrated her hips against his. "I'll get on top and do all the work. I don't think it'll take either one of us very long to come."

He gently grasped her waist to stop her provocative undulations. "Lord, I'm about to lose it right now. But the next time we make love, I want it to be slow and hot and leisurely. I want to see every inch of your body—how it's changed with the pregnancy—and kiss you *everywhere*. I want to do all that tomorrow night, on our wedding night."

She pouted in disappointment. "You're seriously going to make me wait?"

He chuckled at her attempt to sway him. "We're *both* going to wait. It's just one more night, and I promise when I have you naked beneath me, I'll give you as much pleasure as you can handle."

She brightened considerably at the thought. "Oh yeah?"

He nodded and touched his fingers to her damp bottom lip, a wealth of promises shimmering in his eyes. "I'll make you come with my fingers, with my mouth, and when I'm buried deep inside of you. And then, if that's not enough to satisfy that insatiable sexual appetite of yours, I'll do it all over again, until you're content and completely exhausted."

She shivered, knowing he was a man of his word. "You're so bad for teasing me that way."

"The wait will be so worth it," he continued, soothing her with a caress of his palm down her back and one of those *I'm-crazy-in-love-with-you* smiles. "And all that anticipation will make our wedding night even more spectacular."

Oh, yes, she believed him. And she really, really couldn't wait. But she'd have to.

Releasing a resigned sigh, she moved off Jason and let him up from the couch. "Go and get Nick. I have some last-minute wedding stuff to take care of, so I'll meet up with you at the wedding rehearsal tonight."

With a quick kiss to her cheek, he was out the door and gone, leaving her to take a cool shower to douse the heat and desire still thrumming through her entire body.

CHAPTER SIX

"Is IT MY IMAGINATION, or are things with your future mother and father-in-law a bit on the frosty side?"

Jason slanted his best friend, Nick, a quick glance while pulling out a credit card from his wallet to take care of the restaurant's rehearsal dinner tab. He handed the plastic card to the manager standing behind the counter, and the woman began processing the billed charges.

"Ahhh, you picked up on that, did you?" Jason commented in a droll tone.

"It was kind of hard not to notice the strained vibes coming from them, especially Nyla." Nick sent him a sympathetic look, as he was well aware of the history between Jason and his future in-laws. "They were pleasant enough to everyone during the actual rehearsal, but managed to avoid talking to you. I can tell there's definitely something going on."

"Yeah, there is." Jason rubbed at his forehead, feeling the tension of the past few hours gathering at his temples in a stress-induced headache.

He was so grateful for Nick's familiar, and very welcome, presence. Nick was like a sibling to him, and since Jason's relatives back east hadn't been able to make the long, expensive trip for the wedding, Nick was his sole support for the weekend.

As for Nyla and Keneke, it wasn't difficult to figure out the source of their quiet animosity. Jason knew if he didn't do something to diffuse the tension, and soon, there was going to be a huge wedge driven between himself and Leila's family—and eventually, between him and Leila. He might be her husband, but Jason feared that in time, family ties would be a much stronger pull, and he'd end up losing Leila if he didn't do something to strike a balance.

The manager presented Jason with the credit card receipt, and he signed the slip then stepped away from the counter with Nick. "We need to talk."

"Are things okay between you and Leila?" Nick asked, obviously assuming the worst.

"No, we're fine. Great, actually," he added as he thought about the child she was carrying. *Their child,* who deserved to grow up surrounded by their grandparents and uncles' love and affection on a regular basis. "I need to discuss a possible business issue with you. I was hoping we could stay here after everyone leaves, have a drink in the bar, and talk."

"Sure." Nick grinned. "It's not like I have a hot date waiting for me tonight."

Jason rolled his eyes, watching as the wedding

party filtered from the banquet room he'd reserved for the dinner, and out of the restaurant. "I'm sure you'd have no problem finding a willing female if I wasn't asking for your time."

"Hey, I'm here for you and your wedding, not to pick up chicks," Nick said with feigned affront. "At least until tomorrow night. Then I'll be on my own, and I'm sure I can coax some wicked *wahine* to spend the next two days showing me a good time."

Jason chuckled, because Nick was such a predictable playboy. "I have no doubt you will," he replied, just as Leila separated from the group and headed toward them.

Once she arrived, she looped her arm through his and looked up at him, a bright smile matching the happy sparkle in her eyes, which Jason loved seeing. There had been many moments this evening during the rehearsal when he'd caught Leila looking toward her parents with those troubling, uncertain emotions in her gaze. Jason suspected she had no idea where she stood with them anymore, and that had to be a very difficult—and different—position for Leila.

"So, have you told Nick the good news yet?" she asked, piquing his best friend's interest.

Jason had planned to reveal everything tonight during their talk, but he had a feeling Leila wasn't going to let him wait that long. "No, not yet."

"What news is that?" Nick prompted.

"Well, we're not telling everyone, just close family members for now. And since you're like a brother to Jason, you certainly qualify." She leaned close and whispered, "We're having a baby."

It took Nick a few seconds to process what she'd just said. "Wow, that's amazing." He shook Jason's hand enthusiastically, a big grin on his face. "Congratulations, to the both of you."

"Thanks." Leila accepted the light kiss Nick placed on her cheek, then instinctively touched a hand to her stomach. "I think we're both still in a bit of shock, trying to get used to the idea of being a mom and dad so soon."

"The two of you will be incredible parents. And now I know why you look more beautiful than ever," Nick said, and Leila blushed at his compliment. "Pregnancy obviously agrees with you."

"Uhhh, not in the mornings," Jason teased.

Leila gave him a playful jab in the ribs with her elbow. "Other than a little morning sickness, I'm doing great."

Jason grabbed Leila's hand and said to Nick, "Let me have a moment with Leila, and I'll be right back."

They walked out of the restaurant together, and he stopped just outside of the entrance. Jason glanced out at the parking lot, and saw Leila's mother and father talking to one of the bridesmaids.

"What's going on?" Leila asked, seemingly sensing something was up.

He gave her a reassuring smile. "Would you mind

catching a ride home with your parents? I need to take care of some business-related stuff with Nick."

"Sure, I can do that." Uncaring of who watched, she entwined her arms around his neck and kissed him on the lips, softly, warmly, then reluctantly drew back. "I guess I won't see you until the ceremony tomorrow at one, then."

"You're right. There are still a few loose ends to take care of before the ceremony." He watched her bite on her lower lip, saw a rare flash of insecurity touch her features, and sought to soothe any last-minute fears taking up residence in her. "I want you to know if you need anything at all, you can call me at anytime, anywhere. I'll have my cell phone on me at all times."

She nodded, shaking off the uneasiness he'd glimpsed. "I'll be fine."

So why did *he* feel so nervous and uncertain deep inside? The answer to that question came easily. So much still lay ahead for him before he married Leila, and he had no idea what the outcome was going to be. Would Nick agree to his request? Would Leila's parents accept *him* into their family? Would his love for Leila and their unborn baby be enough to make this marriage survive?

Jason was determined to make it work. With the Malekalas. With Leila. For their child who had the power to divide the two families, or bring them closer than ever.

He held her hands in his, grasping her fingers tight. "I love you."

She smiled up at him, and despite all the emotional upheaval they'd both gone through the past few days, there was no denying the devotion shining in her soulful brown eyes. "I love you, too."

Jason clung to that heartfelt reply, knowing he'd need the strength of those words to get him through the next twenty-four hours.

"SO, WHAT'S ON YOUR MIND?" Nick asked ten minutes later, as they sat in a vacant booth in the restaurant's bar nursing a cold beer.

"A helluva whole lot," Jason replied, not even sure where to start. He was still trying to get used to the idea himself, and now he was springing everything unexpectedly upon his best friend.

Nick took a long drink of his beer, his gaze just as direct as his words. "Let's hear it."

A wry grin tipped the corners of Jason's mouth. "You might not like what I have to say."

Nick shrugged, unfazed by the warning. "Try me, and don't assume anything. We've been business partners for years, and friends much longer than that. Whatever's going on, I'll do whatever I can to help."

Jason rubbed his fingers along the condensation gathering on his bottle of beer. He stared across the table at his best friend, hoping like hell this wasn't the beginning of the end of their partnership. "You and I have worked really hard to build Website Imaging into a strong, competitive Internet design company, and you know I'd never do anything to jeopardize that."

"You want out?" Nick guessed, before Jason had a chance to finish what he'd been about to say.

That particular thought had never crossed his mind. "No." Not unless Nick wanted him out by the end of the conversation, which was always a possibility. "I was hoping you'd consider expanding the business."

Nick sat back in his seat, his expression thoughtful. "In what way?"

"By having an office in California, and one here in Hawaii."

Nick's dark brows rose in surprise. "I thought Leila was set to move to California after the wedding. What changed your mind?"

"Leila *is* willing to move to California," Jason said, wanting to make sure that Nick understood that Leila had nothing to do with this business inquiry of his. "She has no idea you and I are having this conversation. It's a decision I came to this week, after finding out that Leila is pregnant and realizing that we really do need to live here, in Maui."

"Because of Leila's family?" Nick asked knowingly.

Jason swallowed a drink of his beer and nodded. "Yeah. For the sake of my marriage, and because I want my kids to grow up surrounded by their grandparents and uncles and cousins. It's the right choice to make." He exhaled a deep breath, and met his friend's gaze straight on. "And as much as I'd like to see this idea of mine work, I'd understand if you'd rather just buy me out and not worry about having a long-distance partner."

Nick barked out a laugh. "Are you out of your flippin' mind?"

The question startled Jason, mainly because he wasn't sure if his friend meant his comment in a good or bad way. "Maybe I am," he muttered.

"We started this Internet design business together, in the small spare room in your first apartment and we built it into the successful company it is today. *The two of us,* Jason," Nick said adamantly. "We're partners, and the fact that you're getting married and moving to Maui isn't going to change that."

Jason's relief was profound. "I wasn't sure how you'd feel about not having daily contact."

"That's what a phone is for, and a fax, and e-mail—"

Jason held up a hand, laughing. "I get your point."

"Good, because the beauty of our Internet business is that location isn't an issue. All we need is a computer. Besides, here in Hawaii, you can tap into a whole new territory we haven't even begun to cover yet."

Jason agreed the potential to grow and expand their company's net worth was huge, and it was exciting to think they'd have that chance.

Now that he'd settled business with Nick, Jason had one more thing left to do before he married Leila tomorrow, to secure his future with her and to convince her parents of his sincerity when it came to their daughter's welfare.

Unfortunately, he didn't think that Nyla and Keneke would be as easy to persuade as Nick had just been.

"DON'T YOU KNOW you're not supposed to see the bride before the wedding? It's bad luck."

As soon as Leila heard her mother's biting remark to the person who'd knocked on the door of her parents' house, she knew the visitor was Jason. Her first instinct was to rush out and see him, to smooth over her mother's less than pleasant greeting to the man who was going to become her husband in a few short hours. But she was standing in the back bedroom wearing just a white, lacy slip, and her mother's comment about seeing the bride before the wedding kept her rooted to the spot.

"Don't worry, I didn't come by to see Leila," she heard Jason tell her mother. "I'm here to speak to you and Keneke. What I have to say shouldn't take long."

That certainly grabbed Leila's attention and aroused her curiosity. It also brought on a swell of apprehension that made her insides twist into a huge, gigantic knot of anxiety.

It was obvious that Jason thought she was down at the cottage getting ready for the wedding, when in fact she'd spent the past few hours with her mother up at the house. She'd needed her mother's help to style her long hair into a softly-curled top knot. But there had been an emotional price to pay for her mother's assistance, since Nyla had taken advantage of their time alone together to ask her if she was certain that marrying Jason was what she truly wanted, and to make sure Leila knew that it wasn't too late to change her mind, despite the baby.

Angered that her mother would still be so uncaring, Leila made it very clear that she wasn't backing out of the wedding. She'd also made it painfully clear that if she was forced to make a choice between marrying Jason, or pleasing her parents, Nyla wouldn't be happy with her decision.

And now, on the heels of that heated conversation, Jason was here to speak to her mother and father, less than two hours before the ceremony. For all she knew, Jason had decided dealing with her parents and their attitude toward him wasn't worth the effort, and he was here to issue them an ultimatum.

Her stomach churned with dread, and she took deep breaths to calm her jittery nerves. Moments before Jason had arrived she'd been just about to leave to meet up with her maid-of-honor and bridesmaids, but she wasn't going anywhere until she heard what Jason had to say.

"You know I love Leila, and while I'm well aware of the fact that I'm not what you expected for your daughter, I want this marriage to work, in every way," Jason began, addressing her parents in a very straightforward manner. "And I'm willing to make changes to fit in to this family. But that means the two of you have to be willing to change, as well."

"What do you expect *us* to do?" Nyla asked defensively.

"Well, how about meeting me halfway for one thing, and stop resenting me for falling in love with your daughter." Jason's voice was deep and imploring. "If you can't manage that for Leila's sake, then think about the baby we're going to have."

Leila literally felt the pain behind his words, and her heart expanded in her chest, aching for him and the simple acceptance he sought from her parents. Unsure how long this exchange was going to last, she sat down on the bed in the room, waiting for him to continue.

"You know I lost both of my parents and I've been on my own for years now. I know how it feels to be alone and without any family. So being a part of *your* family is very important to me. I also don't want our children to feel any strife between us. I need them to know that they are loved unconditionally by their grandparents, no matter who their father is."

"And what about us and what we might want?" Nyla said, her voice softening just enough to hint at her own doubts and insecurities. "We'll never get to see this baby, at least not enough to establish a strong relationship so they know and understand their Hawaiian heritage."

"Trust me when I tell you that you'll see your grandchild on a regular basis. I know it's important to the two of you that your grandchildren grow up learning all about their heritage. I honestly want that, too, and I intend to make it happen."

As Leila listened, she realized the inner strength and courage it had taken for Jason to face her parents this way, to put himself out there. Yet he was willing to take that risk. For her. For *them*.

"All I want from the two of you is to be accepted as part of your family," Jason said. "I hope, in time, you'll be able to do that. And if I can't convince you today that Leila is the love of my life, then I'll just have to spend the next fifty years showing you how much I adore your daughter, and do my damndest to make her happy."

Leila's throat tightened with admiration for this man who would be her husband, and every one of her uncertainties lifted, making her feel light and free and impossibly elated. She loved Jason, with her heart and soul, and she knew that together, they would be able to endure anything.

Wanting Jason to know just how proud of him she was, she threw wedding traditions and superstitions out the window. She grabbed her mother's robe, put it on over her slip, and entered the living room before Jason could leave.

Her mother saw her first and gasped in dismay. "Leila!"

Jason spun around to face her, looking panic-stricken. "You're not supposed to be here, and I'm not supposed to see you before the wedding today."

"I've been here the whole entire time in the back room, and I've heard everything you've said to my parents." She smiled and approached him. "And I'm not the least bit superstitious. Are you?"

His brow furrowed as he thought for a moment. "Well, no."

"Then we have absolutely nothing to worry about." She placed her palm against his jaw and stared deeply into his vivid blue eyes. "I just had to tell you how incredibly proud I am of you for coming here today and facing my parents." And a quick glance in their direction told Leila that he'd earned their respect, albeit begrudgingly. "You are an absolutely amazing man, Jason Crofton, and I'm such a lucky girl to be your wife."

He shook his head and grinned that sexy grin of his. "No, *I'm* the lucky one."

She tilted her head back and laughed. "Then I'd say we make a perfectly lucky pair." She sighed, a smile of pure joy lifting the corners of her mouth. "And since it's about time you made an honest woman out of me and the baby I'm carrying, let's go get married."

CHAPTER SEVEN

As soon as Jason saw Leila walking arm in arm with her father along the pathway toward him, his breath caught in his chest and his heart soared with emotion. He felt overwhelming love, not to mention intense devotion and tenderness. And then there was complete and utter adoration for the beautiful woman she was, inside and out.

She looked absolutely breathtaking in a simple satin wedding dress. The off-the-shoulder design and shimmering white material was a stunning contrast against her smooth brown skin and skimmed along her curves, from her full, lush breasts and hips, all the way down to her satin shoes. She'd foregone the customary wedding veil, which allowed Jason to see her bright eyes and watch her expression as she approached where he stood waiting for her, in the same gazebo where they'd spent their very first evening together.

They were both wearing the traditional leis that Nana had hand-made for them. His, the Maile lei, was constructed of twisted strands of green ti leaves that were intertwined with small white jasmine flowers that gave off the light scent of vanilla. Leila's Haku lei was a crown of white roses and orchids that encircled her head, which matched the lei draped around her neck.

His gaze shifted to Nyla, who sat in the front row and was watching her daughter walk down the aisle between the two sections of chairs and guests attending the ceremony. Then, she glanced up at him, her eyes misty, and gave him a tentative, wavering smile before she returned her attention back to Leila.

It wasn't much, but it was definitely a start, Jason thought gratefully. He'd had no idea how things would end today after his conversation with Leila's parents, but it seemed that her mother was at least trying to make the effort to treat him fairly and decently. He didn't expect their relationship to evolve drastically overnight, but he was satisfied with gradual, positive changes that reflected their willingness to accept him as Leila's husband, and a part of their family.

He thought about what the night still held for him and Leila—mainly, his gift to her that would show how much he cared for her. He'd debated telling her parents this morning about the house he'd planned to buy that was located on the other side of the island, but he didn't want his decision to move to Maui to sway her parents in any way when it came to their feelings toward him. The move was ultimately for

Leila, and she deserved to find out about the change in their future plans before anyone else.

Leila and her father stopped at the bottom of the stairs leading up into the gazebo, and Keneke gave his daughter a kiss on the cheek before he gave her away to her groom.

Keneke looked up at Jason, his expression a bit nostalgic, and rift with emotions. "Take good care of our little girl."

Jason could only imagine how difficult this moment was for Keneke—for any father, really. "I will, sir," he promised, then watched as Leila made her way up the stairs toward him, to *finally* become his wife.

It had been a long, difficult journey to this point in their lives, but as he stared into Leila's brown eyes, everything meshed together seamlessly. He felt whole and settled, in a way that had been missing for so many years, and he knew, without a doubt, that she was the one he'd been waiting for to make his life come full circle.

The ceremony was short and sweet, and when the minister finally announced them as husband and wife, the guests clapped and cheered—including her mother and father. Then Jason kissed his bride, sealing their vows with a warm, tender embrace that simmered with a deeper longing and desire he fully planned to consummate that evening.

They celebrated their nuptials at an outdoor luau reception, complete with roasted *Kalua* pig, *poi,* fresh pineapple, sweet potatoes, and other authentic Hawaiian fare. Her brothers, Mani and Paulo, played in the band, and everyone danced and had a great time. The female guests were amused over the mix-up of wedding favors and actually enjoyed the candied almonds, while the men puffed on the cigars as they congratulated Jason on becoming a married man.

Late into the reception, as the sun was setting over the horizon, Keneke stood up at the microphone and asked for everyone's attention, including the bride and groom's.

"I'd like to propose a toast, to my daughter, Leila, and her husband, Jason." He raised his glass of champagne to the couple, as did all the guests. "Getting used to this marriage hasn't been easy for us for many reasons, but we can clearly see how happy the two of you are, and that you truly belong together. Leila's happiness is all that matters to us, and she's found that with you."

Keneke's gaze sought out his wife's, who gave him a subtle, encouraging nod to continue. "Jason, Nyla and I embrace you with the respect you deserve. We want you to know that from this day forward we consider you one of us. Welcome to the family, *keikikane!*"

While everyone clicked their glasses and drank to the sentiment, Jason cast Leila a curious look that asked her to translate that last word, because he had no idea what it meant and could only imagine what Keneke had just called him.

Leila glanced up at him with tears in her eyes and an amazingly happy smile on her lips. "*Keikikane* means 'son'," she said, stunning him with that admission.

"By the way," Keneke went on, this time with humor in his tone. "Your best man, Nick, told me that it's an Italian wedding custom that however many candied almonds are in the gold box is how many children the married couple will have. We may not be Italian, but I'm a firm believer in customs and traditions and we're not about to dismiss this one. I counted five almonds."

"So did I," someone else yelled from the crowd, and everyone laughed.

"Well, we want *all* those grandbabies," Keneke said meaningfully.

Jason chuckled. "I have absolutely no problem with that request," he replied as he wrapped an arm around his wife's waist and drew her close to his side.

Leila just groaned and rolled her eyes.

Keneke grew serious once more. He raised his glass for another toast and gave them a small, but very significant blessing. "*E Hoomau Maua Kealoha.* May your love last forever."

"Here, here!" the guests cheered.

In that one perfect moment, Jason knew that everything was going to be just fine.

"WE'RE FINALLY MARRIED." Leila exhaled a long sigh of contentment as she and Jason drove away from the reception in his rented sports car, and toward the hotel they were spending the night at before taking off for their honeymoon to the Bahamas the following morning. "After everything we've been through, I can hardly believe it really happened."

"Oh, you'd better believe it happened," he said with a playfully wicked growl. "And tonight I'm going to show you just how married we are."

"Mmm." She reached across the console and gave his thigh a seductive squeeze. "I can't wait." It had been too long since they'd made love, and while Jason had been generous with pleasuring her this week, she ached for that intimate, full-body contact with him.

She rested her head against the back of her seat and glanced at her husband's handsome profile, seeing the smile that seemed to be permanently attached to Jason's face. It no doubt mirrored her own happiness.

The tension and stress of the past week had finally eased for the two of them, and she knew it was a direct result of her father's heartfelt toast this evening at the reception. She was grateful for his peace offering, and it was a wonderful, uplifting feeling to know that they were starting their marriage without any more opposition from her parents.

"It seems my parents are making a valiant effort to make things work for all of us," she said softly. "And I think your talk with them this afternoon made a big difference."

"I know there's still going to be issues, but we'll work through them as they come," he said, and placed his hand over the one still resting on his thigh. "But I do have to say that I no longer feel like an outsider in your family."

Her heart swelled in her chest, because she knew how much her parents' acceptance meant to him. "You're absolutely one of our own now."

He grinned at her. "And it feels damned good."

She laughed, and ten minutes later they pulled up to a house she didn't recognize. Confusion settled over her, especially since she was expecting to arrive at their hotel. Frowning, she asked, "Where are we?"

"I'll tell you in a minute," he promised.

Shutting off the engine, he slipped out of the car and came around to her side. Opening her door, he helped her out of the vehicle so her wedding dress didn't get caught around her legs, then walked with her up to the front porch of the house.

"Oh, I almost forgot. I have a wedding gift for you." Reaching into his pocket, he withdrew a small jeweler's box and placed it in her hand.

More bewildered than ever, she opened the lid and found a key inside. She glanced up at him curiously.

"I bet it opens the door," he said lightly, though she could tell he was anxious for some reason, too. "Give it a try."

"All right." She inserted the key into the lock, turned the knob, and the door swung open. Still standing on the porch, she glanced inside and saw the romantic glow of candles flickering in tall glass votives. They were placed in various places on the bare wood floor, and she inhaled the warm scent of vanilla.

Again, she sought his gaze, searching for some kind of explanation that made sense to this mysterious change of plans. "Jason, what's going on?"

Taking her by surprise, he swept her up into his strong arms, and she gasped and wrapped her arms around his neck to hold on.

A roguish grin appeared, and his dark blue eyes gleamed with heat, sensuality, and something far more sentimental. "I believe it's a custom that the groom is supposed to carry the bride over the threshold of their home."

And then he did just that.

His last word registered in her mind, and her eyes widened in startled astonishment. *"Home?"*

"Yeah, home," he said, his voice dropping to a low, husky pitch.

He put her down, letting her body slide against his until her feet touched the floor. Then he released her, watching her expectantly as she looked around at the immediate rooms—which included a living and dining area and what appeared to be an adjoining kitchen in the flickering shadows. The walls were bare and there wasn't any furniture in the spacious house.

Still shocked, she turned back around to stare at him, and shook her head. "I don't understand. We're moving to California. My things are packed and ready to go—"

He pressed his warm fingers against her lips, quieting her. "And your things will go right here, in this house. I made an offer on it, which the buyer, who'd already moved out, accepted immediately. I was able to rent the place for the night to make it special for you, but it'll soon be ours." The emotions in his gaze shifted. "This past week made me realize that we need to be close to your family. Our babies need grandparents, and I want to be here, too."

"Oh, Jason," she whispered, unable to believe everything he was giving up for her—and wondered if that included his share of his company, as well. "What about Website Imaging?"

"I already talked to Nick, and we're going to work it out so that I have an office here in Maui." He reached for her hands, his expression reflecting his own excitement. "I can still keep my same accounts, and hopefully pick up some new ones here on the island."

"That's…amazing, and so is this place."

"I'm glad you think so." He looked incredibly pleased with her response. "You can get a better look at the house in the morning, but for tonight, only one room matters."

She followed him to the back part of the house. There were more votives along the way, which enabled her to get a glimpse of three bedrooms, two bathrooms, and then they reached the end of the hallway and entered the final master bedroom. The room was all aglow with candlelight, with a trail of beautiful red hibiscus flowers leading to the large four-poster mahogany-framed bed in the middle of the room.

"It took some doing, but I was able to get a bed delivered today," he said, brushing a wisp of hair off her cheek. "I figured you'd like to decorate the rest of the house yourself once its officially ours."

"Jason...I don't know what to say." Overwhelmed by everything, her emotions surfaced in the form of tears that spilled onto her cheeks. "I never expected you to do all this for me."

"I did it for you, and for us." He swept away the moisture on her cheeks with his thumbs, his smile both sexy and tender at the same time. "And because you didn't expect me to buy this place or move to Maui, it makes doing it for you now all the sweeter."

"Do my parents know?"

He shook his head. "Not yet. I wanted this to be a surprise for you, but we can tell them in the morning before we leave for our honeymoon, if you'd like."

She nodded, still a bit stunned. "Who did all this? The candles, the hibiscus..."

"I asked the Realtor to do it." He'd taken off his suit jacket and bow tie at the reception, and now he unbuttoned the front of his shirt. "We had it all planned and I called her right before we left."

Her mouth went dry as he shrugged out of his shirt and the candlelight bathed his skin and the smooth muscles along his chest in a golden glow. "It's very romantic and sweet."

He removed his shoes and socks, and slowly circled around her, building the anticipation of his touch. He slowly, leisurely unzipped the back of her wedding gown, all the way down to the base of her spine as he nuzzled and kissed her neck. "Trust me, there's nothing sweet about what I plan to do to you in this bed tonight."

She closed her eyes as a delicious shiver coursed through her, tightening the tips of her breasts and tickling her belly with heat and awareness. "Yeah?"

"Oh, yeah," he murmured into her ear, and pushed the dress down her arms until it fell into a puddle of satin at her feet. He unclasped her bra, and let that drop to the floor, too, leaving her clad in just a wispy pair of white panties.

Still standing behind her, he reached up and removed the floral wedding lei encircling her head, then released her hair from confinement. The long, silky strands rippled down her back and around her shoulders, and he buried his face in the thick, fragrant mass and inhaled deeply.

He moved away for a moment, and she heard him unzip his pants, heard them drop to the floor to join her dress. Then he sat down on the edge of the mattress and gently turned her around so that she was finally facing him. He gazed at her reverently, and since he'd stripped off all his clothes, his desire for her was unmistakable.

"God, you are so beautiful," he whispered in a rough and aroused tone as his gaze took in the bounty of her breasts, the dip and swell of her hips, and the white panties she wanted gone so she could be as naked as he was.

But he seemed to have other ideas in mind.

Settling his hands on her waist, he spread his legs and drew her forward, so that she was standing between his thighs and she could feel the heat of his breath against the plump curve of her breast. She was dying for him to take her nipple into his mouth, but instead he filled his palms with the mounds of flesh and used his thumbs to scrape across the sensitive tips.

She bit her lower lip, but couldn't contain the moan that managed to escape—a sound of wanting and desire.

He caressed her breasts, kneaded them in his hands, and because she needed *more,* she threaded her fingers through his hair and guided his mouth to her nipple, brushing the aching crest against his damp lips.

"Take me in your mouth," she begged.

He did, making her knees buckle and her breath hitch in her throat as he suckled her breast and used his tongue to tease and flick across the puckered tip. He gave her other breast equal treatment before finally pulling away.

He stroked his palms over her belly, and she quivered from his touch and the adoring look in his eyes.

"I already love this baby of ours," he murmured before he leaned forward and placed a warm, damp kiss on her bare stomach.

Closing her eyes, she reveled in the poignant moment, so amazed at this man's tenderness and ability to melt her heart, and fill her soul with such pleasure and joy.

Before long his hands began to wander, sliding around to her backside and beneath the elastic waistband of her panties. Tugging the scrap of fabric over her bottom, he pushed them down the length of her legs. He stroked her bare thighs and dipped his tongue into her navel the same time his fingers dipped between her legs and caressed her intimately.

Knowing she was close to collapsing into a boneless heap, and unable to stand much more of Jason's slow seduction, she pushed him back on the bed. With an obliging grin, he moved up onto the mattress and she crawled up over him until she was straddling his waist.

"Mmm, taking matters into your own hands, I see," he teased, but he didn't seem at all upset by the switch in roles.

"Well, you're taking your sweet time about making love to me," she complained with a feigned pout and leaned forward so that her mouth was only inches from his and her breasts were crushed against his chest. "We can do slow later, for the next fifty years if you'd like. But right now, this first time with you as my husband, I just want to lose myself in you, in us, and intense, no-holds-barred passion."

She closed the distance between their lips and kissed him, her need obvious. He sank his fingers into the hair at the nape of her neck and returned the kiss just as hungrily.

Scooting her bottom downward, she groaned into his mouth as the tip of his penis pressed against her slick, feminine flesh. Beneath her, she felt him go wild, felt his control begin to unravel, which was exactly what she wanted. With their lips still joined, he grasped her hips and pulled her down as he thrust upward, plunging into her in one long, smooth motion.

She inhaled sharply and sat up, shuddering as every last inch of him filled her up. Before she could catch her breath, he rocked her along the length of his shaft, and that delicious friction against her sex was all it took for her body to come alive and a mindless orgasm to roll through her in waves.

Giving in to the exquisite sensation, she closed her eyes and tossed her head back, gyrating her hips in a steady, rhythmic motion to prolong the pleasure. When it was over, she stilled on top of Jason and looked down at him where he lay on the bed beneath her.

His eyes glittered with a fierce shade of blue, his jaw was clenched tight in restraint, and his chest rose and fell in labored breaths. Deep inside her, she could feel the pulse of his erection and knew he hadn't come yet.

"Come here," he whispered roughly.

She lay her upper body along his, and he wrapped his strong arms around her back. Before she realized his intent, he rolled them over, until he was the one on top and they were face to face, heartbeat to heartbeat.

Amazingly, they were still joined. Heat against heat. Skin against skin. With a slow, sexy grin he smoothed his hand down the back of her thigh, hooked her leg over his hip, and shoved deeper inside her. They both groaned, and he placed a soft, damp kiss on her lips before meeting her gaze once again.

"Hi, Mrs. Crofton," he murmured.

She smiled, certain she'd never felt happier in her whole entire life. She was well and truly Jason's wife. "I love the way that sounds."

"I think you'll like the sound of this, too," he said, his voice low and husky. "*Aloha Au Ia'oe,* Leila."

Her eyes widened as she processed the words he'd spoken to her in her native language, albeit slowly and with concentration on his part. "I love you," she said, and shook her head in disbelief. "How did you learn to say that in Hawaiian?"

His eyes glimmered mischievously. "Your Nana."

She laughed lightly, grateful that her grandmother hadn't taught him other, more unrefined phrases. "You're so full of surprises tonight."

"Only the best kind."

She agreed. Pulling his mouth down to hers, she arched her hips up against his, pushing him closer to the edge of his own release. "Now let's get this marriage of ours consummated."

"Yes, ma'am," he said, and proceeded to do exactly that, christening their new home with hopes and dreams, searing passion, and sweet, everlasting love.

Dear Reader,

A fairy tale. Isn't that how all weddings and the days leading up to them are looked upon? A man and woman fall in love and want to spend their lives together. Nothing could be more perfect. Then – boom! – something happens to send everything into a tailspin that guarantees the day will remain in your memory forever...but for the wrong reason!

In our novella *I Do, Don't I?* Efi Panayotopoulou is one week away from her wedding...or a nervous breakdown, whichever comes first. Everything should be perfect. After all, she's marrying her childhood sweetheart Nick Constantinos, she has a dream of an original designer dress and her family is finally treating her like an adult instead of an overgrown child. Then within the blink of an eye, Murphy's Law goes into effect and everything that can go wrong, does!

We drew heavily from Tony's Greek heritage not only to share some wonderful traditions, but to put our own humorous twist on them. We hope you enjoy Efi and Nick's version of their big, fat Greek wedding! We'd love to hear what you think. Write to us at PO Box 12271, Toledo, Ohio 43612, USA, e-mail us at toricarrington@aol.com and visit our website at www.toricarrington.com.

Here's wishing you your own special brand of happily-ever-after!

Lori & Tony Karayianni
aka *Tori Carrington*

* * *

We dedicate this story to our niece, Eleni Tsilias, and her intended, Giannis. Congratulations on your engagement! Here's wishing you both love, always.

I Do, Don't I?

TORI CARRINGTON

CHAPTER ONE

Day one

"I HATE YOU."

The words weren't said in anger or in true dislike. Rather they were said with a certain wistfulness that made Efi Panayotopoulou smile at her best friend.

"No, you don't. You only think you do." Efi didn't spare Kiki a glance as they hung the fluffy white lace concoction on the back of her bedroom door, then wondered at the breathtaking wedding dress.

Kiki began bobbing her head. "Oh no. I very definitely hate you. Always have, if you want the truth."

Efi backed up until her bed impeded her progress. She plopped down on it, staring unblinkingly at her wedding dress. The mattress moved as Kiki sat down next to her and sighed heavily.

"I mean, just look at you. You have it all. A great family that loves you." She gestured around her. "A room fit for a princess. A great job at your family's pastry shop. And now you're marrying Nick, the most eligible bachelor in Michigan."

Of course, neither one of them mentioned that Nick Constantinos was the most eligible Greek bachelor. Partly because that was a given. Greeks married other Greeks—it was as simple as that. Efi didn't really care what nationality Nick was. She'd loved him ever since she'd first seen him on the neighborhood playground when she was five and he six and he'd just suffered a black eye because he hadn't known a lick of English.

And now, twenty years later, they were getting married.

Efi nudged Kiki. "Good thing I love you so much, or else we wouldn't be friends then, huh?"

She and Aggeliki Karras, aka Kiki, had been friends for longer than Efi could remember. Certainly before they'd attended the same schools together. And long before Kiki had made the decision to go on to university then medical school—from which she'd just graduated at the top of her class—while, after a few college business courses, Efi had gone to work full-time in her family's pastry shop.

Kiki's pretty features softened. "Good thing. I can't imagine you not being in my life, you know, pestering me to complain less and live more."

"Somebody has to, or else you'll end up a lonely

old woman in a black dress growling at everyone you cross paths with. You know, like my aunt Frosini."

They gave the statement the pause it deserved, then they both shuddered. Aunt Frosini was enough to make the bravest soul quake in fear. When she was younger, Efi used to dream that her aunt was the old woman trying to cook Hansel and Gretel in the oven. Or the wicked witch in *The Wizard of Oz*. It was better they didn't see much of Aunt Frosini. She only visited from Crete every couple of years. Of course, she stayed far longer than anyone wanted her to, upsetting lives everywhere she went, spreading poison that didn't do much damage in small doses, but was lethal—mostly to her own well-being since it caused others to contemplate killing her—in large, continuous doses.

Efi had once asked her mother what had turned her aunt so bitter. Penelope Panayotopoulou had said something about goats and family property and a wedding that never was but the story was so outside anything Efi could relate to she hadn't understood much of it at the time. Of course, she'd been ten years old and she hadn't seen goats outside the walls of the Detroit Zoo. That had changed quickly when her father decided she and her three younger sisters needed to understand more of their heritage and instituted annual family trips to Greece, in a small town in Ancient Olympia where his family was from.

While the majority of their time was spent on the Ionian beach, it had been the goats and chickens wandering the hillside town that stayed in her mind. She was just thankful she hadn't seen any of the animals being sacrificed for dinner like her younger sister Eleni had or she might even now also be a strict vegetarian.

Kiki bounced from the bed. "Come on, try it on."

Efi made a face. "Why? You've already seen me in it."

"Yes, but I want to see you in it again. Here."

She eyed the Vera Wang creation rumored to have been the one designed for J.Lo's non-wedding to Ben Affleck. She'd wanted the dress on sight when she and Kiki and her mother had flown to New York six months ago to shop for a dress. But now that it was there, hanging in her room, seven days before her wedding, she was almost half afraid to touch it for fear of getting it dirty.

Kiki picked up one of the *boubounieras*—Greek wedding favors—on the dresser and straightened the white bow. "God, I hate you even more. If that were my dress hanging there, I'd live in it until the day of the wedding."

Efi laughed. "You would not."

"I would so. Not only that, I'd probably wear it for days even after the wedding."

"That would put a crimp in the honeymoon."

Kiki grinned widely. "Who said you can't lift the skirt?"

Efi tossed a bed pillow at her friend.

They heard a car pull up outside, then voices fill the otherwise quiet of Grosse Point, Michigan, a posh, wealthy suburb just north of the bustling metropolis of Detroit on the St. Clair shore. Efi moved to her window along with Kiki and they stared down at what had to be at least twenty relatives getting out of one taxi. There was much cheek kissing and welcoming by Efi's parents. Then Aunt Frosini edged out of the cab and everyone seemed to freeze midmotion; an instant that might not be noticeable to outsiders but everyone there understood too well.

"Speak of the devil," Kiki murmured next to her.

Efi drew a deep breath. "Let the festivities begin."

EFI'S FATHER, Gregoris Panayotopoulou, tapped his knife against his wineglass to gain the attention of the fifty or so relatives seated in different areas of the large house for the first of many pre-wedding dinners for the families of both the bride and the groom. Efi felt Nick's hand on her leg and her knee jerked involuntarily, knocking against the table and nearly upsetting the dozen or so glasses there. Even as heat suffused her cheeks and her thighs, she smiled at everyone when they looked her way.

Her father cleared his throat, offering her a disapproving frown. "Today the *flamboro*, the Greek wedding flag, was hung outside our home, marking the blessed ceremony to take place one week from today."

The guests tapped their own knives against their glasses until Gregoris lifted his hand. "Father Spyros, would you like to say a few words?"

The Greek Orthodox priest seated at the end of the table stood up, the end of his long gray beard nearly dipping inside his glass of retsina as he straightened in his black robes. "I would be honored to speak at this blessed event, the beginning of…"

Efi tuned out and stared at Nick, who grinned wickedly next to her, pretending an interest in what the old priest had to say.

Nick Constantinos was more than handsome. He was of the same make that had inspired ancient Greeks to sculpt and to follow charismatic warriors into battle. From his mesmerizing dark eyes, his slightly hooked nose and his generous mouth, Efi believed she'd never tire of looking into his face. But more than a collection of parts and pieces, it was Niko, now Nick's, charm that made him irresistible. He had but to turn on one of his grins, like now, and she was rendered speechless. Efi slid her own hand over to lay against his thigh. Speechless, maybe. But not paralyzed. She slid her fingers up his hard muscles until the back of her knuckles met his crotch. Nick made a strangled sound and his own knee jerked against the table, upsetting glasses where her jerk had not.

Efi grinned and made sure both her hands were in sight when everyone turned to stare, including her aunt Frosini across from them. Was her gnarled old aunt actually grinning at them as if recalling a wicked memory of her own? Efi lifted a brow.

The priest skillfully reached out and prevented his own glass from toppling over and didn't miss a beat as he continued to drone on in that way that only old priests knew how to.

A little while later, the official introductory speeches at a close, Efi went into the kitchen to help her mother serve the chopped fruit when Nick crowded her into the pantry and shut the door after them.

"You're a bad, bad girl," he murmured, his scent filling her senses even as he filled his hands with her breasts.

Efi made a half-hearted attempt to swat him away. "Me? You were the one who started it. I could have died when the table tottered the first time."

Nick chuckled and kissed her. "It was worth it just to see you blush."

Efi couldn't help but melt against his touch, his kiss making other, greater urgencies known.

"You realize it's been a week since we've made love," he said, kissing the side of her neck.

"Mmm. And it's going to be another week yet."

Nick groaned. "I don't think I can go that long without feeling you around me."

"You're going to have to." Efi said the words even as he backed her against one wall. A couple of cans teetered, so he switched directions and backed her against the door instead. He hiked her dress up even as she spread her thighs to his knowing touch. Just a few minutes. She wanted to feel him inside her as badly as he wanted to be there. To be joined in a way that shut all else out. That reminded her how very much she wanted this man. Not just now, but always.

And in one sweet week, seven short days, they would be finally able to have as much of each other as they desired.

The door moved against her back.

Efi groaned, reluctant to open her eyes and acknowledge that someone was trying to gain access to the room.

The door shook again, then was followed by a strident knock. "Efi? Are you in there?"

"No," she said quietly against Nick's mouth.

He chuckled and kissed her more deeply, working his index finger inside the elastic of her underpants until he stroked her slick flesh.

"Efi, you open this door this minute, do you hear me? *Amesos.*"

Her mother's tone brooked no argument. Efi knew that nothing short of a barricade would stop Penelope Panayotopoulou from gaining access to the room. The question was whether Efi wanted to be caught with her underpants around her ankles when it happened, even if Nick was her groom and they would soon be married. There were just some things you didn't want your mother to see you doing. Ever.

Efi groaned and leaned her forehead against Nick's. "Please tell me these seven days will pass quickly."

"It's going to seem like a lifetime."

"That's not what I want to hear."

"Trust me, it's not what I want to say." He kissed her, his tongue lingering against her lips. "I'll find a way for us to get together."

She joined her hands behind his neck knowing that he would. She'd learned long ago that whatever Nick wanted, Nick got. And she was oh so happy he wanted her.

"Efi, *tora.* Now," came her mother's voice again.

Probably she was listening against the door and heard their exchange.

With a sigh, she straightened herself, then helped Nick do the same. Wearing a bright smile, she opened the door. "I don't know what could have happened," she said, sailing past her mother who stood cross-armed with her grandmother and her scowling aunt Frosini. "Nick came in to help me get some onions and the door just…stuck."

"Hmph," her mother said, pulling her arm in that way that only mothers knew how to do. "You smeared your lipstick while getting those onions. Go clean up in the bathroom before going into the other room or else everyone will know what you two were doing."

Efi made a face.

"As for you, *kolopetho,*" Penelope said, exchanging Efi's arm for Nick's. "Pull another stunt like that and I'll lock you up in the pantry until Sunday."

He grinned at Efi.

"Alone," Penelope clarified.

Nick bowed his head like a chastised child. "My apologies, Miss Penelope."

Efi's mother smiled. "That's more like it. Now go help Mr. Gregoris pour the wine."

"Yes, ma'am."

CHAPTER TWO

Day two

THE SCENT OF BAKING sweet bread wafted around Efi, lifting her mood. Truth was, she hadn't quite seen the week of festivities leading to her wedding day being so…lonely. She'd imagined herself and Nick being joined at the hip, holding hands, as the family swirled around them. Instead it seemed the family was insistent on their being apart. Of course, if the pantry incident last night had anything to do with that, she wasn't going to acknowledge it. What was wrong with her and her groom wanting a little alone time?

"It makes the wedding night that much more… meaningful," her mother had said when she'd asked the question this morning before heading off to the shop at seven.

"The fact that we'll be married should be all the meaning the night should need," Efi had answered back.

But she might as well have been speaking to a granite wall, because her mother was hearing none of it.

So she figured all this maneuvering to keep her and Nick apart was being done for their own good, the way their families saw it.

Better she should have a nice, full orgasm to release the stress.

Is that why brides got cold feet? Following all this well-meaning intervention, and normal nerves that went along with the planning—not to mention the monumental meaning behind the "till death do us part" event itself—she could easily see where a bride might throw up her hands and do the equivalent of quitting her own wedding.

Yes, a solid orgasm would be just what the doctor ordered.

A shiver ran over her skin at the thought of being alone with Nick for an unspecified amount of time. Five minutes, five hours, it didn't matter. Hell, at this point she'd take one minute.

She rolled out a ball of dough against the marble slab until it was a quarter of an inch thick and about two feet long. Then with a pastry knife she cut the rope into two-inch lengths and began braiding those to make *koulourakia,* what amounted to Greek sugar cookies. Her movements were quick and efficient as a result of years of making the sweet. She put the tray of cookies into the oven, then pulled another tray in front of her and began buttering sheets of phyllo dough to make baklava. Even as she sprinkled the walnut, sugar and cinnamon mixture on top of the buttered pastry sheets, she remembered when she'd asked her father if she could add drizzles of melted milk chocolate to the mix. Or, better, raspberry sauce. He'd scoffed and told her no self-respecting Greek would ever put chocolate or raspberry sauce into baklava. And just what was the matter with the traditional recipe anyway? he'd asked. That was the problem with the younger generation. They didn't respect tradition. Always wanted to fix things that weren't broken.

Efi rubbed her nose against her shoulder and looked around the ancient kitchen that was attached to a gloomy showroom beyond. She had a notebook burgeoning with ideas on how to make the shop more modern, more appealing, but it sat gathering dust on the makeshift desk in the corner, receipts nearly burying it. Every now and again she took it out and went over her renovation ideas. My Big Fat Pastry Shop was one idea she had, inspired by another Greek pioneer Nia Vardalos. She wanted to change the beige and more beige color scheme in the showroom to sparkling white and blue. Longed to take out

the wall that separated the showroom from the un-
needed supply closet and add tables where customers
might enjoy their sweets with a view of the street and
Greek Town beyond.

"We're not a restaurant," her father had said. "This
place has run just fine for twenty-five years without the
fancy things you want to do. What do you think puts
the food on the table? Keeps a roof over our heads?"

Efi had offered him a huge eye roll but she hadn't
given up on the idea. In fact, she fully intended to
launch another attack as soon as she and Nick returned from their honeymoon.

The old, rusty cowbell on the front door clanged
announcing a customer. Efi wiped her hands on a
towel and went out to greet the arrival.

She'd no sooner opened the swinging door than
she found herself in Nick's arms.

"Good, I was hoping I'd get you alone," he said
with a wicked grin.

Efi's mood soared as he backed her into the
kitchen, the door swinging closed behind them.
"What are you doing? Shouldn't you be at work?"

"It's lunchtime." He glanced at his watch over her
shoulder even as he worked at undoing her apron
strings. "I only have fifteen minutes. Hurry. If we're
quick, we might even be able to squeeze in some
foreplay."

Efi laughed as they nearly upset a tray where loaves of *tsoureki,* sweet bread, cooled. Then they shuffled toward the preparation table where she pushed the tray of baklava aside so Nick could lift her on top of the cool marble. Good thing she was wearing white jeans where the flour wouldn't show too much. Not that it mattered. Nick was determined to rid her of clothes, period, starting with her jeans.

"Mmm." She reveled in the feel of his mouth against hers. His kiss was sweeter and hotter than anything the shop had to offer, with or without chocolate.

He tugged his mouth away and she made a sound of protest, until she felt his lips against her bared right nipple. She bunched her fingers into his thick, dark hair, enjoying the myriad sensations flicking over her skin in concert with the flicks of his tongue.

Their position reminded her of their first time together. She'd been seventeen and he'd stopped by the shop to pick up a torte for his mother for a party she was throwing on his father's name day. Or at least that had been the story. From what she knew, Nick Constantinos never ran chores for his mother. It wasn't the Greek way. Greek men, it was well known, were coddled by their families until they married, and then the job was turned over to their new brides. She knew many Greek men who didn't know how to boil water, much less iron their own shirts.

Her father had gone to the bank for some financial matters and she'd been in the shop alone. And Nick made no secret that this was the moment he'd been waiting for. The time when he might sample some of the shop's offerings…directly from her skin.

She'd been wholly unprepared for the desire, the longing he'd introduced her to. The feel of his tongue against her belly as he lapped cream from her skin. The liquid that had pooled between her legs that he'd tsked about then set about cleaning up with his mouth.

It had been Efi's first sexual encounter. And it wasn't something she was soon to forget.

And it seemed Nick was determined to make sure she didn't forget this time, either, as he stoked the sparks charging through her veins into a full-out fire.

His fingers were more skilled than they'd been back then. He knew just how to touch her, where to apply pressure, where to pluck and pinch and stroke, making each time her first time.

She fumbled for the catch to his pants, needing to feel the growing length of him, evidence of his want for her. So hot…so hard…

"Condom…back pocket," he ground out, his breath teasing the sensitive skin of her neck.

She took it out and put a corner of the foil packet between her teeth…just as the cowbell on the door outside rang again.

"Efi! Come on out front. I want you to meet someone."

Her father.

"Damn." Nick leapt away and Efi jumped from the table and back into her jeans at the same time, both of them frantically putting themselves back together. If the thought of her mother seeing her in a compromising position was horrifying, having her father walk in…

Efi couldn't even bear to think of it.

She stared wide-eyed as Nick gave her a hard, fast kiss. "I'm going out the back. I'll see you later."

Efi gave him a shove. The door had barely shut behind him when she was swinging to face her father opening the other door.

She smiled at him, hoping she didn't look too flushed or flustered. "Papa. I wasn't expecting you in today."

Efi blinked. If she hadn't been expecting him in today, she certainly wasn't prepared for the person he'd brought with him. She stared at her younger cousin Phoebus, who had always been on the thin side and wore clothes that were much too big for him.

Her father put his arm over his shoulders, dwarfing the smaller man. "I figured now would be as good a time as any to bring Phoebus in to have a look around the place."

Efi's hormones were still running overtime. Especially since Nick had circled the block of buildings and popped up outside the front window, waving at her from over her oblivious father's shoulder.

"I'm not following you," she said to her father. "I thought Diana was going to fill in for me while I'm on my honeymoon."

Diana was her sister, younger than her by a year.

"She is, she is." He patted Phoebus's shoulder hard enough that her cousin winced. "Phoebus is going to be your permanent replacement."

A timer went off in the kitchen behind her, seeming to call an end not only to the cooking time of the *koulourakia,* but to her career as well.

"Pardon me?"

Her father had the good grace to look a little sheepish. "Your mama told me you might have a problem with the…how did she put it? Transition. Yes, transition."

"Transition into what?" Efi couldn't stop herself from asking.

"Marriage, of course. Is that something I smell burning?"

Marriage…

Was her father implying that once she and Nick were married this Sunday, she would no longer be working at the shop?

Yes, she realized, he was.

And that something burning was going to be her in two seconds flat unless he retracted his statement.

Her father mumbled something under his breath as he went back into the kitchen to save the cookies.

Efi took the opportunity to smile at her cousin, then take his arm and lead him to the door. "Thanks so much for stopping by, Phoebus, but my father's a little confused right now. It's an age thing, you know."

Her cousin nodded. "Tell me about it. My grandmother sprinkled sugar instead of salt on the salad last night. Worse, she didn't even seem to notice, saying it was the best salad she'd ever made." He skidded to a halt just inside the door. "Does this mean your father doesn't need me?"

Efi stopped herself from patting him on the head. "That's exactly what it means. Diana will fill in for me until I get back from my honeymoon."

"And then?"

And then what? she felt the urge to scream. "And then I'll be returning here myself."

"But…"

Efi opened the door, then nearly shoved him through it.

"Thanks again, Phoebus. Give your family my best, won't you? I trust we'll see you all at the wedding?"

She closed the door before he had a chance to respond and turned in time to watch her father storm through the kitchen door.

"Burned. Every last one of them."

At that moment Efi couldn't have cared less if half the shop burned to the ground.

"Where's Phoebus?" he asked.

"On his way home. Where he's going to stay."

"What did you go and do that for? I wanted you to show him some of the ropes before you leave."

"There's no need to show him the ropes, because I'm not leaving."

Her words seemed to take a minute to sink in. When her father's own personal lightbulb finally went off, the expression on his beefy, lovable face turned from confused to exasperated.

"Efi, you're getting married."

"Yes, I'm getting married. I'm gaining a husband, not losing my mobility."

He lifted a finger. "Ah, yes, but you'll also become a wife. A mother. You'll have different priorities after the wedding."

"I'll have more responsibilities, not different

ones." She crossed her arms over her apron-covered chest. "Just when had you planned to tell me you were going to replace me?"

Her father scratched his eyebrow with his index finger. "Well...now."

"Ask a stupid question..."

Efi paced the length of the display case then back again. She stared at her father, felt nothing but frustration well up in her throat, then paced away again.

"Efi, listen. Your mother and I discussed this with Niko. We all think—"

"You discussed this with Nick?"

She couldn't believe it. Wouldn't believe it. There was no way Nick was in on this. He knew how much the shop meant to her.

But he also wanted ten kids.

"Well, maybe not with Nick directly. With his parents. And they agree this is what he would want."

"And what about what I want?"

Her father grinned at her and put his arm across her tense shoulders. "Ah, everything will make sense once the wedding is over, just you wait and see."

Somehow Efi got the impression that nothing was going to make much sense ever again....

CHAPTER THREE

Day three

IT WAS A CONSPIRACY, Efi was convinced.

In three days she hadn't been alone with Nick for more than three minutes. And then only because they'd stolen the moments. The more she and Nick tried to be alone together, the more their families worked to keep them apart.

Tonight Nick's family was hosting a dinner at their monstrous house, more his family than hers, and including guests that were still arriving from as near as Toledo and as far away as Cyprus. Every time she blinked, another relative she hadn't seen in over a decade popped up, kissing her and wishing her well and spitting on her.

"Ptew, ptew, ptew." A cousin of hers from Ancient Olympia spat on her as she entered the Constantinos home and shrugged out of her wrap.

Okay, so it wasn't a clear your throat, accumulated a thick wad in your mouth kind of spit. It was more a superstitious gesture to keep a person safe from the evil eye, especially a bride seeing as all eyes were on her now, evil or otherwise.

Still, Nikoletta seemed to put more effort into the spitting than necessary, blowing Efi's bangs slightly back from her forehead.

Efi smiled and hoped there wasn't a spit bubble on her eyebrow. "It's good to see you, Letta. *Kalos erthis.*"

"Kalos sas vrikamai," Letta said automatically, responding to Efi's Greek welcome that meant it was good to be there.

Kiki leaned closer to her. "Well, at least you won't need another shower later," she whispered as Efi discreetly checked her face for spittle before the next long-lost Greek relative greeted her.

"Shush. Your day will come soon enough."

Kiki gave a melodramatic sigh that would have put any of their tragic ancestors to shame. "With no groom in sight outside your own, I don't see how that's possible."

"That's only because you're blind." She looked around for Nick, but didn't see him anywhere. "I've got to make a rest stop."

"Efi!"

Kiki made a face. "Your grandfather, twelve o'clock. You want me to run interference?"

"Too late."

Not that Efi didn't want to see her paternal grandfather. He'd played a large role in her life and her sisters' lives ever since they were young and he'd come to the States after the death of his wife. It was just that his *Grenglish* was atrocious. Oh, she spoke fluent Greek, but her grandfather's interesting mix of Greek and English meant she sometimes had a hard time communicating with the short, energetic man.

"Ah, look at you," her grandfather Kiriakos said, taking her hands and holding them wide. "You look like just your grandmother."

"Thank you, *Papou*," she said, kissing both of his cheeks. "Where's Gus?"

Gus was her grandfather's best friend and also a widower. It was rare when the two weren't spotted together. Although judging by her grandfather's instant angry expression, she had the feeling she might not being seeing the two of them together again anytime soon.

"*Ptew*, he's not fit for you to mention his name, to *kleftis*," Kiriakos said, spitting, although thankfully off to the side rather than on her.

Efi knew the word *kleftis* meant thief, but for the life of her she couldn't figure out why her grandfather would be calling his best friend a thief. Gus owned an antique furniture store not far from the pastry shop and was an upstanding citizen. They'd been friends for over twenty years.

"No matter. We will not let him spoil your special week now, will we?" her grandfather asked, kissing her again.

"I'm sure it's nothing that can't be worked out," she said.

"Never," he said, and moved on.

Kiki took a deep breath. "Well, that was enlightening."

Efi made a face at her friend, then caught sight of Nick behind a short, stout woman bearing down on her and her stomach lightened. "I need to talk to Nick."

Kiki groaned. "God, I feel sick just watching the two of you. You don't mind if I go get some air?"

Efi waved her friend away. "Go for it. Oh, and keep your eyes peeled for any potential grooms. I may be related or about to be related to every attractive, single male in the room, but you aren't."

"I wouldn't marry a Greek if you paid me. I have to live with them. You don't expect me to marry one, too?"

Efi gaped at her.

Kiki grinned and disappeared into the crowd.

EFI CAME TO UNDERSTAND that the difference between her family and Nick's was that the Constantinos family liked to put the *opa* into a party. Sometime after eleven, a trio of musicians set up outside on the back patio with a *bouzouki,* a *baglama* and a clarinet. Warm lanterns had been lit all around and within minutes the sound of a *tsiftetelli,* traditional Greek dance music, filled the fragrant night air. Thankfully it was warm for May, so while a few wore sweaters, the guests for the most part were warmed by drink and the promise of dancing.

By all accounts, the new focus should have allowed her and Nick the freedom to be near each other, if not the opportunity to disappear altogether for a few precious minutes. Instead, the families seemed even more determined to keep them apart. They were all bent on making it clear there would be no more secret meetings in the pantry. No more mysterious knee jerks under the table.

Efi watched the guests spill out onto the back patio and tried to make her way toward where Nick was chatting with one of her uncles when Kiki grabbed her arm.

"Not you, too," Efi complained.

Kiki flashed a smile. "I'm just saving you from dealing with your mother."

Penelope indeed was a couple of feet away closely watching her daughter. Efi fought an eye roll. You'd think she was sixteen and a virgin the way her family was carrying on. Then again, they were probably trying to save themselves from embarrassment. After all, it was hard to host a proper wedding party if the bride and the groom were off somewhere squeezing in a little nooky time.

Efi allowed Kiki to lead her to a corner of the patio. The band launched into their first tune, an old one that almost always got everyone up to dance. Efi laughed as her uncle Iakavo took her hand and led her to the makeshift stage, encouraging her to lead in the traditional line dance.

There were many things she loved about being Greek and this was one of them. She had plenty of non-Greek friends and marveled at the way they celebrated events. Never would you find a bouzouki band at her friend Teresa Galwart's house. Or a lamb roasting over a pit in the backyard of Janice Collingwood's place. There had been a period in her teens where she'd loathed being so different from other families. But somewhere down the line she'd learned to celebrate it.

She looked to where Nick was being pulled into the line and grinned at him, happier than she could ever remember being.

"Jesus. Who in the hell is that?" Kiki asked next to her after cutting into the line.

Efi blinked. "Who's who?"

"Tight red dress at two o'clock."

Efi looked and saw one of her plump aunts kicking up quite a dance.

"I said two o'clock, not four."

Efi shifted her gaze. And as she did she felt her heart drop to the vicinity of her feet.

A breathtakingly beautiful woman of about her own age with long black hair, ruby-red lips and a slinky body Efi had always dreamed of having but never would had her arms held high and was shimmying in a way that marked the end of the line and the beginning of the individual *tsiftetelli* or belly dance portion of the dance where everyone broke off and danced solo.

And it was clearly Nick she was dancing for.

"Aphrodite looks very nice tonight, doesn't she?" she heard her mother ask from her other side where they had moved from the patio and were standing off to the side, as the woman in red took center stage, every man in the place clapping in support of her seductive dance.

Efi gaped. "*That's* Aphrodite?"

The same skinny Aphrodite they had all laughed at when they were kids in Greece? Poor thing, they used to say, named after the Goddess of Love and she had the looks that only a mother could love.

The unfamiliar woman in red began to bend backward in a way that required someone to spot her so she wouldn't fall. Efi watched as Nick offered to be that someone. Aphrodite slithered and shook, taking full advantage of the close contact, the V of her dress deep, her breasts full, her hips all too lush.

Efi had watched Nick do the same thing for countless others, Kiki included, but she had never felt the stab of jealousy that twisted in her gut watching him with Aphrodite. Of course, it could have something to do with the way Aphrodite was looking at him seductively, suggestively, as if she was the direct descendent of her namesake and was putting him into some kind of erotic trance.

Thankfully the song came to an end and the couple in the middle of the patio earned roaring applause.

Unfortunately Efi was afraid the knife in her gut wasn't going anywhere.

"I SAY WE EXCHANGE HER for the lamb and tie her to the skewer," Kiki said a little while later, in the large upstairs bathroom Efi had gone to. She'd meant to be alone, but her best friend seemed uncannily tuned in to her mind-set and had followed, toying with a tray full of guest soaps in the shape of seashells on the counter while Efi tried to repair her makeup in the softly lit mirror.

She sighed. No matter what lighting she was in, she'd never be as appealing as Aphrodite was.

"And Nick. Okay, he'd danced with her once. He didn't need to dance with her again. And yet a third time…"

Efi stared at her. "Shut up, Kiki."

Her friend was all doe eyes and shoulder shrugs. "What? If I were you, I'd have let him know in no uncertain terms that his attention was a little over the top."

"She's my cousin, for God's sake."

"She's a sexpot."

That Aphrodite was.

And as one dance led into three, with Nick gladly playing to her cousin's apparent need for extra attention, Efi had felt as if her heels were growing shorter and her clothes too big until she feared she might disappear altogether.

She swiped a bit of eyeliner from under her lashes and sighed. "I don't know why I'm wasting my time. I'll never look as good as Aphrodite."

"I wasn't aware that's what you were trying to do."

Efi put away her makeup and leaned against the counter, away from the mirror next to her friend.

After a long silence, Kiki asked, "You know her well?"

"Who? Aphrodite?" She nodded. "Yeah. I spent

a couple of summers with her in Greece. The other kids used to call her Scarecrow and she wore glasses and had the biggest nose that side of the Atlantic. My father used to joke you could see her nose coming five minutes before the rest of her arrived."

"Well obviously she grew out of all that."

And then some. "I used to feel sorry for her. Used to stand up for her. Kept her company when the other kids would leave her behind."

"And she thanks you by monopolizing your groom at your wedding party."

They both thought about that for a moment. Then Kiki moved so that she was standing in front of Efi. She gave her a quick once-over, then a more thorough one.

"What?" Efi asked, looking down at her pink dress.

"I don't know. I was thinking this thing is a little too plain."

"It was expensive."

"Fashion is something you buy. Style is something you are."

Style? This *was* her style.

Kiki stuck her right hand inside the bodice of Efi's dress. Efi gasped and grabbed her arm. "What are you doing?"

"Copping a feel, what do you think I'm doing?" She wiggled her fingers against Efi's breast. "I'm trying to improve on your cleavage."

"By groping it?"

Kiki smiled wickedly. "It is said that the more you massage them, the bigger they grow." She glanced at her own modest chest. "So much bullshit, really. Now, would you let go of my hand so I can do my job?"

"Which is?"

"To help my best friend feel better by looking better."

Efi released her grip and watched as Kiki shoved her breasts up then adjusted her bra so that instead of flat skin with the hint of shape under the dress she now had two swells of visible flesh.

Efi moved to put things back the way they were.

"Don't! I'm not done."

"What are you going to do next—roll up the waist of my skirt and make it a mini like we used to do in middle school?"

"That's an idea, but…no."

Instead she tugged on the belt where it was loosely lying against one hip. She tightened it, further accentuating her narrow waist.

"You know, I'd like to breathe again at some point tonight," Efi complained.

"Screw breathing. It's overrated."

Efi laughed and swatted her friend away.

"Here, try these on."

Kiki had kicked off her shoes. Only they weren't shoes, really, but towering skyscrapers with six-inch spike heels.

"Uh-uh. I hate heels."

"And the shoes you now have on hate you."

Efi made a face and considered her low-heeled pumps.

"Forget it," she said, beginning to loosen her belt and put her bra back in order. "I am who I am. And it's who I am that Nick asked to marry. If I go out there the way you want me to, everyone will know I'm jealous. That's not what I want them to remember about the days leading up to my wedding."

Kiki's gaze was on hers in the mirror. "And you? What will you remember?"

Efi didn't want to think about that right now. Hopefully she would remember only the good things and let the rest of it fade away into the blurry recesses of her mind.

CHAPTER FOUR

Day four

EFI SLOWLY AWAKENED to the sound of raised voices downstairs. She plucked her brass wind-up clock from the side table and squinted at it. Just after nine.

She jackknifed upright in bed, nearly putting her sister Diana's eye out with an elbow. Just after nine!

"Hey, watch it," her sister grumbled, then rolled over on the double bed. Diana's room had been commandeered by visiting relatives.

"Sorry." Efi slapped the clock back to the table, tried to peel her eyes the rest of the way open, then decided she could see well enough as she got up, pulled on her pink oversize robe and dashed for the door, tripping over the blankets that comprised her sisters Eleni and Jenny's empty makeshift bed on the floor because their room had been taken over by even more relatives.

She paused in the upstairs hall, listening to the voices downstairs.

"No, you take this back. This isn't ours." Very definitely her mother.

"Look, lady, it has your name on it. It's yours." A man's voice, unfamiliar but obviously impatient.

"It's not mine. That might be my name, but those aren't my things. You've made a mistake. You'll have to take this back to your truck and bring me the right package."

Efi moved toward the stairs and bumped straight into Aphrodite, who had taken over Diana's bedroom along with her parents. She squinted at the other woman who had a good six inches on her and looked drop-dead gorgeous while Efi felt like death warmed over.

"Morning," she mumbled, then made her way around her cousin.

She quickly took the steps in her bare feet, not stopping until she nearly bumped into her mother.

"What's going on?"

The way Penelope and the deliveryman in a brown uniform looked at her, she supposed it might not have been a bad idea to make a pit stop in the bathroom before coming downstairs.

Her mother waved at the deliveryman. "He's trying to make me sign for a package that's not ours."

Efi accepted the package, looked at the return address, her mother's name on the mailing label then

took the handheld computer from the deliveryman
and signed for the already opened package.

"Thank you," the man said with a long-suffer-
ing sigh.

"Don't mention it."

Efi closed the door after him.

"What did you do that for? That's not our stuff."

Efi led the way into the kitchen, ignoring the
twelve relatives of varying ages and sizes milling
about the thankfully large room.

Penelope was on her heels. "Where are your slippers? You're going to catch cold running around
without your slippers."

Efi gave an eye roll that hurt her head, put the box
down on a part of the table that wasn't otherwise occupied by *boubounieras,* food or coffee cups, and
opened the flaps to stare at the contents.

She squinted at the multicolored candy Hawaiian
leis, sure she was seeing things.

At least half of the relatives in the room gathered
to look over her shoulder.

"Told you," Penelope said, pulling out a handful
of the party favors. "Not ours."

She had to give her mother that. The contents of
the box weren't something they had ordered.

Efi fished around inside the box until she came up
with the packing invoice. "300 Greek eye pins" was

typed clearly in the contents column. Essentially small flat blue stones with an eye painted on either side that had been used by the Greeks to ward off evil for eons. Her mother had ordered the pins for the guests to wear to keep evil well away from the church and the wedding ceremony.

Penelope had put the leis back in the box and was now pacing back and forth across the room, weaving around relatives. "Bad omen, receiving the wrong package like this. Bad."

Several of the female relatives nodded in response. A couple of them even crossed themselves and sent a prayer up to the Virgin Mary, while the male relatives merely grunted in response, which could mean agreement or disagreement, depending on how you wanted to take it.

Aphrodite chose that moment to join them.

Efi sank down into a chair, then leaned forward to remove the bag of Jordan almonds goosing her. "We still have three more days to go until the wedding. Plenty of time to get the right package."

"What? What's going on?" Aphrodite asked.

Efi stared at her, wishing she'd die or disappear even as one of their relatives quietly explained the situation to her.

Her mother stopped in front of Efi. "No, you don't

understand. The damage has already been done. The ceremony is cursed."

More cross-signing and Greek prayers went up. And if she wasn't mistaken, Aphrodite looked a little pleased.

"Oh, Mom, stop it already. I'm the one who's supposed to be a nervous wreck. You're the one who's supposed to be trying to calm me down."

Everyone stared at Penelope.

"Since you're not a nervous wreck?" her mother asked.

She had a point. For some reason Efi wasn't nervous at all about the upcoming nuptials. She looked at Aphrodite. Well, okay, maybe a little. "Have at it, then."

She got up, poured herself an extra large cup of coffee, then picked up the cordless receiver, searching for the phone number of domeafavor.com.

"What are you doing?" her mother asked.

"Straightening this out, of course. Somewhere out there a bride is wondering why they got a box full of eyes instead of the leis here." She stared at her mother. "I just hope she's luckier than me in her choice of mothers."

"My daughter, the comedian."

LATER THAT MORNING at the pastry shop, Efi idly wondered if maybe her mother had been right; her wedding was cursed. Or rather, it was beginning to look as if everything surrounding it seemed to be bad news. Forget the leis—not only had she found Phoebus securely ensconced at the shop, her sister Diana appeared to have been training him all morning. Which meant her father's intention to edge her out was going according to plan. With one little caveat: Phoebus couldn't seem to tell the difference between the refrigerator and the ovens.

"I'm going to kill him," Diana said, emerging from the kitchen with soot covering her face and the front of her white apron.

Efi stood at the counter near the register making notes, not officially working. "I'll come visit you in prison."

Phoebus burst through the swinging door to the kitchen, screaming. Efi figured out why as he passed her on his way outside: the back ties to his apron were ablaze. Diana ran after him, but he didn't need her help as he tore off the apron then stamped out the flames, trying to get a look at his own backside to make sure it was untouched.

Efi shook her head. Then again, maybe it wasn't her wedding that was cursed, but her father for thinking he could replace her.

In fact, two of the things that had happened that day didn't bother her, because she'd been against them anyway. The Greek eyes had always reminded her of fish eyes despite the pretty blue stone. She'd shuddered when her mother ordered three hundred for the guests to pin to the front of their dress clothing at her wedding.

As for Phoebus…

"I quit."

Efi looked up from the notebook to find Phoebus facing her. "Bully for you."

"Tell your father it's going to take a hell of a lot more than he's paying me to put my life on the line."

"Consider it done," Efi agreed.

And with that Phoebus exited a second time. Diana stood holding the charred remains of his apron.

"Papa is not going to be happy."

Efi shrugged. "He'll get over it."

"And what about me?"

She wasn't sure she was following her younger sister.

"What if Papa's right and you won't want to return to the shop after you get married? I can't work here. I've got one more semester and I become a nurse. I don't want to run this shop."

Not her sister, too. "I'm not going to change my mind about the shop, Di. I'm coming back to work right after my honeymoon."

Her sister stared at her long and hard then thrust the ruined apron at her and untied her own.

"What are you doing?"

"Going after Phoebus, of course."

"Why?"

"Because I'm not willing to take the chance, that's why." She took her purse from behind the counter. "Besides, I don't want to hear it from Papa when he finds out Phoebus quit."

"But the guy has absolutely zero ability in the kitchen."

"Yes, well, from what I hear it took you three months to learn how to set the oven timer, so I'm willing to cut the guy a little slack."

Diana moved toward the door.

"Wait."

Her sister waited.

Efi left the two aprons on the counter, and moved to stand between her sister and the door. "I've got errands to run, so you can't leave."

"This is just a ploy to stop me from going after Phoebus."

Maybe. "I'm not the one on the clock today—you are. So you stay, I'll go." She picked up her notebook.

"And Phoebus?"

"Call him."

With that, Efi left the small, dim shop that she

wanted to change into a showplace and stood outside, the midday sun warming her. She shouldn't have come downtown. Then again, the choice had been between staying at home being fussed over by her mother and the relatives who had taken over their house, listening to them talk about curses and omens and bad events that had happened in their family since the beginning of time, or coming to the shop and discovering she was being replaced.

She fished her cell phone out of her purse—there was only one person capable of making her feel better.

Nick answered on the first ring.

"Meet me at the apartment. Now," she said, wondering why she hadn't thought of this before.

"I'm there," he responded, his voice sending anticipatory shivers up and down her spine.

THE SIMPLE APARTMENT on the fringes of Grosse Point was large and airy and one of the few things she and Nick had agreed on until they could afford to make a down payment on a house. The furnishings, of course, had been another matter. He'd wanted everything large and covered in leather and dead animal pelts, while she worshipped the very ground Martha Stewart walked on. So they'd compromised and the apartment that they would spend their first full night in Sunday after the reception smelled of a rich burgundy leather recliner, and was dominated by a pink-and-white-striped sofa with flowered throw pillows. The dining room was left empty because her grandfather Kiriakos had said he wanted to buy them a set.

The bed, however…the bed was her dream, the water bed Nick had wanted having been ruled out because it was against the lease in the third-floor apartment. Efi let her purse drop to the foyer table then walked toward the door that hid the wrought-iron creation in the other room. Covered in white eyelet lace and tons of pillows of varying sizes and shapes it looked like a picture snipped out of a magazine. And considering she'd designed it from just such a picture, she couldn't have been happier.

And, of course, despite Nick's grumbling about it being too feminine, he'd quickly realized the other uses for the iron posts.

Efi smiled as she ran her palm over one of the iron posts in question. In twenty-four hours the place would be packed with relatives, but now it was empty. Tomorrow night was the official *krevati,* which in Greek literally meant "bed" but also symbolized the making of the marital bed by single women in the family and other traditions designed to bring the newly married couple happiness and fertility. Of course, the event would be followed by food and drink and dancing in the apartment.

No one need know that only a day before, the bride and groom had already "baptized" the bed in their own intimate way.

Efi began stripping out of her clothes, anxious for Nick to be there so they could have those all-important few minutes together they'd been trying to steal in what seemed like forever.

One whip of the coverlet and the decorative pillows went flying. She climbed between the Egyptian sheets, the material silky against her bare skin, then drew the sheet up to her chin. Changing her mind, she draped it to lie against her stomach, then struck a pose of lazy invitation, waiting for the moment Nick would walk through the door.

She heard his key in the lock and swallowed in anticipation. A quick crunch of her hair and she smiled in wicked pleasure.

Her cell phone chirped from where she'd put it on the bedside table. Damn, what a mood breaker. She groped to turn it off. Probably her mother. She flipped the receiver open to punch the silence button, only to find that it was Nick's name in the display screen…

And looked up to see her mother standing in the bedroom doorway…

CHAPTER FIVE

Day five

THE IRONY OF THE SITUATION wasn't lost on Efi, although she was hard put to find any amusement in it. Just the day before she had been caught by her mother in bed waiting for Nick, her excuse that she'd stopped by for a quick nap making not a dent in what she and her mother knew was the truth. Namely that she was hoping to finish what she and Nick had started in the pantry those days ago.

And now, some thirty hours later, in the same apartment, both sides of the family were crammed into the small place, on the same bed—however remade and minus her—the single women decorating it with rose pedals and *koufetta,* sugar-coated almonds. Efi wasn't all that sure how she felt about Aphrodite being one of those women, her long dark hair silky and swaying as she bent over the bed. She supposed it was a good thing her cousin didn't know which side of the bed she was going to sleep on or else she might find a series of strategically placed pins protruding from the mattress.

At any rate, Kiki seemed as tuned in to Aphrodite's suggestive intentions as Efi and thwarted the beautiful woman at every turn. If Aphrodite tried to make eye contact with Nick, Kiki stepped in the way. When Aphrodite tried to test Efi's perfume on the dresser, Kiki took the bottle out of her hands and put it back down. The moment Aphrodite positioned herself so she was in front of the women, Kiki edged her out of the way. At one point Kiki jostled Aphrodite so hard the other woman nearly fell headfirst into the connecting bathroom. Efi thought it good that she hadn't fallen, because Kiki likely would have locked her in for the duration of the *krevati*.

The *krevati* simply meant "bed," but in this context, the marital bed was prepared by the single women. Rose petals for romance. Sugar-covered almonds to indicate the bitter sweetness of love and life. Even her cousin Helen's baby was rolled across the mattress for fertility reasons, the six-month-old crying the entire time (which Efi hoped didn't mean her own babies would be as irritable). Then the rest of the family filed through and put envelopes of money on the sheets. Some of the envelopes were given rather than a gift.

Next came yet another party.

Efi helped her mother and her aunts put together a buffet-style meal in the kitchen, wondering if she could withstand yet another party, Greek or otherwise. Her head ached and she feared her feet were deformed for life, given the nonstop series of different heels she'd had to wear over the past week. But at least tonight was the official end of the festivities. At least until the wedding and reception on Sunday two days away. The only thing planned for Saturday was a quiet dinner with her and Nick and their parents. She found she was looking forward to it, especially once someone put a CD on and one of her uncles grabbed her hand and urged her to lead in the start of the dancing.

The size of a room didn't matter to her relatives. Give them a closet and they'd find a way to dance without anyone being seriously injured. While not as extravagant as the Constantinos party with the bouzouki band, the atmosphere emerged even more personal, what with the close confines and the more casual dress. "The ceremony is only two days away! Opa!" seemed to be exclamation of the night. And it could mean one of two things: it's almost over, thank God! Or our kids are beginning their life together, amen!

As she stumbled over a rug, Efi preferred to look upon it as the former rather than the latter.

"May I?"

She blinked up to see Nick holding out his hand for hers. Instantly all her weariness eased away, replaced by a burst of strong love and gratitude. If ever she forgot what all this was for, she had only to look into Nick's grinning face and remember.

He took her hand and led in the dance, Efi easily following, and taking the lead from him herself in a way that earned whistles and cheers from the family, their dance seeming to reflect their life to come. The struggles. The love. The fact that one of them would take the lead, but it wouldn't always be the same one. They were partners in this particular dance of life, and if their harmonic steps now were any indication, they would have a very sweet life indeed.

And Efi wanted Nick so badly she ached with it.

"May I?"

Aphrodite indicated she wanted to break in between them. Nick instantly moved to release Efi's hand to take her cousin's, but Efi held fast and instead reached to include her on her left side, between her and her uncle Spyros. Aphrodite didn't appear pleased, but Efi really didn't care. Nothing was going to come between her and her groom. Especially not a little attention-hogging tart like Aphrodite.

Almost immediately afterward Kiki cut in between her and Aphrodite, putting the other woman even farther away from Nick. Efi smiled at her best friend in gratitude. She hadn't chosen Kiki as her *koumbara* for nothing.

A little while later Efi was in the kitchen helping with some of the clean-up and the cutting of fruit to put out which would officially call the drinking to an end and thus the night. She peeled a banana then pushed her hair from her forehead with the back of her hand.

"I'm going to have a talk with that girl," she heard her mother mumble next to her.

Efi blinked at her. "Who?"

"Your cousin Aphrodite, that's who. She's going after Nick like she's a bitch in heat."

Efi gasped, surprised by her mother's comments. Penelope Panayotopoulou was usually level-headed and polite to a T. It wasn't like her to engage in kitchen gossip when the subject was in the other room.

Every bone in Efi's body relaxed. Up until that moment she'd been afraid she was experiencing a bout of jealousy she couldn't quite figure out how to handle. Something irrational and unreasonable that she would have to just grin and bear until it finally passed. But with her mother's comments, she was shown that she wasn't the only one noticing her cousin's unwanted advances on her groom.

"It's hard to believe it's the same Aphrodite I knew when you were kids," her mother continued, arranging the fruit Efi cut on silver platters. "That girl had been afraid of her own shadow. Now she's looking to cast her shadow in places she shouldn't."

"I don't think she's that bad," Efi said. She stopped. "Well, okay, maybe she is."

Her mother waved a strawberry at her. "She did the same thing back home, you know."

Efi raised her brow. Gossip was rarely as good as what you heard when it came from back home.

"She broke up the wedding of her best friend. Uh huh. Caught her canoodling with the groom in the back of a pickup truck the night before the wedding."

Efi's throat tightened.

"She's engaged to him now."

She stared at her mother. "She's engaged?"

Penelope waved vaguely. "Well, from what I understand she was. She found out just yesterday that her fiancé went back to his first bride. They're to be married while she's here."

Efi's head spun with the information. Aphrodite had been engaged to a man once set to marry her best friend. And now she was making moves on Efi's groom.

She met her mother's gaze and they looked at each other for a long moment.

"I think I'd better get back out there."

"I think you'd better get back out there."

They said their thoughts at the same moment, then Efi left her mother to finish up the fruit, passing her watchful aunt Frosini on the way out. Her aunt seemed to look through Efi in a way that made her shudder to the bone.

Sure enough, there was Aphrodite, head thrown back, sexily laughing at something Nick had apparently just said to his *koumbaro* Alex. Her cousin was draped over the arm of the chair he sat in. A chair Efi herself had helped him pick out.

"Excuse me," she said to Aphrodite, nearly shoving her from the arm, then smiling widely. "Oh, I'm sorry. Here, let me help you over to the couch."

The young woman's eyes flashed as if she understood exactly what was going on. And Efi was more than happy to confirm her suspicions. She was in the right. Nick was her groom and Aphrodite had no right to openly flirt and try to engage him as if he was the only single man in the room.

The music had switched over to old American songs. A slow one came on and she walked over to where one of Nick's younger cousins, Pericles, was holding up the corner, barely having spoken all night. The gangly, shy guy wore glasses that made his eyes look twice as large. Efi smiled at him and led him to where Aphrodite was standing looking miffed, her arms crossed under her ample breasts, in the opposite corner. She motioned for them to dance.

"You think Perry will know what to do with her?" Nick asked, sweeping Efi up into his arms to join the other couple on the dance floor.

"Unlike yourself, you mean?"

He blinked at her.

"Never mind," Efi said, snuggling closer to him, breathing in his subtle cologne, reveling in the feel of his arms around her and his body against hers. She wasn't going to let anything ruin this one moment.

Nick grazed her ear with his lips. "We can lock ourselves in the closet," he murmured.

She laughed softly. "And have half the family banging on it? No, thank you."

"We could sneak outside. My car's parked up the block."

"They'd be on our heels before you could start the engine."

He sighed. "You're right."

"There is some good news, though," she whispered.

He pulled back to look at her.

"In two more days there's not going to be anyone trying to keep us apart."

In two days they would be husband and wife.

The thought sent goosebumps shivering up her arms.

In the midst of all that had been going on, she'd somehow lost sight of the light at the end of the tunnel. The reason their families were going to such great lengths to keep them apart. The motivation behind the loud celebrations.

She and Nick were getting married.

Efi watched the slow, wicked grin spread across his handsome face and her breath left her body. God, what she wouldn't give to see that grin every moment of every day for the rest of her life.

And judging by the hardness pressing against her belly, she had a pretty good idea that he felt the same.

"Wish for another slow song," he muttered.

"Why?" she asked innocently.

"Because we're going to look awfully awkward dancing slow to a fast one."

CHAPTER SIX

Day six...

THE DAY BEFORE HER WEDDING.

Efi automatically jerked upright in bed, only to realize there really wasn't anywhere she needed to be. At least not at 8:00 a.m. So she nudged her sister Diana's elbow over and away from her ribs and rested her head back down on the pillow, watching the sun dapple the walls of her room through the branches of the big oak outside her window.

In just over twenty-four hours she would be Mrs. Nick Constantinos. She twisted her lips, not sure she liked the sound of that. Okay, how about Efi Constantinos? She settled more comfortably against the mattress. Yes. That sounded much better.

She couldn't remember a time when her name and the length of it hadn't caused her problems. Filling out any sort of form was a chore because inevitably there weren't enough spaces to fit Panayotopoulou. On her bridal magazine subscription they had cut her name so she was Efi Panayotopo.

Not that Constantinos was that much shorter. But it was connected to Nick. And that alone was enough to make her feel all warm and mushy inside. Not to mention sexy. Merely imagining waking up to Nick curved against her backside or with her cheek smushed against his hard chest made her shiver all over. Never again would they have to worry about relatives lurking on the other side of the door or tracking them down to make sure they weren't doing anything they shouldn't be doing. They would be married and a healthy sex life would be expected…along with lots of little grandchildren named after their grandparents.

Okay, she'd traveled a little far down that particular imaginary road. Right now all she wanted to think about were periods of unbroken, hot monkey sex between her and her husband on that white bed decorated with rose petals and sugared almonds.

She blinked, bringing into focus the opposite side of her room. Wedding gifts had been arriving throughout the week from relatives abroad and closer who couldn't make the wedding. Her mother had initially begun stacking them in the dining room. Until she'd caught one of her aunts skillfully trying to re-wrap a gift she'd opened to see what was in it. In fact,

Penelope was convinced that a gift or two might even be missing, along with a crystal ashtray, a figurine of the Greek goddess Athena and an oven mitt her mother was sure Aunt Frosini might have burned in some sort of strange old village ritual. So the gifts had been moved to Efi's bedroom, along with the rest of the *boubounieras,* a great number of the bridesmaid dresses, and umpteen other items connected to the wedding, making her room look like a bridal shop. She glanced at Diana sleeping next to her and Eleni and Jenny sleeping together on the floor near the gifts. Well, almost like a bridal shop, anyway.

The smell of freshly brewed coffee reached her nose and she followed it like a woman in a trance, slipping from the bed, putting her feet into her slippers and grabbing her robe, never breaking her leisurely stride. She wrapped her fingers around the door handle.

"Are you sure you're ready for this?"

She looked over shoulder at where Diana peeked at her from barely open eyelids.

"I was born ready for this," she said.

She swung open the door to find nearly every one of her female relatives on the other side, her mother leading the way with a makeshift tambourine by way of a metal pie plate and they launched into an old Greek wedding song that could be translated as "Tomorrow we're going to the chapel and we're going to get married…"

Efi broke out into a grin, glanced at where Diana groaned and pulled her pillow over her face, then led the way down to the kitchen, the group dancing and singing and banging on metal pans behind her.

EFI WAS ACCUSTOMED to the way Greeks like to celebrate. It didn't take much. A normal dinner was often reason enough to overindulge in wine and food and to dance until you couldn't dance anymore. But when it came to the really big events, like her wedding, the Greeks knew how to celebrate in a way that made her giddy with wonder.

If they were back in the old country, she knew that traditionally the men would be walking up and down the town streets singing and calling out for everyone to join in the ceremony the following day. Of course, doing so in Grosse Point, Michigan, would probably get them arrested for disorderly conduct at best, public drunkenness at worst, so the group's activities were contained to the bride's and the groom's respective family homes.

Even Aunt Frosini's dark, scowling presence couldn't detract from the events. Thankfully she hung back from the main crowd, content watching everything unfold before her.

Efi thought there was probably some sort of civil safety ordinance about having so many people in one place. Everywhere you looked there were people. A good many of them had stayed in their house from the night before, others came over at the break of dawn to join in the festivities. While each day of the week leading up to the actual day of the ceremony held some sort of significance, from the *krevati* on, there would be nonstop eating and drinking and dancing until the family saw the bride and groom off after the reception…and sometimes it didn't even stop then, but continued on with the family minus the couple of honor.

Efi had participated in events for other family members, but it was different now that she was the object of attention. From being told how beautiful she was, how much she glowed—followed by the requisite three spits, of course, to ward off the evil eye—to be waited on hand and foot lest she break a nail or something in preparation for her big day, everyone went out of their way to make sure she was happy.

Even her father had closed his shop for the weekend, something she hadn't known him to do except on Christmas day, and even then he often went in to fill some special orders for his best customers and for the family.

Of course, he wasn't here amongst the women. Instead he was probably at Nick's parents' house helping organize the men's celebration.

At somewhere around 10:00 a.m., the telephone began ringing and never seemed to stop. A constant stream of good wishes poured in from family and friends, near and far.

Only, as Efi watched her mother take this particular call, she got the unsettling impression that the caller wasn't a well-wisher. Penelope's face drained of color and she gripped the phone so tightly her knuckles were white.

"I don't understand," she said in her thickly accented Greek. "Could you please repeat what you just said?"

More than a few people in the room seemed to tune in to the situation and motioned for the others to hush.

Efi moved to stand next to her mother, resting her hand on her arm.

Slowly Penelope hung up the phone, her hands trembling.

"Your grandfather's been arrested."

No MATTER HOW RESOLUTELY they asked the family to stay put, it seemed the entire household of female relatives, along with the males from the Constantinos house, stood outside the metro Detroit police station, cars double-parked, others letting their passengers out at the curb in the front. Efi had a denim shirt and jeans on over her nightgown, her youngest sister Jenny not even going that far, putting a hoodie on over her pj's, which nowadays could have been considered clothing.

"Damn fool of a man," Efi's mother grumbled as they waited at the front desk for the officer to get her grandfather's paperwork.

"Ladies, ladies!" a female police officer was shouting to get the attention of Efi's many relatives where they crowded the small lobby. "All those without business, you'll have to wait outside."

"We have business," one of Efi's aunts insisted.

The female police officer looked an inch away from putting them all into holding cells until they settled down or listened to her.

"All those without immediate business, outside. Now," she said, her tone brooking no argument as she swung her cuffs.

Like a bunch of angry hens, Efi's aunts and cousins quickly filed out of the station, leaving a blessed calm in their wake. That still left her parents, Nick and his parents, and her sisters at the desk. The female officer eyed them, then sighed and went back to work.

The officer with the paperwork stepped to the desk. "He's been arrested for grand larceny," he stated.

Efi's mother shook her head. "What does that mean, exactly?"

The officer stared at her. "It means he crashed his car through the window of a local furniture shop and made off with some of the goods. When the responding officers caught up with him, he was dragging a dining-room table on a blanket on the street behind him."

Her wedding gift of a dining-room table...

Efi closed her eyes, wishing the nightmare away.

Her father looked around. "Where's Gus?"

Everyone looked around, as if by doing so they could make her grandfather's best friend, and very likely the owner of the furniture store in question, materialize.

"I'll go get him," Nick offered, earning him a grateful gaze from Efi.

He left and she turned her attention to the officer.

"How do we get him out?" she asked.

"Thankfully it's been a light day. He's already gone before the judge." The officer then named a bond amount that made her mother gasp.

Her father took out his checkbook.

"I'm sorry, sir," the officer said. "I'm afraid I'm

going to have to ask for either cash or a cashier's check. We don't take personal checks, for obvious reasons."

"What obvious reasons?" her father asked.

The officer merely stared at him.

"Are you calling me a liar? Saying I don't have the money to cover the bond?"

Efi touched her father's arm. "Why don't you let Diana go to the bank and cash the check, Papa? There's a branch just up the block."

A half hour later they were leaving with her grandfather.

"Damn thief," he was saying, apparently about his best friend. "He's the thief and it's me they arrest."

"*Papou,* you crashed through the front of his shop." And he'd been dragging a dining-room table behind his car.

Efi found it amazingly easy to envision her grandfather doing just that, going twenty miles an hour down the street in order not to do much damage to her wedding gift, even as broken glass fell from the hood of his old Lincoln.

"I should have crashed through all the windows, the *klefti,*" he said vehemently.

Nick pulled up to the curb, then rounded his car to help Gus out, her grandfather's lifelong friend and the owner of the shop he'd vandalized.

"You son of a bitch!" her grandfather shouted, advancing on the other man.

"They let you out?" Gus countered. "They should keep you locked up for good. You're a danger to society!"

And just like that the families fought to keep the two men apart as officers coming into the building slowed their steps, wondering whether or not intervention would be needed.

"Would you two stop it!" Efi stepped between them. "You're acting like children."

"Children?" Gus said to her. "Who are you to insult me? It must be in your blood, this blatant disrespect."

"Don't you talk to my granddaughter in that tone, you old goat!"

Efi stared at her grandfather. "Yes, you're right. I am your granddaughter. Your granddaughter who is set to get married tomorrow and whose day you just ruined with the stunt you pulled."

Her grandfather had the grace to look abashed.

Gus snorted. "None of this would have happened had he just paid what the furniture was worth."

"Worth? You marked the price up three times retail because you knew that was the piece I wanted to buy for my granddaughter! The girl who is named after my wife, God bless her soul."

"Others were interested in buying the set."

"Others aren't your best friend!" her grandfather said. He lifted a hand showing two fingers. "Twenty years we're friends. Twenty years I drink wine with you, treat your kids like they're my kids, help put your son through college, and this is the thanks I get?"

"You? What about my shop? Do you know how much money it's going to cost to repair the damage you've done? Forget the window—the pieces that were in the display are destroyed."

"Stop it!" Efi shouted. "Just stop it!"

Everyone stood and stared at her, Nick included. He lifted a hand to rub his chin, half hiding his grin.

"Both of you go home. Now. And think long and hard about what you've done."

"I've—"

"Quiet! I'm not finished." Efi cleared her throat, trying to get her own emotions under control. "I want you both to think about what happened today. And tomorrow I want you both at my wedding ready to apologize."

"Apol—"

"Shush! Not a word." She looked at her parents, who seemed frozen to the spot, watching her.

Her father cleared his throat. "I'll take Dad home."

Nick's parents considered Gus. "And we'll take him home."

Efi nodded her thanks.

Her father began walking away with his father. Efi could just make out her grandfather saying, "First we have to stop to get my car and the furniture. I want to get it set up in the apartment before tomorrow…."

Efi shook her head when she and Nick finally stood on the sidewalk alone.

"What a nightmare," she whispered, watching as the last of her eccentric family finally disappeared down the street.

Nick was toying with something at the neck of her shirt. "Cute. Can I see the rest of it?"

She realized he was referring to her nightshirt, the one with Betty Boop on it proclaiming how good it was to be bad.

Efi swatted Nick's hand away. "After tomorrow you'll get to see as much of it as you want to."

Not that she intended to wear the old nightgown to bed with her new husband. Well, at least not for the first month or so. She'd bought all sorts of sexy new nighties to keep him entertained.

Although given the way he was looking at her and her Betty Boop nightshirt, she wondered if she hadn't wasted her money.

He bent down and kissed her leisurely, seeming to forget they were standing in front of a police station.

"You do realize we're completely alone," he said, kissing her again. "No families hassling us to do something." Efi melted against him as he kissed her again. "No one looking over our shoulders…"

She pressed her hand against his chest with the intention of pushing him away. Instead she leaned closer. "You realize we're at risk of being arrested for indecent public display of affection, don't you?"

"Mmm. All things considered, I can think of worse things," Nick said, kissing her more deeply.

The shrill beep of a car horn.

Efi lazily blinked to find her father's car at the curb packed full of her relatives.

He'd come back for her.

"Shit," Nick said, smiling down at her.

"You can say that again."

"Efi! Get in the car this minute!" her mother yelled.

"You'd think we were teenagers and they'd forbidden us from seeing each other," she said, kissing Nick this time.

"Instead we're getting married tomorrow."

Getting married… She and Nick…

Efi smiled and kissed him one last time before going to join her family in the car.

CHAPTER SEVEN

Day six continued...

STRANGE THAT EVEN as the arrangements for her wedding came together, Efi's very life seemed to be coming apart at the seams.

Efi stood in front of her bedroom mirror plucking and pulling at her new dinner dress. Forget that she couldn't seem to sneak a few much-needed moments alone with her groom. But worse, every time she turned around, she ran into her cousin Aphrodite, who seemed overly curious about "the groom." While her nonstop questions might sound natural coming from anyone else, the constant "how did you two meet?", "where does he work?", "how many children does he want?" came off a little too...personal for Efi's liking.

"Oh, stop it," she muttered to her reflection. "Your cousin is not trying to steal your groom."

She only wished she believed her words.

Only one more day to go, she whispered to herself. And she and Nick would be husband and wife.

She started. Is that how she viewed marriage? As a type of ownership? Put a ring on Nick's finger and he was taken, her property, off-limits to Aphrodite and others? If that was the case, then what about the 50 percent divorce rate? The high incidence of infidelity?

Her mind started to spin and she put her hands to her head as if to stop it.

She'd always looked at Nick's and her exchanging of vows as having to do with love, happiness and creating a life together. A union forged out of mutual love for each other, not a way to brand him as hers.

There was a brief knock on her bedroom door. She'd locked it earlier in case her cousin had a few questions she'd forgotten to ask her. She'd felt sorely tempted to push her out her second-story window when she'd asked how Nick kissed.

She automatically started to unlock the door, then asked instead, "Who is it?"

"Diana."

She released a heavy sigh then opened the door to her sister.

"Mom sent me up to get you. She thinks you should be there when the Constantinos family arrives."

Something else she wasn't particularly looking forward to. "Thanks," she said, although she really didn't feel it.

Oh, she and Nick's parents got along well. And she was looking forward to the quiet night over the weeklong series of parties. But somehow she always felt something was going unsaid. Something the older couple felt about their only child marrying her, the oldest of four girls. She usually came away from any meeting with them feeling as if she were lacking, somehow. As if they'd taken a thorough inventory and she'd come up a few supplies short of what they wanted in a daughter-in-law.

She began to edge around her sister.

"Is everything okay?"

"Hmm? Sure, everything's fine. Why wouldn't it be?"

"I don't know. You look a little frazzled. And not bride-to-be frazzled, either. You look a little pale."

She actually felt pale, if that were possible.

But that wasn't the thing she needed to hear before going down to help welcome her groom and his family when they arrived.

"Thanks, but I'm fine." She hoped.

She hesitated at the top of the stairs, her fingers squeezing the top rail. "Have you seen Aphrodite?"

Diana looked toward her bedroom door. "Mom said she went out earlier. Why?"

Efi tried to ignore the burst of gratitude that the other woman wasn't there. "Nothing. She asked to borrow a pair of earrings and I thought I might give them to her."

"I'll do it."

"No, that's all right. I'll do it later."

Efi's step was lighter as she took the stairs. She knew it was silly, her worrying about her formerly ugly duckling cousin and her whereabouts, but considering everything going on just then, she didn't think it a major sin to be happy about her absence.

"That color washes you out."

Her mother's words stopped her in the doorway to the dining room. "Gee, thanks, Mom. Between you and Diana I'm about a breath away from locking myself in my bedroom and letting you handle this dinner."

Penelope fussed at her dress until she apparently figured out Efi wouldn't change the dark navy into another color with a few pulls and tucks. "You should have worn pink. Pink is a good color for a bride. Navy looks like you're going to a funeral."

"If you don't stop I will be attending a funeral. Yours."

Penelope tsked her and her father rustled his newspaper where he was already sitting at the table.

"Are we going to eat anytime soon?" he asked, blissfully unaware of the color of her dress and their impending guests.

Her mother took the paper from him and folded it up. "Straighten your tie."

Efi watched her father stare at the item of clothing as if he'd forgotten he had it on and was afraid it might come to life and strangle him. Still, he did as her mother asked.

The doorbell rang. Efi stared at her parents and her parents stared back at her.

"All right, all right, I'll get it," Efi said with a sigh.

Only, when she opened the door she half wished she had stayed locked in her bedroom. Because standing in the doorway, hanging off her fiancé's arm as if she belonged there, was none other than Aphrodite.

EFI WAS AWARE she was banging the china louder than the situation called for an hour later in the kitchen, but she couldn't help herself. Even though she was standing there staring at the small pan, the Greek coffee boiled over anyway, covering the burner in thick, bubbling brown liquid.

Great.

"Finally I can steal a kiss."

Nick snuck up behind her, his hands skimming over her hips, his mouth resting against her neck.

Efi shouldered him away.

"Ouch." He moved to stand next to her, rubbing his chin where she'd connected in a satisfying way. "What was that for?"

While Aphrodite had disappeared upstairs the minute Nick and his parents had come inside, the damage had already been done. She might as well have been sitting at the dinner table with them, her long legs peeking through the strategic slit in her skirt, her hair sliding over her shoulder so she could push it back with sickening ease.

"Don't you think it a little convenient that Aphrodite just happened to be visiting your cousin Aspa and was on her way here just as you and your parents were leaving the house?"

Nick blinked at her as if he didn't have a clue what she was talking about.

"And just when did Aphrodite and your cousin become such good friends, anyway?"

Nick remained standing, staring at her as she mixed another batch of coffee and put the pan on the burner. When she looked at him, she found his handsome face holding a wide grin.

"You're jealous."

Efi felt the tremendous urge to elbow him in the stomach. So she did.

But she got zero satisfaction out of his loud whoosh.

"I am not jealous," she lied. "I'm just watchful." She waggled her finger. "I don't trust that girl."

"Aphrodite says you've been close ever since you were young."

Sure, when she was a gangly scarecrow who was afraid of her own shadow. "Close being a relative term."

She felt Nick's arm around her waist again and resisted the urge to push him away again. "You really are jealous, aren't you?"

"Well, how would you feel if a great-looking guy jiggled his wares in front of my face and I wiped saliva from my chin as a result?"

Nick raised a brow and she made a face, silently admitting that the imagery wasn't the most effective she could have come up with.

She waved her hands. "I mean, you can't tell me you didn't notice she's got a killer body."

"I noticed. I am a man, after all."

"And, as a man, you, of course, have to appreciate the body's form because, after all, it is natural, right?"

His grin widened. "Hey, you can't ignore what's in front of you."

"And if Aphrodite stripped down in front of you, you wouldn't be able to ignore that either, right?"

Nick's grin disappeared. "Whoa. Now you're putting words into my mouth."

"No, I'm trying to help you notice the big foot you

put into your own mouth." She turned from the stove and poked her finger to his chest. "Going by your reasoning, a guy is only a guy and just as he can't help looking if something's put in front of his face, neither can he resist sampling."

Nick held his hands up. "Okay, this is where I get off this ride."

"Oh, no you don't," she said, grasping his arm. "You're not going anywhere until we have this out."

"You're being irrational, Efi. There's nothing to have out until you're thinking more clearly."

"My thought processes are just fine, thank you very much. It's yours I'm having trouble understanding."

"What was I supposed to do earlier when she asked to ride back here with us? Tell her to walk?"

Efi was about to respond when the sound of raised voices from the other room interrupted her. She and Nick looked toward the closed kitchen door.

Had their parents heard them arguing?

Efi began to lead the way to the other room then remembered to take the coffee off the burner before it boiled over again. She pushed the wooden barrier slightly open as Nick watched from over her shoulder. Nick's mother practically had spittle on the sides of her mouth, while her father looked an inch away from using the butter knife he grasped in his hand.

"You go see what's going on," Efi told Nick. "I'll get the coffee."

But the moment they rejoined their parents, the room had fallen silent, everyone staring at the crumbs left over from dinner on the tablecloth in front of them.

"So…" Efi said quietly. "Tomorrow's the wedding…."

She met Nick's gaze where he sat between his parents across the table from her. He looked at her as if trying to figure out where she was going with her comment, considering their conversation in the kitchen. And perhaps she was trying to lead him somewhere. Perhaps she was looking for him to make some sort of public proclamation that she was the most beautiful, most desirable woman in the world. All right, maybe not in the entire world, but at least when it came to him. Was that too much to ask? Especially when that's the way she felt about him? She couldn't imagine herself being attracted to any other man, no matter how many body parts he jiggled in front of her.

"That's why it's important that we come to an agreement now," Nick's mother, Mimi, said.

Efi squinted at her. "Agreement? What agreement?"

She watched Nick shift uncomfortably. "Mother…"

"Don't talk to your mother in that tone of voice," his father, Stamatis, said.

What way? She wasn't aware that Nick had said anything in any certain way.

Or had he and she wasn't getting it?

"If you had any reservations, you should have brought them up long before tonight," Efi's father said.

"Reservations? What reservations?" Efi's stomach felt leaden with dread.

"In the village where we're from, now is the time for the families to discuss such matters," Stamatis said, puffing out his chest like some sort of rooster lording over his hens.

She watched her father's chest puff out in response. "Yes, well, that explains why no one's ever heard of your village." He snorted. "Village? It's no more than a dot on a map. If it even rates a spot on a map."

Uh-oh...they were trading insults. Not a good sign. The two families had always gotten along well. In fact, both of them had seemed pleased by the engagement, even if his parents found some unnamable something lacking in her. They'd celebrated together. Talked of children. Of shared family vacations in the future.

Now they looked a blink away from physical violence.

"Reservations? What reservations?" she asked more loudly this time.

They all looked at her.

Efi fought the urge to gulp.

Maybe this was it. Maybe the Constantinos had finally named that unnamable something.

Her father gestured widely toward the couple to his left. "Extortion. What they're doing is nothing short of extortion."

Nick's mother's face turned red. "It's a longstanding Greek tradition that the terms of an acceptable dowry are worked out before a couple marries."

"The night before?" Efi's mother said.

Dowry? Had Mimi Constantinos just mentioned the word dowry? But that was something reserved for historical romance novels, wasn't it? The rich duke set to marry an even richer duchess until the poor shopkeeper's daughter catches his eye.

Why was she getting the impression she was cast in the role as the poor shopkeeper's daughter?

"We're not in Greece. We're in America," her father pointed out.

Efi suddenly felt faint.

Silence. Then Efi's mother held her hands out palms up. "All right, okay. This is nothing we all can't handle like rational adults." She stared at her husband next to her. "We knew this was coming."

Her father sat back in his chair. "We knew nothing. We suspected these bloodsuckers had their eyes on my money all along."

Efi gasped. So far as she knew, the Constantinos had money of their own. Plenty of it.

"Papa!" she said.

"It's the truth." He glared at her.

Mimi's hand fluttered to her neck. "I don't think what we're asking for is unreasonable."

Nick cleared his throat. "And just what did you ask for, Mother?"

His father spoke, "That they buy you a house. A respectable house in our neighborhood."

"Or at least provide a sizeable down payment on one," Mimi clarified.

Efi wasn't aware of any discussions being held involving a house.

"Something we were already prepared to do. It was to be our wedding present to our daughter," Gregoris said.

Efi stared at him, tears burning her eyes. "You were? Oh, Papa!" She grabbed his hand and squeezed it.

"But that's not enough for them. They have a list," her mother said.

"A list?" both she and Nick said at the same time.

Mimi moved a napkin that was hiding what indeed appeared to be a list. And a long one at that.

Efi raised both brows.

Nick reached for the list, grabbing it before his mother could stop him. "Buy Nick his own accounting firm." He stared at his parents. "I don't want an accounting firm. I'm happy where I am."

"Now you are happy. But in five years when you have three kids to feed? Will you be happy then?" his mother challenged.

Efi reached across and took the list from him.

A family vacation for ten Constantinos relatives—to celebrate Nick's and her union—to Greece during the high season of summer this year, four-star accommodations…

A new dining-room table for the Constantinos household to accommodate the new family members, to be bought at one of the most exclusive antique shops in Detroit…

An amount of cash to Nick's parents as a show of respect…

Efi's head swam with the words in front of her eyes.

Her father was right: this was blackmail.

"It is only fair," Stamatis said, straightening his tie. "Our son is going to support your daughter for the rest of her life. It is only fair he be compensated for this role."

"And how does a trip to Greece and a new dining-room table—not to mention cash for you—compensate Nick?" Efi couldn't stop herself from asking.

"We raised him," Mimi said.

"Christos kai panayia." She muttered the Greek curse, getting up from the table so fast she knocked over her coffee cup. "My father's right. You are trying to blackmail us."

Nick began getting up. "Efi, this is something our parents should be discussing. We should stay out of it."

She stared at him. "Are you in on this…attempt to extort money from my family?"

"Such disrespect for the man who's going to provide for you and your children?" his mother asked.

Efi stared at her. "I don't need anyone to provide for me, thank you very much. I plan to work for what's mine."

Mimi Constantinos gasped as if the notion was inconceivable.

"Isn't it enough that we're paying for the wedding, including that overpriced party you threw the other night?" her father asked.

Her parents had paid for the Constantinos party? The one with the band and the dancing Aphrodite? She'd known her parents were paying for the wedding, and had even felt a bit guilty about some of expensive things her mother insisted on getting, but she hadn't a clue that they were also springing for the

Constantinos' expenses. For all she knew, her father had also paid for their family to come over from Greece.

She suddenly felt ill.

"I'm going to leave the room before I say something I regret," she whispered, then turned on her heel.

It didn't help her mood one whit when she found Aphrodite standing smiling at her from the top of the steps.

"Stay away from my man," she told her cousin before she stormed into her bedroom and slammed the door.

CHAPTER EIGHT

Day six continued...

A STRIDENT KNOCK at her bedroom door. "Efi, open the door. Now!"

Over the past hour, the plea had been made first by her mother, then by her cousin Aphrodite, and now by her sister Diana who, it was safe to say, probably only wanted access to the room because it was now hers, as well. The house was filled to capacity with relatives and unless her sister wanted to take up residence in the bathtub, Efi's room was it.

"Come on, Efi. You're acting like a twelve-year-old."

She stopped her pacing and strode toward the door and opened it. Diana appeared shocked, as did her mother, her aunt Frosini and every other female relative standing outside the door.

Efi grabbed her sister's arm and hauled her inside, slamming the door closed after her.

"Hey! That hurt."

"You think you know pain? Try feeling what I am right now."

Her sister gave her a record-breaking eye roll. "Come on, Efi. While I won't pretend to know what happened tonight, from what Mom says, you're blowing everything way out of proportion."

Efi stared at her younger sister. "You want to stay in the room or do you want to go back out into the hall?"

Diana made a face.

Efi returned to her pacing.

Her younger sisters Eleni and Jenny had already moved their makeshift bed to their parents' room, to give the bride a quiet night's sleep as well as leave plenty of room in the morning for all the women who would be fluttering about getting ready for the ceremony.

Efi stopped and stared at where her sister stood with her arms crossed over her chest. "Can you believe what they're asking for?"

Diana looked genuinely puzzled. "Who?"

"Who? Who? I'll tell you who. The Constantinos, that's who."

No lightbulb went off behind her sister's eyes.

"I thought Mom briefed you on the night's goings on?"

"She told me you blasted Aphrodite."

"That's why she thinks I've locked myself in my room?" She walked toward the door and shouted at it. "This is not about Aphrodite!"

She hoped her mother and the relatives who had their ears pressed against the wood suffered some hearing loss.

Efi stood with her hands balled at her sides and gave a frustrated shout. "Only the Greeks would find the shallowest, most damning reason for my actions."

Diana sank down on top of their currently shared bed. It was just then that Efi remembered her sister would be inheriting the room with the view of the front lawn rather than her middle room with a view of a tree and the house next door.

Even Diana had motivation to see Efi gone.

"So if Aphrodite isn't to blame, what is?" Diana asked.

"What is?" Efi began pacing again, her entire body seeming to vibrate with suppressed emotion. "For starters, let's begin with Nick's parents trying to blackmail Dad for millions."

Diana's brows shot up.

Efi scowled. "Okay, not millions. But it might as well be, considering the list they presented him with tonight."

Diana sighed. "That's nothing new, Efi. A dowry is part of Greek tradition."

"We're not in Greece." She spoke the words slowly, with deliberate clarity. "And a dowry is maybe a thousand or two to put toward a down payment on a house, or a dining-room set…"

The mention of the furniture made her close her eyes and groan as she recalled her grandfather's bizarre behavior earlier in the day. Her grandfather still refused to apologize, and Gus, his best friend of the past twenty years, refused to drop the charges. The next time the two met would probably be in court.

She heard a sound on the other side of the door and stared at it.

"And yes, I'll admit, I have some issues with our cousin." She couldn't even bring herself to say Aphrodite's name. "I mean, how tacky can you get, openly targeting your cousin's groom the nights leading up to her wedding?"

Diana cracked a smile. "Tacky as tacky can get."

That earned a bit of a smile in return as some of the frustration ebbed from Efi's muscles. She sank down next to her sister. "You can say that again. It was all I could do not to slug her when I saw her with Nick earlier."

"What do you mean you saw her with Nick?"

Efi shrugged. "I guess she found a reason to go over to the Constantinos household, you know, because of a newfound friendship with one of Nick's cousins, and she needed a ride back here. Conveniently enough, Nick and his parents just happened to be coming here for dinner. So when I opened the front door…"

"Ouch," Diana said with a flinch.

"Yeah, ouch."

"You know Nick would never do anything, don't you?"

Efi stared at her wedding dress still hanging on the back of the door. Did she know? She wasn't sure. All she had to do was remember the way he'd danced with Aphrodite, the way he allowed her cousin to get her way, to make it appear as if she was making some headway with him, and Efi began feeling like a dowdy old maid all over again.

"Efi? You do know that, don't you?"

Efi shrugged. "Yeah…I guess."

"No, you *know*. Nick loves you. Always has, always will."

"Yeah, but he's had to go without for the past two weeks."

She realized what she'd said as she and her sister stared at each other. Then they burst out laughing.

Diana pointed a finger at her. "You know, that actually may be to blame for your mood tonight. Lack of sex has a strange impact on a person."

They heard what sounded like a gasp on the other

side of the door. And Efi had to agree with what she guessed was her mother's response. "Diana, you may only be a year younger than me but I'd prefer it if you do not refer to sex in any manner around me until you're at least forty, okay?"

Another eye roll.

"I don't know." Efi rubbed her stocking feet together, glancing at her shoes near the door where she'd kicked them across the room earlier. "Maybe this is what they mean when they talk about cold feet." She looked at her sister. "Do you suppose Nick is going through the same thing?"

Out of the long line of people who had tried to convince her to unlock her bedroom door, Nick hadn't been one of them. Of course, she knew her mother probably hadn't let him anywhere near the stairs, much less her bedroom door, but still…

He had to know something was wrong. Didn't he?

Or did he take their relationship so much for granted that he believed no matter what, she would be at the church tomorrow on time?

Diana put her arm across her shoulders. "So are you done with your temper tantrum now?"

Efi squinted at her. Then she nodded and smiled. "Yes."

"Good. Mom says there's plenty of leftover *ka-rithopita* and I'm dying to dig into it. Let's go."

Efi motioned for her sister to lead the way. She followed her to the door, opened it for her…then slammed it straight after, immediately driving the lock home so she was once again alone in the room.

It wasn't all that long ago that the idea of her mother's walnut cake seemed able to solve any dilemma. But now her problems loomed a little larger than a handful of walnuts, cake and syrup.

SOMEWHERE AROUND MIDNIGHT the knocking finally stopped, the women probably surrendering to sheer exhaustion. The last word had come from her mother.

"We all know what you're going through now, Efi. Get some rest. Everything will look better in the morning."

Efi looked toward her dark window and the fringed purple lampshade reflected in it and sighed. She couldn't imagine anything looking better in the morning. Not the way she felt.

What had begun as a volcanic eruption had dissipated, but the lava flow had coated every inch of her insides so that she felt numb and…well, just plain different. In the course of twelve hours she had gone from a giddy bride to a reluctant bride with a heap of doubts.

She reached for her cell phone on the bedside table. Still no call from Nick. A thousand calls from

Kiki, who had joined the women outside the door at around nine, but nothing from the one person she needed to hear from most.

She clicked the phone closed and put it back down.

If her family was to be believed, tomorrow her entire life would change. Overnight she would go from a young woman with dreams of taking over her father's pasty shop and turning it into a sweet lover's dream, to a wife with nothing to look forward to but her husband's dirty socks and the children, being a drain on him as he worked for her and their family for the rest of his natural life. Not exactly how she had envisioned their life together.

And just how exactly had she envisioned it?

She realized with a start that she really hadn't given it much thought beyond the wedding, the honeymoon and their cozy little apartment.

She pushed from the bed and wandered to her wedding dress. Somehow it seemed sullied by the day's events, the ivory white dimmed by her thoughts and the ache in her heart. She fingered the delicate lace, then before she knew what she was doing, she stripped out of the dress she'd worn for dinner and shrugged into the yards of white fabric. She couldn't do all the back buttons on her own, but she could do enough of them to hold the dress in place. She opened her closet door to access the full-length mirror on the inside and stared at her reflection.

She'd seen herself in the dress no fewer than a dozen times while making up her mind to buy the expensive piece and during alterations. But where her mind had been clouded by visions of being a princess on her wedding day, now her mind seemed frighteningly clear. It was just a dress. Nothing more. Nothing less. A dress that seemed to hide too much in the light of its glaring whiteness.

It was then she realized she couldn't go through with it. As much as she loved Nick, she couldn't go into that church tomorrow and pledge her everlasting devotion to him, without reservations, without doubt. There were too many questions floating around in her mind. Too many things she needed to know. Too far a place for her to get to before the ceremony.

Where that morning she'd been a girl feasting on the dream of a wedding, now she was a mature woman considering the consequences of her actions.

If she let Nick's parents do what they wanted to do to her father, she'd never be able to look them in the face again. And Nick? He hadn't seemed shocked by their requests. In fact, he'd suggested that they allow their parents to hammer everything out.

Efi smoothed her hand down the pretty lace bodice. Is that what the future held? A life as the docile wife chained to home and hearth while her husband dictated the direction of their lives? Was she facing years of holidays and Sunday dinners sitting across from in-laws who saw her as a big price tag instead of appreciating her for the person she was?

A sense of panic so overwhelming ballooned in her chest she thought she might burst with it.

She stepped toward the door, listening to the other side of the wood. She didn't hear anything, but that didn't mean no one was there. She quietly unlocked the door and inched it slightly open to find Kiki, her mother and her sister lying on makeshift beds in the hall outside. Kiki met her gaze and began getting up. Efi quickly closed the door again.

Essentially they were blocking her in. Ironic that she had been the one to initially lock herself in. She had little doubt that if she didn't come out first thing in the morning, they would go in search of a battering ram and crash the door in to gain access. After all, no matter how she felt, or what she was going through, the show must go on.

She rushed toward the front windows and pushed the right one all the way up, staring at the ground below. When she was a teen she used to sneak outside by way of the branches of the old oak. But it had been a number of years since she'd done it.

"Oh, the hell with it."

Bunching up the skirt of her wedding dress, she swung one leg over the ledge, then the other, maintaining a death grip on the window. Her heart beat thickly in her chest as she reached for the nearest branch, fell short and tipped slightly forward.

Oh, God.

She took a deep breath and tried to calm her fear as she reached again. This time she slipped completely from the window and cried out as she frantically grabbed for the tree, catching a branch right before her feet would hit the ground. She swung there for a moment or two, looking around and hoping no one heard her, then let go.

And found herself standing in the familiar cradle of Nick's arms.

"It took you long enough," he said, grinning down at her.

CHAPTER NINE

Very early day seven—W-Day...

THE NUMBNESS EFI HAD FELT permeating her every cell now melted into a dull, throbbing ache. She sat in the car next to Nick, finding it strange that it wasn't all that long ago they were anxious for some alone time so they might fool around. But now that they had it, they couldn't be farther away from each other physically or emotionally.

She didn't know where he was going. Didn't care. All that mattered was that no one was following them, neither of them had their cell phones with them, and time stretched ahead of them like a gaping hole.

"How did you know I was going to climb out the window?"

Again she caught a hint of Nick's grin. But only a hint, because he seemed to be struggling with more than a few demons of his own, given the shadow of concern in his dark eyes.

"I know you," he said quietly. "Or have you forgotten that?"

Yes, she guessed she had forgotten that. She should have expected that he'd be waiting outside for her to drop from her bedroom window. Instead she'd been preoccupied with the fact that he hadn't called her, hadn't tried to bust her door in. And all the while he had been waiting outside for her.

Unfortunately, knowing that now didn't help with what had gone between. The hours of soul-searching, of moving through frustration and anger to a sense of numbness and ultimately an eerie kind of clarity that made her forget she was wearing her wedding dress on the day before her wedding and Nick had seen her in it.

"You're having second thoughts," he said simply.

She looked at him.

"Refer to my earlier reference as to how I know that."

"Because you know me," she said quietly.

She felt his gaze on her while he slowly navigated the empty, winding residential streets of Grosse Point.

"Or do I?" he asked.

Her heart gave a hiccup. If even Nick was questioning his belief in her, then they were in more trouble than she feared.

He ran his right hand through his hair in a way she'd never seen him do before. It was an anxious move, one that spoke of uncertainty and doubt. And made her feel all the more confused.

"Where are we going?" she asked, noticing the way he sped up, leaving the neighborhood and heading for I-94.

"Somewhere we can talk."

THAT SOMEWHERE ENDED UP being a downtown hotel.

Efi's throat tightened and she felt terribly near tears when Nick got out, registered them, then came back out to help her from the car.

"I don't think I'm in the mood for sex right now, Nick."

He eyed her. "Funny, neither am I."

She searched his sober features, wondering just how everything had gone so wrong in such a short period of time. Had it really been earlier that day outside the police station that she couldn't get enough of kissing him, of touching him, of wanting him, restless for him to be her husband?

"Come on. I think it's a good idea if we have a talk."

She didn't move.

He sighed. "Look, I'm not about to go home just yet, and I don't think you are, either. So this is as good an idea as any others I've had." He hiked a brow. "Unless you have one?"

She didn't.

She put her hand in his, feeling the instant jolt she always felt whenever they touched. The realization was both comforting and bewildering. If she doubted everything with her mind, shouldn't her body and its messages follow suit?

Within minutes they were in the nicely appointed hotel room. It boggled the mind to think that she was in the same room with Nick with a bed in it and she wasn't trying to tackle him to it.

She looked down to realize she was still wearing her wedding dress.

"Where are you going?" Nick asked.

"To change out of this thing."

He, too, seemed to realize what she was wearing and it looked as if he'd just swallowed a goose egg whole.

Efi carefully climbed out of the dress in the bathroom and pulled on one of the white Turkish terry-cloth robes from the back of the door. She thought about draping the dress over the bed, but thought the term "big white elephant in the room" all too appropriate and instead managed to hang it on two hangers in the closet.

All too soon she stood facing Nick again. He stared at her as if he didn't know her. And, she suspected, for all intents and purposes that was probably the same way she was staring back at him.

"Well…"

"So…"

They both spoke at the same time, then awkwardly looked away.

Neither said anything for a long stretch. How long, Efi couldn't be sure, but as they stood across the room from each other she felt the gap between them grow larger and larger.

She forced herself to sit on the end of the bed and cleared her throat. "Are you thinking about not going through with this tomorrow?" she asked.

Nick looked shocked by her question. "No, no." His brows drew together. "Are you?"

"No, no," she said equally quickly.

Although given the swiftness of their answers, she doubted the honesty of them.

Both of them were clearly having second thoughts about tomorrow. They just hadn't reached the point where they were willing to admit it.

The mattress dipped low when Nick sat down next to her. Close enough to touch, but far enough apart that they wouldn't.

"This isn't as easy as we thought it was going to be, is it?" he asked, staring at their reflection in the dark television screen.

Efi shook her head. "No, it isn't."

He rubbed his face with his hands. "Do you think this is a matter of cold feet?"

Efi stared down at her stocking feet much as she had earlier when she'd wondered the same thing. "I don't know."

"Me either."

She smiled softly. "Well, that clears things up, doesn't it?"

She felt his gaze on her profile and turned her head to find him studying her.

"You know you always were a smart ass."

"And you always were a mule," she said back.

They'd said the words to each other countless times over the years, but it was usually while they were rolling around on the closest available object, whether it be the back seat of his car or the couch at his parents'—the sentiments were exchanged while in the throes of passion and with affection.

While that affection still existed, it was more serious now somehow. As if they were both realizing the weightiness of the words.

Nick cleared his throat. "About Aphrodite…"

Efi threw her head back and groaned. "No, I don't want to hear it. What's happening now…what's going on…" She held his gaze. "This isn't about Aphrodite, Nick. Sure, I may have been jealous. But deep down I'd like to think I'd known you would never do anything with her."

"I kissed her."

Efi's heart pitched down to rest next to her bare feet.

Nick sighed. "No, actually that's wrong. I didn't kiss her. She kissed me."

"Did you kiss her back?"

"No. But I didn't push her away immediately either."

"Because you thought you might like to kiss her?"

He didn't say anything for a long time.

"Nick?"

"What?" he blinked at her. "Oh. No. When she cornered me at my parents' house inside the bathroom and kissed me I was thinking that I should probably want to kiss her. But I was surprised that I didn't."

Efi swallowed hard, trying to portray a measure of dignity. "Oh?"

"All week long, the guys have been talking about how hot she is. About how I could have her at the drop of a hat. And how you would never have to know anything about it."

Efi really didn't want to hear this. She'd known her cousin had had designs on Nick, but she hadn't known about the rest. And she didn't want to know either.

"Look, Nick, you don't have to explain anything…"

"Yes, yes, I do. Because it was in that bathroom, facing a very attractive woman who apparently wanted me badly, and having her kiss me, that I realized that you're the only one I want."

Efi's throat tightened with emotion. "And that's why you're having second thoughts about the wedding? Because you want me?"

"Yes."

He wasn't making much sense to her. Then again, her own feelings weren't making much sense to her either, so she figured they were pretty much equal.

Except for the Aphrodite kiss. He was way in the hole when it came to that one.

"So I've explained some of what's been going through my mind. How about you?" he asked.

"Your parents."

He stiffened.

Efi's shoulders slumped.

She knew how she would react if he said anything negative about her parents. They were her family, her rock. They were the two most important people in her life up until now. If he so much as said one negative word about either of them she'd probably freak.

But she needed to say this about his parents.

"What happened tonight…what they said…asked for… Well, it came way out of left field for me."

Nick remained silent.

"Did you know they were going to ask for what they did from my father?"

"No."

"But you were okay with it?"

"Yes." He blew out a long breath. "No."

"Then why did you tell me to butt out?"

"I told you to butt out? I didn't tell you to butt out."

"Yes, you did. You told me that perhaps it would be better if we let the four of them work things out."

"Yes. That I did say."

"That's telling me to butt out."

He looked at her for a long moment. "Yes, maybe you're right." He rested his forearms on his knees and clasped his hands together between his legs. "Look, the truth is I didn't know what to say. I don't know. Maybe it's different with your family, but I grew up an only kid. I didn't have any siblings to throw in with. To distract them away from me. It was only just…me. And somewhere down the line I learned that it was easier to go their way than to face a disagreement with them."

Efi smiled softly, longing to push a stray lock of his thick dark hair back from where it rested against his brow. "Until it came to me, that is."

He quickly looked at her. "How do you mean?"

"They didn't want you to marry me."

His spine snapped straight. "I never told you that."

"You didn't have to. I figured it out all by my lonesome."

Nick looked hurt.

"Listen, what your parents thought about me way back then is neither here nor there now," she said quietly. "What's important is that when I needed you to back me up, or at least give me the room to speak my piece, you told me to stick a sock in it."

"I did not."

"Essentially, yes, you did."

He deflated again. "Okay, maybe I did."

Efi pulled the robe more tightly around her, feeling suddenly cold. "All this *is* more complicated than we thought it would be, isn't it?"

He nodded but didn't answer.

"Can I ask you a question, Nick?"

He indicated with his gaze that he was waiting.

"Do you want me to stop working after tomorrow?"

One of those wary expressions kids wore when they'd been asked if they'd washed their hands before dinner crossed his handsome face. "I don't know. Do you want to stop working?"

Efi fought the urge to roll her eyes. "I'm not one of your parents, Nick. There's no wrong way to answer the question."

"Oh, yeah? Then why do I feel like there is?"

"You want me to stop working, don't you?" she asked, surprised.

He turned his head to stare at his hands. "Okay, I admit it—I want to support you. You're going to be my wife and I want to provide for you. For our family."

Efi absorbed his honest answer, a part of her touched by his proclamation. "You know earlier, when I put my wedding dress on, I realized how much I've been looking at this, our marriage, through rose-colored glasses."

He shifted to face her more fully as if something she'd said struck a chord with him. "How so?"

She shrugged and faced him more fully as well. "I don't know. So much energy has gone into planning the wedding, into shopping for dresses, juggling relatives and guests, wrapping *boubounieras,* going to parties…well, I don't think either of us have much talked about what comes after. I mean beyond the obvious. Yes, we'll have our apartment. But aside from that?"

She'd warmed to her subject, finding a string she thought she could follow until it led to the answers she so desperately needed to find.

"I didn't understand until right this minute that you'd wanted me to stay home."

"Do you want to work?"

She stared at him. "Yes, I want to work. What in the world am I going to do all day at home by myself?"

"Raise our children?"

"Children? What children, Nick? It's not like we're going to start popping them out one after another the day after tomorrow."

"Why not?"

She gasped. "Are you serious? You really want my full-time job to be looking after our kids?" She held a hand up. "And where's the plural coming from? Let's start with one—a few years down the road—and see what develops from there."

He looked confused. "But I thought that's what happened. You get married, you have children and…"

Efi waited.

When it appeared he wasn't going to continue, she asked, "And what, Nick?"

He looked at a loss for words. "What what? I don't know. We go on family vacations to Greece. Buy a house in the suburbs. Go to soccer games…"

"And you have a career."

"No, I work."

Efi squinted at him. "Is that really how you view your job?"

"What, you think I enjoy crunching numbers all day, every day?"

"What, you don't think there's something wrong with spending your life doing something you don't like?"

"I didn't say I didn't like it. I said I don't enjoy it."

Efi shook her head and turned her hands palms up. "I love my job at the shop."

He blinked at her. "Really?"

His genuine shock surprised her. "Really."

His expression was so dumbfounded she almost laughed. Almost.

She nudged him in the arm. "Hey, I have an idea. I'll work and you stay home and take care of the kids."

Shock turned to insult. "What?"

She hadn't been serious, but his reaction insulted *her*. "What's so wild about that? People do it all the time nowadays."

"Not people I know."

She didn't know any that did it that way either unless the guy had been laid off or outsourced, but hey, if she loved her work and he didn't...

She leaned back on her hands. "What would you do for a living if you could do anything in the world you wanted to do?"

Back to shock.

"Come on, Nick, the question's not that difficult. Surely you've thought about doing something else."

"Never."

"Never?"

He averted his gaze. "Well, okay, maybe I thought about being an attorney at one point."

"Then why didn't you become one?"

"Because my grades weren't quite up to snuff for a scholarship and I didn't want to ask my father for the money."

"So?"

"So what? Do you know how much law school costs?"

"So? We'll get a student loan."

Her use of the word "we" where moments before it had been her and him caught them both off guard.

Efi smiled at the same time Nick did. Just like that they had become a couple again. Not the same devil-may-care couple that looked only to where they might catch a few minutes alone to heat up the bed-sheets, but rather two individuals who wanted to share everything together.

"We're 'we' again," Nick said.

Efi smile widened. "Yes, I guess we are."

"Does this mean we're on again for tomorrow?"

Efi's heart skipped a beat. While neither of them had ever vocally said the wedding was off, they'd understood that if things hadn't changed between them, it wouldn't have been right for either one of them to go through with the ceremony.

"We need to get a few things straight first," she said, tracing patterns on the bedspread increasingly closer to his leg.

"Such as?"

"Such as I don't stop working at the pastry shop."

He slowly nodded. "Okay."

"That we need to talk further about the children issue."

"But we agree now to have at least two."

"Over a period of years. And not right away."

He considered her. "I can live with that."

Now came the tough one. Efi cleared her throat and pushed forward with it. "And that you put me above your parents."

A painful expression came over his face.

"Nick, it's not what you think. Right here, right now I promise you I will never try to come between you and your parents."

He searched her face. "Then why do I need to put you above my parents?"

"Aside from the fact that I'll be your wife and the mother of your children?"

He nodded.

"To guarantee you don't allow them to come between us."

He thought on that one.

"And I promise to do the same thing with my par-

ents." Although her parents had never tried to come
between them or made any outrageous requests of
him or his family, she thought wryly. "I'm not saying it's going to be easy. Far from it. Your parents are
used to getting what they want from you."

"And I'm used to giving it to them."

She leaned forward on her arms, putting their
faces inches apart and allowing her to stare at his de-
lectable mouth. "Yes, well, now I'm the one you
should be giving all that to."

"Efi?" he asked after staring at her mouth for a
long time.

"Hmm?"

"I'm finding I want to give you much more."

She smiled and kissed him lingeringly. "Oh?"

He groaned. "Mmm. Much more."

"Then what are you waiting for?"

CHAPTER TEN

Day seven...

EFI SAT IN THE BACK of the car that was to take her to the Assumption Greek Orthodox Church. Her father had hired the brand-new black Mercedes and the inside smelled of fine leather, newness...and of nerves.

She toyed with her white gloves, readjusting the sugar cube her mother had tucked inside her right one to guarantee a sweet marriage and life with Nick. Somewhere pinned to her slip where no one could see was one of the Greek eyes that were supposed to ward off evil. She'd never gotten through to the company that had sent the wrong package, but somehow Kiki had scared up a box and her mother had handed the eyes out to everyone on hand, then sent her sister to the church ahead of time to hand one out to everyone else entering the church.

"Marriage is hard enough without having to worry about outsiders interfering," she'd said.

Efi wasn't sure what had happened while she was locked inside her room last night, then at the hotel later with Nick, but this morning she'd discovered a disheveled and glum Aphrodite who, when she wasn't flanked by one of her parents, was flanked by both of them. And whenever she made a move, one or the other would yank her firmly back. Family gossip had it the family was going to arrange a marriage for her back home to an older widower who would know how to keep her in line.

Efi had almost felt sorry for the girl.

Almost.

"Miss, are you ready?"

Efi stared at the driver in the rearview mirror. "No."

He gave her a brief nod.

She'd been sitting in the car for a good ten minutes. Her family had already left for the church, upon her insistence. All that was left to do was for her to get there herself.

Efi rested her hand against her stomach, trying to calm the butterflies there. But far from the strange restlessness she'd experienced last night, this was more nerves than anything. That case of cold feet she suspected most brides experienced before they were to be joined with the one they loved in front of God and everyone.

Or was it?

She heard the click of her swallow over the sound of the car's air conditioner. Last night…

Last night she and Nick had talked in a way they never had before. But everything was far from settled. While they'd made some very good headway, there were still so many things to discuss, so many things to work out. Like if her father refused to allow her to do what she wanted with the shop downtown, she wanted to open her own place nearer Grosse Point, or perhaps even farther north in Royal Oak. That's something she should have discussed with her husband-to-be, right? And what if she'd awakened something in *him* that made him second-guess his own choice of careers? What if he wanted to quit his job and go to law school?

Another swallow.

The door next to her opened and she started.

She'd thought everyone had already gone ahead to the church. Instead she found her aunt Frosini climbing in next to her.

"You're about to make the biggest mistake of your life," the old woman said.

THE DAY WAS SUNNY and warm. The church was packed to overflowing. The best man and woman stood outside with the groom and the two families, waiting for the bride to arrive. For all intents and purposes everything was going according to plan. Only the groom knew the true extent of what had happened the night before. And despite the memorable way he'd come together with the bride, she hadn't said one way or another whether she would be at the church on time.

They'd both returned to their respective homes early that morning and he hadn't been left alone for a moment since. Initially he'd been asked where he'd been, why he hadn't called, but all that was soon forgotten as the festivities leading to where he stood now began. His own father had actually serenaded him. He hadn't known Stamatis Constantinos to sing a note in his life, yet he had gotten down on one knee and sung of a son of whom he was proud and a future that was sure to be bright.

Of course, Nick knew that when he and his new bride returned from their honeymoon he'd have to begin the long process of weaning himself from the influence of his parents, to learn how to put his own direct family—Efi—first. But for this one morning, his last as solely a son, he allowed himself to enjoy being the center of his parents' attention. Even after he'd told them that Efi's parents were not to be asked or expected to give anything to the bride and groom that they wouldn't do normally.

His mother had gasped at the news and fidgeted with her necklace. But his father had merely grinned at him in a way that Nick still wondered about. He'd expected anger, or perhaps even a long discussion where his father might try to convince him what they were asking for was reasonable. Instead Stamatis had grinned at him.

Much as he was grinning at him now.

And now it was Nick fidgeting not with his necklace but with his necktie.

Nearly everyone he knew in his lifetime was gathered for the event. Everyone but Efi.

He felt something on his left shoulder and looked to see Efi's aunt Frosini brushing lint from his suit jacket. She grabbed his chin in her bony fingers and gave him a jostle and a smile, then walked away, her black dress broken slightly by a sky-blue scarf she carried rather than wore.

Strange old woman, Aunt Frosini. For the past week he'd gotten nothing but evil looks from her. He'd feel the hairs at the back of his neck stand up on end and turn around and find her staring at him, as if wishing him some sort of ill will. But now he couldn't help thinking he'd been given a nod of some sort, a vote of confidence that perhaps he hadn't had before, but had somehow earned between then and now.

Or maybe she knew something he didn't....

He squared his shoulders. It was just nerves, he told himself. Efi was coming. Of course she was coming.

Wasn't she?

He looked at his watch. She was already more than forty-five minutes late. While it was tradition for the bride to keep the groom waiting—some sort of dominance thing, much like the stepping on the foot directly after the ceremony—wasn't forty-five minutes too long?

He leaned toward her father. "Who's with her?"

Gregoris Panayotopoulou stared at him beneath his bushy brows. "What do you mean who's with her?" He swept his arm wide. "Do you not see everyone here?"

Nick fought a sudden rush of panic. "No one's with her? She's alone?"

"The driver's with her."

"The driver…"

"Of the car I rented for the occasion."

A stranger…

He reached into his pants pocket for his car keys, only to find them not there. He'd given them to his *koumbaros*—his best man, Alex—for safekeeping.

"Give me my keys," he said, pushing Alex from where he was talking to Kiki in a way that told him there might be another wedding not far in the future.

"Why? Did you forget something out of your car?"

"Just give me the goddamn keys!"

Alex began handing them over. "I wouldn't go just yet."

"Why?"

His friend grinned just as he heard the strident honking of a car horn. "Because your bride just turned the corner."

EFI TOOK HER FATHER'S HAND and climbed from the back of the car. Her pulse beat slightly faster, but nothing she couldn't handle. Her family and friends applauded her appearance as her eyes swept the crowd looking for Nick.

"Are you ready?" her father asked, beaming down proudly at her.

She kissed him on the cheek and nodded.

Then the group parted, opening a path to where Nick waited for her at the bottom of the church steps.

Her heart skipped a beat.

So breathtakingly handsome, this man who was going to be her husband in a few short minutes.

She began walking toward him on her father's arm, her gaze catching on a spot of bright blue as she walked.

Aunt Frosini...

"You're about to make the biggest mistake of your

life," the old woman had said when she'd climbed into the back of the car at the house.

Efi had been afraid she was going to play into all her fears about her coming nuptials. Instead, the old woman had shared with her a story so similar to hers they could have been the same woman.

It seemed when her mother had said Frosini's plans for marriage to a man back in their home village had fallen through and had involved land and goats she had been only partially right. There had also existed an Aphrodite in Frosini's life. A woman, a relative, who had tried to steal her groom from her.

Only ultimately she hadn't had to steal him. Because Frosini had readily given him up.

"I allowed fear to guide my actions," she'd told Efi in the back of that air-conditioned car, the driver trying to appear not to be listening but listening nonetheless.

She'd taken Efi's hands and stared deep into her eyes. "Marry Nick, *agape mou.* Marry Nick and complete the circle I broke so long ago."

Now Efi smiled at the old woman who had lived her life as a single woman, an outcast in Greek society, a person forever relegated to be someone's aunt or pain in the ass.

A woman who had drawn a map for her that led straight to her heart.

Efi's father stopped and she blinked to find she stood at the foot of the steps, looking into Nick's dark, dark eyes. She saw hope and happiness and love. She also saw the same fear of the unknown she felt in the pit of her stomach like a pool of mercury.

Nick held out his hand. Efi looked at it, then back up at him. And when she put her fingers in his, she did so knowing that whatever they faced, they would do it as a couple. In every sense of the word…

Dear Reader,

Having been raised in a primarily Irish family, I hadn't had much experience with Italian weddings… until my own. My husband and I actually had a very small, outdoor wedding, with our closest friends and family at a beautiful mountaintop shrine in Maryland. Yet my very dear mother-in-law did manage to bring a bit of her big Italian family culture into our private, but perfect, wedding.

I honestly had never seen nor heard of a *"boursa"* until she presented me with one she'd handmade for me. A silk and lace purse with bits of blue ribbon, this "purse" was something I was to carry at my reception, to gather gifts of cash from well-wishers. As I said, our wedding was pretty small…so the purse wasn't exactly bulging. But I did treasure it, and have held on to it for my own daughters.

My husband's family also brought a big platter of Italian cookies for the reception, decorated with *"confetti"*…the Jordan Almonds that do, as my mother-in-law informed me, represent the bitter and the sweet of life. Fortunately, the number of colourful almonds mixed in with the delicious cookies did not indicate the number of children we would have…I have three. Not three dozen.

I hope you enjoy this story of a non-Italian woman being welcomed into a big Italian family, with all the love, laughter – and food! – that goes with it.

Happy reading!

Leslie Kelly

* * *

There Goes the Groom

LESLIE KELLY

CHAPTER ONE

IT WAS A BRIDAL GOWN fit for a princess.

Carefully shifting the mountain of silk and lace on her lap, Rachel Grant stroked the delicate material against her fingers, nearly cooing at its softness. Any bride's dream, the dress was traditional in style, with a square neck and tight-fitting long sleeves. A slight sheen in the fabric gave evidence to the quality of the silk, and the lace was so delicate, she was afraid to breathe on it for fear it would disintegrate.

Its pure white color represented the ultimate virgin bride, which made Rachel shake her head. Was there such a thing these days? If so, she hadn't seen much evidence of it since she'd moved here to Chicago to open this bridal boutique with her aunt.

"Who cares?" she whispered. "I'll wear white, too." Then she sighed, acknowledging a few depressing truths. Not only was she pretty far away from a wedding dress of *any* color, considering she hadn't had so much as a date in six months. But also, white wasn't so far off for her. Nope, her only sexual experiences had been high school, back-seat-of-the-car type things where clothes never came fully off for fear of an unexpected pair of headlights.

And since moving to Chicago she'd been about as sexually active as a post-menopausal divorcée.

"Maybe you have to get married to get laid in this town," she muttered, returning her attention to the fabulous dress.

She carefully touched the tiny seed pearls decorating the bodice, telling herself she was merely testing the sturdiness of the sewing. Marveling again at their miniscule size, she peered at the small white roses which accentuated the waistline just above the scalloped layers of lace falling away into the ten-foot long train.

Beautiful. Perfect.

Too bad it belonged to the Nazi Bride of Taylor Avenue.

"Are you checking that over again?"

With a guilty start, Rachel jerked her rapt attention off the mounds of silk and lace, spying her aunt Ginny standing in the doorway to the front of their shop, Wedding Daze. She'd thought she was alone, and had been unable to resist one last, covetous look at the gown, which had arrived earlier this week for one of their clients. "I thought you were already gone. Don't you have to go to the bank?"

Ginny nibbled her bottom lip. "I forgot the money."

Rachel didn't say a word. God love her aunt, whose soft blond hair was showing its first strands of gray, and whose gentle brown eyes were now out-lined by tiny laugh lines.

Ginny was only fifty—and a robust, healthy fifty at that—so that forgetfulness wasn't due to her age. It was just part of the loveable woman's personality. She sometimes said she'd forget to put her clothes on every day if she weren't so self-conscious of her mammoth bustline, which had, according to Ginny, been leading the way through her life since age twelve. Unfortunately, the fifty-year-old had been blessed with Grandma Josephine's hourglass figure, with emphasis on the *top* of the hour.

More unfortunately, so had Rachel.

No, she wasn't in the quad-D sizes, but it sure was tough working around all these beautiful, strapless bridesmaid gowns when the last time Rachel had gone strapless was to her sixth grade dance. And that had been pushing it, particularly since her elementary school boyfriend's nose had been just about eye-level with Rachel's throat. If he'd leaned any closer while they danced, he may as well have used her breasts as a chin rest.

"I think I forgot to take my Ginko Biloba, which is supposed to help me stop forgetting," Ginny said with a helpless sigh. "How can I be expected to re-member to take something for my bad memory, if my memory's too bad to remember to take it?"

Rachel chuckled, acknowledging again why they made such a good team in their fledgling—but thriv-ing—shop. Rachel handled the financial, record-keeping side of the business while Ginny usually focused on the seamstressing and creative stuff. Whenever they took over for each other, the weaknesses inevitably showed. Unfortunately, neither of them were the neatest, most organized people in the world, as evidenced by the back room, which looked like the inside of a white-lined box, with satin, tulle and lace strewn as far as the eye could see.

"I'll take care of the deposit."

Ginny shook her head. "Absolutely not. It's right on my way. Besides you're…busy."

Busy. Busy feeling up another woman's wedding gown. Which was only moderately less embarrassing than feeling up another woman's man. Or another woman.

"I can't say I blame you for drooling over that dress," Ginny said. "It's one of the loveliest I've ever seen."

"I'm not drooling," Rachel replied. I'm *lusting*.

Only over the dress, though. Not over anything else belonging to the Nazi bride. Particularly not her fiancé, who, to Rachel's continued surprise, was a member of a popular, much-loved local family. The Santoris owned an Italian restaurant a few doors down, and were the most warm, welcoming, full-of-life people she'd ever known.

All except Lucas. The Nazi's groom. Oh, he was gorgeous all right, like his brothers. Maybe even a little bit more so, since his brown eyes flashed a hint of danger, unlike his fun-loving, raucous siblings—

at least the ones Rachel had met so far. Raucous Lucas was not. He was sarcastic and moody, an attorney who was about as warm and welcoming as a case of frostbite. Which made him just about perfect for his psycho-bride, Maria Martinelli, who faced a mutiny—if not murder—at the hands of her own harried bridesmaids.

Not to mention her dressmaker.

She'd heard rumors that Luke had once been a charming, flirtatious playboy. According to the mutterings of some of the women on the block, the flirtatious part of him had disappeared the day he'd gotten himself engaged to the daughter of the don of the neighborhood. Rudy Martinelli's ties ran not only to the east coast, in New York, but all the way back to Sicily.

Interesting choice the D.A. had made. Daughter of a man much of Chicago considered a kingpin of crime.

"Seems a shame it's going to be worn by such a she-devil," Ginny murmured. "I bet it would look glorious on you. Have you…."

Oh, no, Rachel wasn't a strong enough—or pathetic enough—woman for that. She wasn't about to start trying on other women's wedding gowns. Doing so would definitely put the exclamation point on the sentence, "Rachel Grant: Loser."

Clearing her throat, she said, "I'm just giving it a last once-over before the bride comes in for her fitting tomorrow. The way she was squawking over hating to have to wear a traditional dress to please her father makes me think she's going to be more unpleasant than usual."

"I think I'll call in sick tomorrow," Ginny said with a heavy sigh.

"Not if I call in sick first."

"Do you think Maddie would…"

"Maddie swore she'd quit if she ever had to deal with the Nazi bride again. Remember?" And they couldn't afford to lose their part-time seamstress. Not if Rachel wanted to have any personal life at all. Wedding Daze had been swamped in the few months since they'd opened and Rachel was only now getting some weekends off because of Maddie's part-time help.

"Come to think of it," Ginny said, nearly bouncing on her toes in excitement, "I have an appointment for my annual GYN exam tomorrow. I made it months ago." She clapped her hands together and lifted her smiling face upward toward the ceiling, as if sending up a prayer of thanks that some guy was going to be poking a big metal object up her…. "So I can't be here."

Rachel groaned. Because that left her. She was the lucky one who got to deal with the Nazi bride. Rising, she regretfully hung the dress back up and zipped it back into its protective cover. "I guess I get to do it. Lucky me."

"Maybe she'll be in a good mood," Ginny said, not sounding optimistic.

"Yeah, and maybe Prince Charming is going to walk through the front door and sweep me off my feet."

"It's possible."

"But it's not very likely," Rachel said with a sigh. "I might get hit on every day, but not by men who could be called Prince Charmings."

"Sure they can," Ginny said with a cheeky smile. "Unfortunately, they're *other* women's Prince Charmings."

Rachel knew exactly what her aunt meant. "More often other women's Sir Scumbags. I swear, if one more groom with cold feet makes a move on me while his bride's in the fitting room, I'm going to go postal on him."

Ginny winked. "Just don't do it near the stock. Blood really doesn't come out of white satin." Turning to leave, she blew Rachel a kiss. "See you tomorrow. After my appointment."

"What time is your appointment?"

"What time does the Nazi bride come in?" Ginny didn't have the guts to turn around and look her in the eye for that one.

"Ginny…"

"Oh, all right. It's at eleven. So I'll be in after lunch."

Nuts. Maria Martinelli's appointment was at ten-thirty. Which Ginny probably darn well knew, judging by the way her shoulders shook with laughter.

Somehow, that laughter lightened Rachel's mood, even after Ginny left. She liked seeing Ginny happy, particularly since the two of them were each other's only family. Ginny had been a second mother from the time Rachel's mom had died ten years ago. After losing Daddy last year, there'd simply been nowhere else she wanted to be than with her only living relative—and very dear friend. The fact that Ginny now lived in Chicago had made the prospect of going into business with her even more exciting. Because Rachel had always longed to visit the big city, so different from her small hometown in North Carolina.

Hearing the bell tinkle over the front door, she smiled and shook her head. Ginny had probably forgotten the deposit *again*. "Maybe you should tie it around your wrist," she called as she entered the front of the store. "Or put it in your bra!"

But she didn't see her buxom aunt. Instead, she spied an eager-looking groom. One with whom she was all too familiar. She groaned softly, recognizing fat-fingers Frank Feeney, whose nice-but-stupid fiancée, Cassie, had left a half-hour ago.

"I'm sorry, we're closed," Rachel said, stiffening as she tried to stare the guy down. "Cassie's gone. You missed her."

Turn around. Turn around and walk out so I don't have to knee you in the groin because you accidentally *touched me one too many times.*

But he didn't. Instead, to her complete dismay, he came all the way into the store, shutting the door—which Ginny had obviously forgotten to lock—behind him. "Well, that's too bad," he said, licking those thick sausage-link lips that matched his thick sausage-link fingers. "But maybe you and I can have a nice chat, anyway."

A nice chat. The last time this guy had tried to have a nice chat, he'd asked her to help him make sure he was ready to be faithful to one woman for the rest of his life. He'd had the perfect suggestion on how to do it.

By having Rachel strip naked for him to see just how long he could resist her.

"I don't think so," she said, her jaw as stiff as her shoulders. "Now I'm going to count to ten, and if you're still here, I'm going to pick up the phone, call your fiancée and tell her what a jerk she's marrying."

The threat didn't appear to phase him. Neither did the numbers she whispered as he stepped ever closer in the shadowy confines of the store. She began to count aloud. "Three, four…."

"Don't be coy," he said, his steady steps never faltering.

For the first time, Rachel felt a twinge of concern. It was past closing time so she couldn't expect anyone to wander in. She had no after-hours appointments scheduled. And the semi-darkened interior, lit only by the lights in the back room, would make it difficult for anyone passing by to see a thing going on inside. "Eight, nine."

"You don't want to do that," he said, his confidence nauseating. "You don't have to play hard to get with me."

Hard to get? As if she'd let this man *get* her?
Not in this lifetime, mister.
Moving her hands behind her back, she felt

around on the counter for the phone. Or a weapon. She found nothing. No scissors, no wickedly sharp, metal letter opener—if they really made those things anywhere but in old black-and-white film noir movies. Finally, though, her fingers closed around the hard base of a plastic bride-and-groom cake topper.

Better than nothing.

But just in case, she also lifted her leg slightly to warm up her knee for action. Then she gave him one final warning glare.

"Ten."

I'M GETTING MARRIED.

Hitched. Tying the knot. Settling down. Goin' to the chapel.

Putting his head in the noose.

He shook off the thought and tried to focus on the truth. *I, Lucas Santori, am getting married.*

He still couldn't believe it. In less than three weeks he would be a married man. Nineteen days until a wedding. A ring. Two ecstatic families. A Knights of Columbus Hall decorated in white, green and red to honor the flag. Tureens of Italian wedding soup and platters of homemade raviolis and red gravy. His two grandmothers arguing over which of them made the best brachiole. Tables overflowing with Italian cookies and confetti—candy coated almonds. A bride carrying a borsa, the white silk bag stuffed to overflowing with cash-filled envelopes. Anisette toasts and cream cake and Rudy Martinelli crying and red-faced as he danced with Maria to the sweet-enough-to-make-you-puke song "Daddy's Little Girl."

Then the crowning moment when the deejay would have them turn to the crowd and would say, "Ladies and gentlemen, meet Mr. and Mrs. Lucas Santori."

Ball and chain, here's my friggin' leg.

Walking down Taylor Avenue on this warm and sunny May afternoon, it seemed impossible that it had really come to this.

Why in God's name had he proposed to Maria Martinelli? When the hell had he fallen in love with her? More importantly, *had* he fallen in love with her? The last couple of months had gone in such a blur, he really couldn't say. He'd fallen all right, but not necessarily in love. Just into an engagement he never would have predicted six months ago.

It had started as a blind date with a neighborhood girl, the daughter of one of his father's boyhood friends. She'd seemed a lot like the women in his family. Friendly, nice, traditional. No, she hadn't inspired any great passion. Which hadn't seemed such a bad thing, since she was a good Catholic girl. Luke hadn't even tried to push their relationship to a more physical level. Somehow, now, with the wedding just a few weeks away, it seemed damn near criminal that he hadn't ever *cared* about their lack of intimacy. That didn't bode well for their sex life.

They'd dated. He'd liked her. His family had been

wildly enthusiastic—as had hers. Then for some un-fathomable reason, he'd found himself putting a ring on her finger, wondering who the insane person was who'd taken over his vocal cords.

And she'd turned into Bride-zilla.

"Joe, it's your fault, you sorry sonofabitch," he muttered, knowing his older brother's blissfully happy marriage of one year and his wife's pregnancy had given Luke sappy visions of the same thing for himself.

"And yours, Tony." Oldest brother Tony was married, too. He and Gloria had two sons and promised the continuation of the Santori way of life, right down to Tony managing the family pizzeria for their Pop.

A guy passing on the sidewalk paused and gave him a strange look, obviously having heard him talking to himself on a public street. Luke merely shrugged. "I'm getting married."

The guy nodded, an expression of understanding—and sympathy—appearing on his face. As he began to walk away again, he muttered, "Three words of advice: run like hell."

Run? Run out on Maria?

Well, that didn't sound so bad. Particularly since he barely recognized the demanding, shrill woman she'd become in the past couple of weeks, so unlike the quiet, traditional, soft-voiced one he'd dated at first.

But running from her father, affectionately called Chicago's godfather by folks in the neighborhood?

Suicide.

Luke knew Rudy wasn't *really* mafia. But he was old school, meaning, easily insulted and not very forgiving.

This errand to the bridal shop was a prime example of Maria's irrational behavior lately. She couldn't make her fitting tomorrow—yet another dental appointment like so many others she'd been going on recently. The woman was going to have more crowns than the Windsors if she kept on at this rate.

But instead of calling the dressmaker to reschedule, she'd begged Luke to go to the shop in person to let them know about the cancellation, claiming the shop owner didn't like her. Which was why he was now strolling down the block from his parents' restaurant—where he'd stopped, as he often did, for a beer after work—toward the boutique.

From what Mama said, the shop owner would likely still be there, working her fingers to the bone. The Santori clan had all but adopted the newcomer to the area, which surprised him, since the sweet-faced little southerner was so unlike his mother, sister or sisters-in-law. But for some reason, Rachel Grant was practically all the women in his family talked about these days.

Probably because they were all too nice to talk about what was *really* on their minds: his upcoming marriage to a diva who made Cher look like a sweet, selfless girl-next-door.

"What have I gotten myself into?" he whispered, shaking his head as he again mulled over the mess he'd made of things.

When he pushed the door open and saw the curvy blonde dressmaker in the arms of a beefy guy in a brown suit, he figured his day had gone from bad to worse. Bad enough he'd just acknowledged he might be facing a marriage without passion.

Much worse, he'd apparently walked in one someone else's amorous moment.

CHAPTER TWO

LUKE STIFFENED when he entered the store and saw Rachel Grant being held by another man. Anything would be better than walking in on a lover's tryst when his own love life had been pretty damned barren lately, so he'd expect a little discomfort. Not anger. Since he was only casually friendly with Rachel, seeing her in another man's arms *couldn't* have been what made his blood start pounding hard in his temple and something like fury seethe through his veins.

Wondering for a brief moment what on earth would have inspired the reaction, he finally chalked it up to embarrassment. *Maria, from now on, do your own dirty work!* Interrupting lovers' trysts wasn't in the groom's job description.

The tryst thing probably wasn't a bad supposition, considering Rachel's incredible, traffic-stopping figure, and her smile which had left Lucas speechless on more than one occasion. Not to mention the emptiness of the shop and the sinfully seductive lingerie hanging on display in one corner of the quiet, closed bridal boutique.

Then Rachel whacked the guy upside the head

with one of those plastic bride and groom statues that went on top of a wedding cake, and all hell broke loose. The bride separated from the groom, who went flying into a rack of wedding shoes. There he sat, like a wooden soldier in a white satin canoe.

The plastic bride—broken and smeared with some red stuff he quickly identified as blood—stuck sideways out of the thick, sandy-colored hair of the jackass in the brown suit.

And Rachel Grant heaved with anger.

"Ow, you hit me!" the amorous guy said, his yelp loud enough to be heard out on the street.

"I gave you fair warning, now get out before I call the police. You can feel free to explain to your fiancée why I am no longer able to do her fittings."

"I'm bleeding." As if shocked by his own words, the guy touched a fingertip to his temple where a miniscule scratch was visible. Then he disentangled the plastic bride's arm from his hair and threw her to the floor.

"I'm sorry I hurt you, Freddy," Rachel conceded, a grudging tone in her voice. "But I had the right to defend myself."

Luke's jaw clenched, as did his hands. His pulse began to throb in his temple as he realized he most certainly hadn't interrupted a tryst. He'd walked in on an *assault*.

"I think I'm gonna need stitches."

"Be glad it wasn't one of the cake knives or you'd be bleeding like a stuck pig," she snapped, obviously having used up her tiny bit of sympathy for the whining assailant.

The man didn't look very glad. In fact, he began to look entirely pissed off. Luke realized the time had come to step in when the stranger's two hammy hands curled into fists and he leaned toward Rachel in a threatening manner.

"Stop right there, *Freddy,*" Luke murmured, his voice steady and even. Probably only those who knew him well would recognize the tone and realize he was damn near furious.

He dealt with some scummy people in his job at the Chicago D.A.'s office, and had prosecuted some really bad ones. None angered him as much as those who abused women or children. "Lay a finger on her and you'll be spending your wedding night in intensive care."

The bastard finally turned around and saw him standing there. So did the blonde—Rachel. Initially, the man's scowl betrayed his annoyance at being interrupted. Then, when he saw the fury on Luke's face—not to mention his tall, threatening form—his eyes widened in fear.

Sighing visibly, Rachel stepped back to lean against the checkout counter. She began to look a little stunned, as if her bravado had been used up and she'd realized this bastard might have hurt her had Luke not arrived on the scene.

"You okay?" Luke asked as he strode across the

store to her side, taking her arm to steady her since she suddenly appeared a bit wobbly on her feet.

She nodded.

"You want me to call the police?"

"This is none of your business," the other man blustered. "Besides, it wasn't what it looked like."

"Yes, it was," Rachel said, bringing a hand to her face and pushing a long strand of her pale blond hair off her cheek.

Her hand shook. But her voice didn't.

Luke glanced at the counter. "Where's the phone?"

"Don't," the man said, sounding desperate. "I'm sorry, I obviously misread your signals."

Rachel Grant's spine snapped straight and fire appeared in her eyes as she stared the man down. Obviously her quick flash of uncertainty had evaporated. "Signals? What signals would those be? The dozen times I've told you 'no'? The afternoon last week when I said I'd rather stick flaming pins in my eyes than have anything to do with you?"

Luke waited, letting Rachel decide how to handle things. He had to hand it to her, she wasn't getting all hysterical or weepy, the way a lot of women might after being physically manhandled by a letch who couldn't take no for an answer. In fact, she was holding up remarkably well.

He'd met the woman several times at his parents' place, but he hadn't formed too deep an impression of her—beyond acknowledging her beauty and her

smile, which made everyone around her feel warm
and happy. Including him. And, of course, that if he
hadn't been stupid enough to go and get himself engaged to someone he wasn't even sure he liked anymore—much less loved—he would definitely have
wanted to get to know her better.

Now, however, he was seeing past the thick blond
hair, the wide blue eyes, the pretty face and the curvy
figure. She was tough. Smart. Good under pressure.

"Please, I just got cold feet. I love Cassie and I
didn't mean any harm," the now-sweaty and red-
faced Freddy said.

Rachel paused, then muttered, "Go, before I
change my mind and let him call 911."

She was also forgiving.

The guy left so fast Luke didn't even have time to
give him a little shove for good measure. He thought
about going after him, or calling his brother Mark,
who worked on the Chicago P.D. Two things stopped
him from doing it: the man's "cold feet" remark—
since his own felt like frigging icicles these days.

And the sound of Rachel Grant's harsh, ragged
breathing.

Once they were alone in the store, he hesitated,
wondering if he should leave now, giving the woman
a chance to pull herself together. Another part of
him—the big brother part who'd rip out the throat out
of any man who tried something like that on his baby
sister Lottie—instead reacted with pure instinct.

He held out his arms.

And she dove right into them.

RACHEL COULDN'T SEEM to stop shaking. She wasn't prone to hysterics, and her eyes weren't full of tears. Concern hadn't given way to fear, nor was she shocked by what had just happened. But she couldn't stop the shivers racing up and down her spine, making her legs weak and her breaths choppy.

The ugly scene with fat-fingers Freddy hadn't come as a complete surprise, given the man's persistent come-ons at earlier meetings. Still, she'd never expected him to put his hands on her against her will. And her worst nightmares hadn't prepared her for a sloppy kiss from those big, squishy lips, which looked like two fat, bloated worms ready for the fishhook.

Yuck. The memory made her shiver some more.

When she'd moved to Chicago, she'd never imagined having to defend herself against a man who was about to pledge to love, honor and cherish a nice, friendly woman like Cassie-the-twit. She'd certainly never expected to get more attention from men at work than she'd ever had helping manage her father's dry cleaning business in North Carolina. Why would she, when the only male customers she ever saw were engaged to be married?

Grooms were supposed to hit on strippers. Women who popped out of cakes at bachelor parties.

Not dressmakers who'd measured their brides for their wedding gowns.

"Shh, it's okay, don't cry," she heard, the soft male whisper tickling the hair at her temple as his warm breaths touched her cheek. "He's gone, honey, he can't hurt you anymore."

She supposed the slow, deep shudders wracking her chest seemed like sobs to the big, solid man she was pressed against.

Very big. Very hard. Very warm.

Absolutely delightful.

Awareness washed over her. Awareness of the breadth of his firm body, just beneath her fingers, which were tightly clenching his shirt. The dress shirt was unbuttoned at the neck, and Rachel's mouth was an inch away from the tanned skin of his throat. She inhaled his spicy, masculine scent, watching the way a few springy, black hairs on his chest moved beneath her slowly released exhalations.

His heartbeat was strong. Rapid. She could feel it since they were pressed tightly together. Rachel's breasts suddenly felt heavier, more sensitive, almost tingling as he shifted a tiny bit, so their bodies scraped even more delicately against one another.

Their hips touched, as did their thighs. His trousers brushed against her bare calves, and one of her feet had slid between both of his. If they were sitting, she'd be straddling his thigh. The thought made pure warmth and liquid heat ooze through her body, to settle with insistence between her legs.

Oh, God, what was happening to her? Comfort had changed to something else—something heady and wicked and dangerous. She was mentally cataloguing how seductively perfect it felt to be in his arms, how much she suddenly *wanted* this man.

This man. Luke Santori. The man she'd decided must have been adopted because of how unlike his easy-going brothers he was.

Boy, had she been mistaken. How on earth could she ever have thought Luke was cold when his whole form gave off such sizzling heat? Not to mention the tender, sweet way he stroked her back, making soothing sounds against her temple. Saying more soft things she couldn't quite make out, beyond the word "safe."

Safe? Good Lord, she was nowhere near safe. This was the Nazi bride's groom and here she was curling into him like a stripper against a pole. She jerked back, bringing her shaky fingers to her mouth, trying to regain control of herself.

"Rachel?"

She gave him a slow nod, silently telling him she was okay, though, in truth, she was anything but.

"You sure you don't want me to call Mark?"

"Mark?"

"My brother. He's a cop and his station's not too far from here."

Another big hunky Santori brother to fill up every molecule in this suddenly small-feeling shop? *No, thanks.* Her senses were already on overload, pushing her into dangerously aware territory. Territory she had no business even glancing at, much less curling up against.

Engaged man territory.

"I don't think so. I'm okay, and I somehow doubt he'll be back. Especially if his fiancée starts questioning him about the cut on his head." Still feeling too close, too affected by a man she had no business being affected by, Rachel stepped away, retrieving the poor little groom figurine, who'd landed among the white satin wedding shoe display.

"Who was that guy?" Luke asked, leaning one hip against the counter and crossing his arms in front of his chest.

"The husband-to-be of one of my customers."

He frowned. "Nice."

Hearing his sarcasm, she for some reason felt compelled to elaborate. "It's not as uncommon as you think. Grooms with cold feet seem to think the dressmaker's their last chance for a fling." She grinned wryly. "I suppose they consider me a safer bet than risking communicable diseases at their bachelor parties."

A flash of something like anger made his eyes blaze and his jaw tighten. "This has happened before? Why don't you have a panic alarm or something?"

She shook her head. "Nothing like *this* has happened before. It's usually harmless flirtation. But it's still annoying."

"It's more than annoying." His jaw remained tight, his pulse visible in his temple. "What if I hadn't shown up here?"

"I didn't feel in any real danger."

Until you walked in.

"Do you know self-defense?"

"Like karate or something?"

He nodded.

"Uh…no. But my knee can do some damage. And I think my fingers are bony enough that if I punched a guy in the throat I could make it pretty darn hard for him to breathe."

Rolling his eyes, grabbed her hand and lifted it. "Oh, yes, you should really register these things as lethal weapons."

Only his obvious disapproval kept her from yanking her hand away in shock. Because she was apparently the only one of them who had felt the amazing flash of electric heat when their fingers had touched.

"I think Freddy's neck was too fat for you to find his Adam's Apple," Luke said, still tsking, but now sounding slightly amused. "A finger in the eye is probably a safer bet."

"I prefer the good old knee to the groin."

"With nutless cowards like him, you might have a hard time hitting the target."

His disgusted words startled a laugh from her lips. "Poor Cassie."

"Cassie?"

"His fiancée."

Finally realizing Luke was still holding her fingers, Rachel slowly pulled them away. She also sent a silent message to her heart to quit its ridiculous

super-sonic beating and get back to its regular, uninterested, professional-woman rhythm.

"Thank you," she finally murmured. "I'm glad
you showed up."

He met her steady stare and nodded to acknowledge
her thanks. Then they both fell silent. Just…staring.

He looked at her as though he'd never met her before, and she couldn't tug her gaze away from his
dark brown eyes, sparkling with warmth and energy.
Not cold. Nowhere near cold.

"You *do* know who I am, right?" he finally murmured, filling what had been a long, though not uncomfortable, silence.

"Sure." She cleared her throat, figuring her wildly
swinging emotions were causing that warble in her
voice, and the weakness in her legs. "We've met at
your parents' restaurant."

"I wondered if you remembered. Every time I see
you, you look the other way or walk out the door."
His words, though, light and teasing, held a hint of
accusation.

She couldn't deny it. She *had* avoided him, thinking she was doing it because she didn't like the third
Santori brother, who wasn't as playful and friendly
as his two older siblings.

The happily married ones.

Now she suspected she'd been avoiding him for
another reason. Because she found him *too* attractive.
Definitely too attractive for a man scheduled to marry
someone else in less than a month.

Reading about him in the papers had made him even more interesting to her. Lucas Santori was a hotshot in the D.A.'s office and was often mentioned by the media for his anti-crime crusade. And of course, she couldn't help but hear about him from his very proud parents, who liked to brag about their sons who fought bad guys—as cops, soldiers, or, in Luke's case, prosecutors.

"How's Maria?" she asked, trying to busy her hands with some useless paperwork on the counter. Receipts, order forms, ad copy…none of which seemed to have any words right now, just dark, blurry specks on which she couldn't concentrate. He didn't reply right away, and she looked up in curiosity.

Lucas seemed a bit stiffer, as if he wasn't comfortable talking about his fiancée. Considering Maria was as well liked as your average everyday serial killer, Rachel could understand why.

"Getting jittery. She's actually the reason I came down here," he finally admitted.

"Oh? Don't tell me the wedding's off and I'm going to get stuck with that twenty-thousand-dollar dress."

Luke's jaw dropped open and his eyes widened. "Twenty…"

Grimacing and cursing herself for her big mouth, Rachel forced a laugh and shook her head. "I was exaggerating."

Though not by much.

"She's, uh, not going to be able to make her appointment tomorrow."

Another cancellation. Why was she not surprised? "What if it needs alterations? We're not dealing with the normal turnaround time here, since she changed her mind so many times before settling on a dress."

"I'm sorry."

"She *does* remember the wedding is less than three weeks away, right?" she asked before she could stop her runaway tongue.

"How could any of us forget?" Luke asked, sounding almost mournful.

She chose to chalk his tone up to standard pre-wedding guy-talk. Not anything more personal. Certainly not an indication that Lucas wasn't exactly thrilled about his upcoming marriage.

Even if he was, it was none of her concern.

"It'll all come together," she said, wanting to comfort him for some reason. "Everyone is stressed this close to the big day. It's perfectly normal."

"Speaking from personal experience?"

His gaze shifted to her left hand and she instinctively curled her ringless fingers. Forcing herself to focus on totaling the day's receipts, she said, "Just from being in the business. Not personal experience. I'm completely unattached."

Now, why on earth had she needed to volunteer that tidbit? Lord have mercy, this man was making her jumpy and uptight. She couldn't control what was coming out of her mouth…odd for Rachel, who was usually adept at hiding her true thoughts since the customer always had to be right. Even a customer who insisted on a strapless gown when she had no breasts to hold it up, or a halter one when her rolls of back fat were hanging out all over the place.

If asked for her opinion, she gave it as carefully as possible. If not, she kept her mouth shut.

"No wonder my mother likes you," Luke said, breaking into a rueful smile.

Oh, he looked amazing when he smiled. So amazing she lost track of the short column of numbers she'd been mentally adding.

"Why?" she couldn't help asking.

"Well," he said, a twinkle visible in his brown eyes, "because she's a consummate matchmaker. With very available sons."

"The engagement *is* off?" she squeaked out, shocked into asking the question. Of course, she realized her mistake a half a second after the stupid words left her silly tongue.

He stared at her. Hard. "I meant my brothers. The twins."

"Oh, of course."

Candy apple red. The color of her first car. Her favorite lipstick. And now, her face.

Luke apparently noticed. He continued to stare, his gaze questioning as he studied her cheeks, her hair, her lips. Then finally, sounding almost confused, he asked, "Why did you assume it was me?"

She could tell him one of a number of truths. She could admit she found him incredibly attractive. Could tell him she'd been trying to convince herself she didn't like him when, in actuality, she probably liked him more than a nice woman who respected other women's boundaries should.

Or she could tell him it was a natural assumption, considering he was marrying a cast iron bitch.

Instead, she lied. "Oh, I didn't. I was joking."

Lame, Rachel. Very lame.

Finished with the receipts, she rubber-banded them together, stuck them in a manila envelope, and carried them to a shelf loaded with shoeboxes of varying size, shape and condition behind the counter. After checking the dates, she found this month's box, opened it, and put the receipts inside.

"Now, there's an effective filing system," Luke murmured, sounding amused.

She glanced over her shoulder. "Don't I know it. But only for one more day. We have a desk with built-in file drawers being delivered tomorrow and I'm going to get organized if it kills me." Then she looked around, unable to hide a sigh. "Which means I need to get to work. I have furniture to move around before it shows up, and I need to clear a big place on the back room floor to put things together."

She hadn't been hinting around for his help. She *hadn't.*

"Can I give you a hand?"

Drat. Okay, maybe she had. But only because she could use some help. Not because she, uh, wanted him to stay or anything. Any pair of hands would be useful.

Especially big, strong male ones, connected to thick, muscular arms that looked like they belonged on a lumberjack rather than an attorney.

Okay, bad thought. She obviously wanted him to stay for all the wrong reasons. *Say no. Say no and get away from him now before you get in any deeper.*

Once again, however, her tongue moved without any interference from her brain. "Thanks. That'd be great."

CHAPTER THREE

RACHEL REALLY *had* needed his help. Luke kept reminding himself of that over the next hour as they emptied boxes and folded them out of the way, rearranged an old bookcase and disassembled some shelves. Slowly but surely they made space in the tiny, crowded back room of the dress shop.

Tiny. Crowded. Dangerous.

"Whoops, sorry," she mumbled when she slipped on a scrap of lace, bumping against his side.

That was the dangerous part.

"It's okay," he said, biting the words out from between tightly clenched teeth.

Liar. In no way was it okay.

Because the enforced proximity had made the two of them brush against each other more than once. Each contact—though innocent—shocked him, until he remained on edge, expectant, waiting for the next brush of her hand, or slide of her shoulder against his. Or just the feel of her long, silky hair flitting across his skin when she tossed it back to get it out of her face.

It was the heat of the closed-in space, the unexpectedness of it, that was all. It had nothing to do with the sunniness of her smile, or the throaty warmth of her laugh. It was completely unconnected to those clear, sparkling eyes or the slight southern twang in her voice.

But even as he told himself that, he wondered if he was wrong. Because he had never reacted this way—with such instant awareness—to anyone before.

Not until today. Three weeks before his wedding. *Hell.*

He should have followed Mr. Brown Suit out the door. Instead he'd stayed. And gotten himself into some completely unexpected trouble. Not merely because of his cold feet or her killer smile. No, what had really done him in was that he liked her. Really, truly, liked her.

"So, earlier, when you said you need space to 'put things together' you weren't talking about the actual furniture, were you?" he said as they finished a final trip to the Dumpster in the back, now filled with scraps of wood and shoeboxes.

She nodded.

He persisted. "As in assembling?"

"Yes." Seeing his skepticism, she fisted her hand, put it on her hip, and tilted her head back. "I know how to use basic tools."

He followed her stare and noted the rinky-dink toolbox. His three-year-old nephew had sturdier looking stuff in his toy box. "You're going to use that?"

"I'll be fine," she insisted, her tone allowing for no

further argument. Then, as if realizing she might have sounded ungrateful, she added, "I so appreciate your help, even though you really didn't have to stay…"

They'd gone over that a few times already. "Forget it. I'd be willing to bet you put in some overtime hours on my behalf in recent weeks."

She glanced up, appearing puzzled. "I don't know what you mean."

"Well, I know there's been a lot of…*indecisiveness* with my family."

The confusion disappeared from her face, and she chuckled. "Oh, you mean the four different bridesmaids gown styles? The three shades of pink? The two types of headdress?"

"And the partridge in a pear tree," he said, unable to hold in a rueful chuckle.

Her eyes sparkled as she laughed with him. "It's not so bad. Weddings are pretty…"

"Torturous?"

She tsked. "I was going to say energetic."

"Yeah. Like the electric chair." Electric chair. Condemned man. Kinda fit the direction of his thoughts these days.

"Pessimist," she said with an amused frown.

"Optimist."

Her eyes narrowed and she said, *"Man,"* as if getting the last word with the ultimate insult.

He couldn't help replying, with equally exaggerated disgust, *"Woman."*

Their playful bickering brought a feeling of pleasure deep inside Luke's body as he acknowledged how relaxed he felt in this woman's company. He hadn't felt this way for a long time. A *very* long time. *Why didn't I meet her six months ago?*

"I hope this desk isn't too big," he said, looking around the circle they'd managed to clear in the back room.

"It's huge." She didn't sound worried. Again the optimist. "I think my aunt pictures it doubling as a back-up sewing table, but I plan to keep it perfectly neat and for business only. She'll probably be disappointed when she sees how organized and professional I'm going to make this place."

He raised a brow, unable to help it. Given the woman's shoebox filing system, he wondered just how organized she was going to be.

Rachel seemed to sense his skepticism and she frowned. "I *am* organized and businesslike."

"Uh-huh."

Her eyes narrowed. "*Very* organized."

He didn't say a word, merely letting his gaze fall on the teetering pile of bridal magazines in one corner and the haphazard stack of packing boxes in another. They hadn't been shoved there during the rearranging, but had remained exactly where they'd been when he arrived.

Following his stare, Rachel blew out a long breath and swept a strand of hair off her face. It was a nervous habit, one that caught his eye every time. When she was deep in thought—or nervous—she shoved her hair out of the way as if it was an unwelcome shroud instead of the pure spun gold that looked softer than any silk gown in this place.

He gulped the image away, returning his attention to the job at hand.

"Okay," she admitted, her tone grudging. "Organization has never been a strong suit of mine. Or Ginny's. But my father did teach me a lot about bookkeeping and management. If you looked at our books, I'm sure you'd be very impressed."

"As opposed to being terrified when I look around this maze and wonder if I'm going to stumble over a dead body back here?"

"Well, *that* was gentlemanly," she said with a half-smile, not sounding offended.

"I'm not the gentleman of the family."

"I know."

"Zing right back."

She flushed. "I mean your brother Joe seems to hold that title. He's so polite and all."

Joe? Luke almost laughed. "Joe considers himself a hammer jockey. I think he'd be crushed if he thought women didn't consider him rugged and dangerous."

"Meg certainly doesn't."

No, Joe's wife of one year, Meg, considered him her other half, which, to anyone who knew them, appeared absolutely true. They were so blissfully in love it made his teeth hurt to be around them. He still really needed to deck his brother for that, consider-

ing the trouble Joe's sappy "happily married" talk
had caused for Luke lately.

"By the way," Luke said, remembering her words,
"I think I've been exceedingly polite this afternoon."

Rachel winced in embarrassment. "I'm sorry,
you're right, you've been wonderful."

Their stares met. Held. The air—already stuffy—
grew more heated, until finally Rachel cleared her
throat and added, "And so is your family. Your
sisters-in-law and your sister Lottie have been real
angels to deal with."

He let her get away with changing the subject to
a very innocuous one. Because they had no business
thinking *wonderful* thoughts about each other. No
business at all. "Thanks. They are all pretty great."

She nodded. "And determined. Gloria says she'd
get the last of her baby weight off or else she'd wear
four body girdles, but there was no way she'd let me
order a bigger size bridesmaid gown than her pre-
pregnancy one."

Lucas flinched just at the thought of women and
their torturous contraptions of beauty. "Tony's wife.
She's as bossy as a real big sister."

"I know. With the two adorable little boys. I guess
they're keeping up the family tradition."

"Well, God help them if they have five of them
like my parents did."

"I've never heard your parents complain. In fact,
to hear your mother tell it, her boys are'a'da best men
in all-a-Shee-ca-gooo."

She did a lousy job of imitating his mother's thick Italian accent, particularly with the twangy, musical lilt to her voice, but he didn't have the heart to tell her. Especially because she looked so darn cute when doing it. "How about you? Lots of siblings?"

She shook her head. "Only child." Her eyes clouded a little. "My father died last year, and my only family is now Aunt Ginny, who's been a surrogate mother—and friend—for a long time."

He nodded and remained quiet for a moment, in silent understanding. Then, wanting to lighten the moment, he shook his head. "So, no sisters or brothers. Meaning you never had the joy of the big hand-me-down marathon during Labor Day weekend before back-to-school."

Raising a brow, she said, "No, I'm afraid not."

"Fortunately," he explained, "I was always the same height as Joe, even though he's a year older. So jeans that were too short for him got passed down to Mark or Nick."

The words were an opening he hadn't intended, and she reacted to them. Her gaze traveled over him, from head to toe, as if assessing his height, his build. Her lips parted as she drew in a deep, slow breath, and he nearly groaned when she slipped her tongue out to moisten them. The atmosphere thickened yet again. No matter how many times either of them tried to retreat behind a wall of friendly, casual conversation, they kept coming back to this. This unexpected attraction. That was the only word for it—it wasn't just awareness. It was attraction. On both their parts.

Which left him with only one choice. No more retreating behind words or laughter or desks. It was time to get out of here for real.

And after making his excuses and brushing off her thanks, that's exactly what he did.

"I'M ALMOST THERE. I'm so close," Gloria Santori said, her face mottled red with exertion as she hissed the words between clenched teeth. "A little more. One…more…inch…. Yes, yes, oooh…"

"For cripe's sake, Gloria, you sound like you're doing a porn movie."

Surprised into a laugh by the caustic tone of Luke's sister, Lottie, Rachel looked around the fitting room of the shop to see everyone else laughing as well. Even red-faced Gloria—who'd been trying desperately to fit into her bridesmaid gown—chuckled. Then she shot her sister-in-law a glare. "Oh, look what you did. Now I have to suck it in all over again."

So far, the entire afternoon had been like this—fun and raucous, silly and companionable. Like it always was when with the Santori clan, though, this time, only the women of the family were around. Rachel was enjoying herself tremendously just sitting back and watching the interactions of this close-knit group.

Closest to Gloria—who was already turning blue from lack of oxygen as she tried again to zip up the too-tight dress she refused to have let-out—sat

Luke's mother. Mrs. Santori wore a brightly colored, flowered sundress that made her look much too young to be the mother of six adults. In the months since she'd met her, Rachel had never seen the Santori matriarch in anything but a dress. And, as usual, she wore a small pin with the colors of the Italian flag. The woman's jewelry always reflected her ethnicity. Sometimes it was something as simple as a pin made of dried pasta.

Luke's sister, Lottie, sat beside her mother. Slumped back in her chair in boredom, her long legs were sprawled out in front of her and crossed at the ankle. She'd inherited her family's dark hair and eyes, like her brothers, but thankfully not the masculine features that made her older siblings so striking. Instead, she had her mother's soft, round face, and wide smile—though her biting wit and scruffy clothes labeled her the tomboy Rachel suspected her to be.

Sitting on the other side of Gloria, with her swollen feet resting on another chair, sat Meg, Joe's wife. She watched the goings-on with a Madonna-like smile, absently rubbing her large stomach and asking the baby within to give her kidneys a break or to get his foot out of her rib cage.

Both of Luke's grandmothers, one of his aunts and two of his female cousins had come in earlier. Since they weren't part of the bridal party, however, they'd been much easier to deal with, and had already departed.

Rachel blessed the day the Santori women had decided to give all their wedding patronage to her fledgling shop. They'd put she and Ginny in the black within two months of their grand opening.

The only one absent from this family event was the bride. Who, to be honest, nobody seemed to be missing.

"Mary mother of God," Mrs. Santori said with a definite huff, "Gloria, you're going to pop the seams. Let Rachel do her job and give you an extra inch."

Four would be better. But Rachel kept her mouth shut.

"Yeah, the size tag will still say eight," Lottie said. "You said that was all you wanted, to fit into a size eight. You never said it couldn't be an *altered* size eight."

Gloria cast a hopeful glance toward Rachel, who hurried to agree. "Oh, absolutely. The size on the tag is the only one that matters." Then, not untruthfully, she added, "I work with these dresses all the time and they all run much smaller than standard sizes."

The oldest Santori daughter-in-law finally stopped trying to tug the zipper up her back, and lowered it instead. She immediately heaved a deep breath, her face returning to its normal color. "Oh, thank God. I was about ready to try water pills and laxatives."

Luke's mother made the sign of the cross. "And how would that have affected the baby?"

Gloria twirled around as Rachel went to work with the measuring tape and pins. "I stopped nursing last month." Giving Rachel a mischievous grin in the mirror, she added, "Baby Mikey is six months old now, and Tony isn't the most patient man in the world."

If Gloria had thought she'd shock her mother-in-law, she'd obviously guessed wrong. Mrs. Santori merely smirked. "So, I guess you never tell my Tony they are fine to play with when they're not full to bursting like a pair of water balloons?"

Lottie snorted. Gloria grinned. Rachel chuckled under her breath. And Meg, growing pale, murmured, "Uh, water balloons?"

"All done," Rachel said, before the conversation turned to breast-feeding and breasts and Santori men playing with said breasts.

Rachel couldn't go there. Not even in her mind. Not without feeling all tingly, just at the thought of being touched by one of those men in particular. The one whose bride should have been here, the center of attention, right now.

"So what was Maria's excuse for not showing up this time?" Lottie asked, not hiding a frown.

Her mother pursed her lips. "She has a dentist appointment."

"Huh. You know, it kinda says something about a bride if she'd rather get a root canal than get fitted for her wedding dress." The other women mumbled and Meg coughed into her fist, but Lottie appeared unrepentant. "Oh, come on, you know it as well as I do. She's about as interested in getting married as I'm interested in staying a virgin until my wedding night."

Mrs. Santori grabbed the gold cross hanging around her neck and raised her eyes heavenward. "Lottie!"

The young woman flushed a little, shifted in her chair, and re-crossed her legs. "Sorry." Not too sorry, because she persisted. "But it's true. I hear her latest demands are that there be no mother's cakes and no Italian food of any kind at the wedding? She's decided to call in some French caterer at the last minute?"

Mrs. Santori blanched and her lips tightened. But she merely shrugged. "It is not our wedding."

Lottie shook her head in disgust, then shrugged. "I guess we can look on the bright side. Today sure has been a lot more pleasant than it would have been if she was here."

"That's not nice to say about your brother's fiancée," Mrs. Santori said with a hard stare.

"I know. But we're all thinking it, aren't we?" Lottie retorted, glancing around at all of them, as if daring them to deny it.

Mrs. Santori didn't answer. Neither did Gloria. Or Meg.

Rachel continued to work, staying out of this family discussion. But she couldn't help feeling very, very curious.

Maria didn't seem too anxious to get on with this wedding, judging by her complete disinterest in her own gown. Lucas's family didn't seem too happy about things, either.

Which left her wondering…how, exactly, did the groom feel about his upcoming nuptials?

CHAPTER FOUR

LUKE TRIED TO KEEP his mind off Rachel Grant the next day, knowing it was not only wrong but also dangerous to be thinking so much about a woman other than the one he was supposed to marry in a short time.

But he couldn't get her out of his head. Her smile. Her husky voice. The unconscious grace in her movements. The affection in her eye when she spoke of people she cared about—like Luke's own family. The resolution in her voice when she talked of using her delicate little fingers as lethal weapons against offensive oafs like the one yesterday.

"Get out of my head," he whispered as he parked his SUV outside his parents' restaurant after work.

She wouldn't. She certainly hadn't gotten out of his head throughout the long, sleepless night before, or today at work when he'd had a hard time concentrating on a thing anyone said to him. His co-workers chalked it up to pre-wedding distractions. Hmm. He guessed wondering if he'd made a terrible mistake and proposed to the wrong woman a few months be-

fore meeting someone who could be the *right* one—
would be distracting for anyone.

Why hadn't he met Rachel first?

Or not at all.

No. He couldn't even *pretend* he wished that. Especially on days like today, when he'd spent all
morning on the phone with Maria, who'd suddenly
decided she hated every single thing about their wedding plans, from the food to the dress to the music.

He'd bowed out of the food and the music. But
he'd pinned her down on the dress, rightfully saying
there was no time to order another one.

Yet even as he'd said it, he'd been worrying more
about Rachel—and how the rejection of a twenty
thousand dollar gown might affect her business—
than he had about his high-strung fiancée.

"Eyes front," he muttered under his breath as he
got out of his car and walked around it to the sidewalk. Ten steps to the awning; a few more until he
was inside with his parents, his brother, the regulars.

But his eyes weren't obeying his brain. They
shifted, looking left. Up the block. Toward the bridal shop.

A panel truck was double-parked at the curb in
front of Rachel's building. Watching a uniformed
deliveryman exit the store, pushing a large dolly, he
remembered the desk she'd been preparing for last
night. She'd gotten her delivery. Which meant she
was sitting up there again this evening, with her little screwdriver and her small hammer out of her

Tonka Toy toolbox, about to set up a desk that probably weighed more than she did.

"Not your concern," he reminded himself.

But his feet didn't listen to his brain any better than his eyes did. Because he suddenly found himself turning away from the restaurant, and striding a few doors up the street.

When he got to the boutique, he figured he'd just peek inside, make sure Rachel had help with her task, then slip away. Nice and easy. A look, that was all.

But she didn't have help. Luke couldn't contain a groan when he saw her in there, trying with all her might to tug at an enormous cardboard box.

"Dammit, Rachel," he muttered.

His hand reached for the doorknob, but his subconscious tried to talk him out of it. *Don't do this.*

He almost obeyed the mental voice. Then he muttered a curse and consigned it to the depths of his subconscious, where it could party all night long with his conscience. And he walked into the darkened shop.

She immediately looked up, a flash of concern on her face. Probably understandable, given what had happened the previous evening with the s.o.b. in the brown suit.

When she saw and recognized him, he expected the concern to fade away. It didn't. If anything, she seemed more disturbed. Her frown deepened, then she quickly dropped her eyes, shielding her expression behind her bangs and her half-lowered lashes. She said nothing for a long, thick moment.

"You look like you need some help," he muttered, answering a question she hadn't even asked.

She'd been asking more than that one question with her discomfort and her silence. And he'd been less than honest about his one answer. But it would do for now.

"My aunt wanted to stay, but I was afraid she'd hurt herself so I told her I had help."

Unbuttoning the sleeves of his dress shirt, he rolled them up as he walked across the store. "You really do need to start locking the door after hours."

"I was going to, but since the delivery man left this monstrosity right in the middle of the floor, I would have had to walk across it to get to the door."

"The monstrosity you were about to try to wrestle into the back room all by yourself." Shaking his head, he squatted down and tested the weight of the box, lifting one corner. Then he grunted. The thing had to have a couple hundred pounds of pressed wood sections inside. "The guy couldn't even bring it into the back for you?"

She made a tiny little sound, almost a clearing of the throat, but probably more like a groan of embarrassment. "It won't fit."

He sat back on his haunches, following her stare. She was right. The box wasn't going to fit through that narrow doorway.

"I was trying to open it, figuring I could just carry it piece by piece."

"You should've stuck with your shoe box system." Then, not bothering to ask if she wanted his help, he tore open the end of the carton and began pulling components out.

"Lord have mercy, are those the directions?" she asked as a wad of paper about the size of Chicago's phone book came tumbling out.

"'Fraid so."

"Wow, I hope you're good with your hands?"

There was a loaded comment. Because yeah, if he did say so himself, he was damn good with his hands. As well as other body parts. All of which were dying to prove the point to the woman staring at him in wide-eyed innocence.

Maybe not *complete* innocence. Her bottom lip disappeared between her teeth and a flash of embarrassment crossed her face. She'd obviously just realized how her words had sounded.

"Uh, I mean…I hope you're handy in the…"

Bedroom? Oh, most definitely.

She cleared her throat, appearing more and more uncomfortable. "Do you know how to handle tools?"

He couldn't help responding, "I've been known to effectively use a tool or two."

Why he wanted to bait this woman—to ratchet up the awareness factor even higher than it already was—he had no idea. But he couldn't resist. Especially when the embarrassment faded from her face, only to be replaced by a look of heated amusement. Not to mention a spark of devilment.

She knew what was going on here. Knew full well.

"So, have you been complimented on your prowess?" Her words were whispered, almost purred. A smile of pure mischief played on those full lips of hers, making Luke's heart skip a beat.

He quirked a brow. "I'm not one to boast."

She waited.

"But I suppose I've received some enthusiastic compliments in the past."

Not lately. Not anytime lately. He'd been less sexually active in the past six months than he'd been in the preceding six *years*. Which had to explain why he'd had such a basic, hot reaction to Rachel, even when their conversations had been merely cordial and friendly.

This definitely wasn't one of those innocent moments. They both knew they'd moved beyond cordial and friendly. Into dangerous territory.

They fell silent and in that silence exchanged a wealth of words. Neither of them moved or breathed. Until, finally, Rachel broke the connection by glancing toward a rack full of wedding gowns. "Well, I suppose you'll be a handy husband for Maria to have around, then."

That effectively doused whatever the hell they'd both been thinking. Luke sucked in a ragged breath, then slowly let it out with a nod. "Right."

Returning his attention to the job at hand, he grabbed for an excuse—any excuse—to end their private interaction. "I think you might be right. I might not be the man for this job."

Oh, how he wished he could be. But not now. Not

when another woman was wearing his ring and her damned wedding dress was likely one of the ones hanging in the back room right now.

"Maybe you should leave," Rachel murmured, apparently feeling just as guilty and uncomfortable—if only for the direction of their thoughts—as Luke.

He shook his head. He had nothing to feel *really* guilty about. Yet. And he intended to keep it that way.

Luke wasn't a cheat. He wasn't a slimy prick like the brown-suited guy who'd hit on Rachel the night before. Which meant, he would keep his physical distance. At least long enough to figure out what he was going to do and what his intense interest in Rachel really meant.

Was he just another groom with cold feet? He immediately thrust that idea out of his mind. Because he'd been completely faithful, in his actions and in his brain, until the minute he'd found himself alone with Rachel the night before.

Meaning, sharing another private evening with her was probably a very bad idea. "I think we need to call in reinforcements. This is a job for one of the other Santori men."

"Oh?"

Nodding, he pulled out his cell phone and called his brother, Joe. As usual, his good-natured sibling didn't hesitate before agreeing to swing by the shop on his way home. "One down," he said as he cut the connection. Then he dialed another familiar number.

"Who now?" she whispered, looking uncomfortable at needing this much help. Hell, for all the woman had done for the women of his family lately, putting together a desk was the least they could do. *They.* Plural. As in, no-way-in-hell-was-he-going-to-be-alone-with-her-again. Which was the real reason he'd asked Joe to come help.

Well, that and the fact that Lucas could reduce a witness to a squirming mess on a witness stand, but could hardly tell a monkey wrench from a tire iron. He'd definitely been exaggerating about his prowess with certain tools.

Of course, they hadn't *really* been talking about the kind that came in a big metal box. And they both damn well knew it.

"I'm hungry," he explained as the phone began to ring. "Pepperoni and green pepper okay?"

She nodded. "But only if it's on me."

"You gotta be kidding. You don't really think my parents charge me, do you?"

Her eyes narrowed. "Then we'll order Chinese."

"You think my mama's not gonna find out from my brother Joe if I order Chinese carry-out when I'm four doors up from the restaurant? I don't know about you, but I don't particularly want to be on the receiving end of one of her lectures." He shuddered. "Or worse, her martyred silent treatment."

Her chuckle made her blue eyes sparkle in the late-day sun slanting through the front windows of the shop. "Okay. Pizza. But only if you'll let me run next door to buy the six-pack of beer to go with it."

"Deal," he agreed, knowing Santori's didn't deliver beer. Then, before she could leave to go to the liquor store next door, he said, "But better make it a twelve-pack. I have the feeling once the word gets out that I'm up here doing something involving tools and grunt work, we're going to draw a crowd."

RACHEL BOUGHT a case of beer. And it was a good thing. Because within an hour of Luke's arrival, his father, two of his brothers, one of his sisters-in-law, and his sister were crowded into her small shop. She had to wonder who was holding down the fort back at the restaurant, and assumed Luke's mother and one of the cousins who worked in the kitchen were covering for a while.

As usual, the Santoris were loud. Good-natured. Rowdy. The brothers gave Luke unending grief about his lack of prowess with a drill. In return, he told them he was going to make sure they got called for jury duty. Their father stayed out of the fray, for the most part, watching with an indulgent smile, occasionally muttering something in Italian under his breath.

Never having had any siblings, Rachel found herself fascinated by the interplay between them all. Tony, the oldest, walked with a swagger and tried to take over. But Joe, who owned a construction company, would have none of that. He became foreman, with thick, stocky Tony doing a lot of the lifting. Luke gave advice, read the directions and was pretty much in the way except for the heavy lifting.

With those muscles, he was more than capable of helping out in that department.

Rachel, Meg and Lottie stood watching and chatting while the brothers manhandled all the components of the desk into the back room. The men took occasional breaks to enjoy the pizza and beer, then proceeded to put everything together. But even as she enjoyed spending time with the women of the family, she found her attention returning again and again to Lucas.

He was different tonight than she'd ever seen him, either when they'd first met at the restaurant, or here in the shop last night. Seeming content to help with the muscle work, he then sat back and handed his brothers whatever tools they pointed at. He laughed a lot, flashing a dimple in one cheek, one she'd never even noticed before. His smile made his eyes crinkle at the corners, and, for the first time, she saw he had tiny laugh lines there.

This was the man she'd heard talk about. The charmer, the joker. The flirt who'd given Meg a loud, smacking kiss right in front of her husband, just to get a rise out of Joe when he'd arrived. The man who'd been conspicuously absent the first few times Rachel had met him.

Moody and snappish, he'd still been incredibly attractive. Flirtatious and smiling, the man was downright deadly.

"You'd think they went out and chopped down the tree for the wood to make this damn desk," Lottie said, sounding both disgusted and amused as she helped herself to a second bottle of beer. "They're so proud of themselves."

Meg had been drinking milk. "Give them their glory. Joe's been complaining that he does nothing but paperwork these days. He likes getting his hands dirty."

Hands. Strong hands. Masculine hands. Competent hands. Rachel couldn't stop staring at them.

Apparently Meg was having the same reaction. "My God, we should've sold tickets," she murmured as she watched the room full of testosterone at work.

Meg's stare remained focused squarely on her husband. Rachel's, however, was directed at the man beside Joe. At Luke's thick arms, revealed by the rolled-up sleeves of his dress shirt. His sweat slickened skin over taut muscles. Those powerful hands carefully turning the furniture and the thick legs straining against his dress slacks as he moved a finished section out of the way.

"If the shirts start coming off, I'm outta here," Lottie said, "because the two of you are going to float me away with your drool."

Rachel flushed a little, wondering what the other women would think of her drooling over any of the men here, all of whom were attached.

"Good grief, Lottie, I know they're your brothers, but you have to admit, they're a darn fine-looking bunch," Meg said.

Lottie just rolled her eyes, and Rachel drew in a

deep, relieved breath. Apparently the other two had thought nothing of her rapt interest in the exertions of the men in the room. Of course, they assumed she was joking along with them, admiring guys the way women always admired guys. Even *other* women's guys, as long as the hands-off-bitch-he's-mine thing was a given.

It was. Always. Rachel had never poached on another woman's territory.

So why, God, could she not remove her attention from Maria Martinelli's fiancé?

She returned her attention to Lucas, wondering what he was staring at with such keen interest. Following the direction of his stare, she spied the mountain of fabric samples on the sewing table. Then, almost certainly unaware of her intense scrutiny, Luke did something that revealed so very much about the man carefully contained within his professional facade.

As if unable to help himself, he reached out and ran the tips of his fingers across the top sample, a shimmery, peach-toned pile of silk, almost the color of blushing skin. His touch was slow, deliberate. She could almost see the physical pleasure he took from feeling the cool softness against his skin. His eyes closed briefly and his lips fell open as he pulled in a slow, deep breath and rubbed his fingertips together with the silk between them.

Still not knowing he was being watched, he placed his entire hand on the material, spreading his fingers, then tightening them, allowing the material to pool between them. A lethargic smile crossed his lips as he spread his fingers apart again and opened his eyes.

No one else had noticed. No one else watched. Only Rachel. And she couldn't say a word. Not even when he looked up and caught her staring with shocked intensity.

He didn't look away, didn't laugh off the moment with an embarrassed joke. He made no verbal or silent apologies for the fact he'd just revealed about himself.

That he was a sensual man. A man who took pleasure in physical things. Seductive things.

It had only been one stroke, one touch, on an inanimate object several feet away, yet Rachel almost felt as if *she'd* been touched. Caressed. Enjoyed in a basic, primal way that had temporarily stopped time for this powerfully built, fascinating man.

She could only imagine how he would touch a woman. How he'd slowly devour her, savor the feel of skin on skin, taking his time to enjoy every new sensation. How he'd delight in all the textures and contours of her body. The tastes. The smells. The soft wetness.

She swallowed hard as a warm, lethargic pleasure oozed through her. The heat in his dark brown eyes told her so much more than words ever could have. His thoughts matched her own, she knew it beyond doubt. And still he didn't look away.

"Too bad they're not working in the front room,"

Meg said, sounding as if she was far away, rather than right beside her. "We would have had women paying to line up for a peek in the front window."

Oh, yes, Rachel would have paid to watch this. Him. There wasn't much she wouldn't have paid to attain this incredibly intimate knowledge of the man beneath the elegantly tailored suit. There was much more to Luke than the expensive clothes and the brilliant reputation. He had depths she'd never have suspected. Seductive, sensuous ones, and they appealed to a deep part of her she'd never really acknowledged.

All that coiled masculinity combined with that wickedly potent sensuality had brought out every feminine instinct she possessed. This was desire flowing through her. Want. Immediately recognizable, even though it was almost unfamiliar.

It had been a long time since she'd truly wanted to touch a man. To suck the salty flavor of his skin. To kiss the line of his jaw. To encircle a hard erection in her hand. To stroke and taste and have and take.

Take. That's what she wanted to do. This wasn't simple awareness of him as an attractive man, like last night. Something about tonight had made her cross the line from interest to desire.

And she knew what it was: that touch. That one deliberate, sensuous, evocative touch of his hand on the silk.

She wanted his hand. She wanted to *be* the silk.

"Rachel?"

Giving her head a hard shake to clear it—and

seeing Luke do the same thing a few feet away—she turned her attention to his sister-in-law. Meg was watching her curiously and she wondered if the other woman had noticed how hard she'd been staring at Luke. She almost lifted her fingertips to her mouth to make sure there wasn't any drool there, as Lottie had teased. Because, God help her, she'd sure been doing some mental drooling. Not to mention fantasizing.

She forced a small laugh. "I haven't met Mark and Nick yet, but I imagine the five of them together could stop all the traffic on Taylor Avenue if they just walked outside and took their shirts off."

Lottie made a sound of disgust. "Ewww. Those are my obnoxious, bossy, arrogant brothers you're talking about."

"I still can't imagine what it was like growing up the youngest girl with all five of them," Rachel said, giving Lottie a pitying look. "Did you ever have a boyfriend brave enough to come to your house?"

Lottie stuck out her bottom lip in a disgusted pout. "Not after Mark and Nick got all the guys at St. Raphael's believing Papa had been Mario Puzo's inspiration for *The Godfather.*" She shot Luke a glare. "And that Luke's wicked temper had inspired the character of Sonny."

Luke snorted a laugh. "Haven't you heard? I'm the lover of the family, not the fighter."

"That'd be Nick," Meg murmured. The Marine.

"Nah," Tony said, obviously listening as intently

as Luke had been. He gave them a salacious grin, wagging his brows. "*I'm* the lover. Just ask Gloria."

"Not listening," Lottie snapped, sticking her fingers into her ears and humming a loud tune.

Then Joe piped in. "As for the Godfather? I think we're talking about Rudy Martinelli. Luke's new Daddy-in-law."

Oh, great. Perfect. Like she needed a reminder that the Nazi bride was the daughter of a mafia don. And Rachel had just been making twenty-nine kinds of love to the woman's fiancé in her head.

Luke stiffened, nearly imperceptibly, at the mention of his future father-in-law. So did Rachel. Because as easy as it had been to sit here feeling like a part of this big, loud, loveable family, she had absolutely no right to feel that way. Maria was the one who should have been here, laughing over the brothers, lusting over Luke, getting friendly with her future sisters-in-law.

This was all wrong. Especially the lusting part.

Which she intended to stop. Now. Right now.

Just as soon as she could put the mental picture of Luke running his hand over that piece of flesh-colored silk out of her mind.

Which might happen around about…never.

CHAPTER FIVE

"DID YOU EVER WONDER if you were doing the right thing by getting married?" Luke sipped at his beer, as if the question was a casual one, rather than one of vital importance to his sanity right now.

His brother Joe, who sat across from him at a table at the restaurant, immediately shook his head. "Never. Why?"

"Just wondering. You and Meg were such a whirlwind, I guess we never really talked about it."

Joe didn't even pause to think about it. "I knew she was the one the first time I laid eyes on her." Then a half-grin crossed his mouth. "Well, at least the first time I met her in person. I'd seen her picture a few times before that."

Luke saw the speculative gleam in his brother's eye, but was too wrapped up in his own confusion to question him about it. He'd been looking for advice…not to exchange more tales of true love and all that schmaltzy crap with his totally-mad-for-his-wife brother.

He and Joe had stopped by after work, as usual,

not for a bite, but just to connect with the family. Meg would be here soon, and Gloria and Lottie were already in the kitchen. Mark hadn't been around much lately because he'd been working on a case requiring a ton of overtime. But most other weeks, he'd have been sitting right next to Luke. They'd all be sharing the pitcher, letting off steam, basking in the warmth and security of being part of a dynamic group who knew no other way of life than to interact almost daily with the family.

Funny, Luke had once tried so hard to escape the Santoris. He'd been the only son who went away to college, and had surprised everyone by continuing on to law school. Yet now, since being back in Chicago, all he longed for was the big family madness which had sometimes driven him nuts as a kid.

Driven him nuts, maybe. But his family had also been the most important part of his existence. Going away to school hadn't been the start of a new, bigger life. It had made him long for the more intimate one he'd been running from. A life many of his friends— from small families or broken homes—had envied, even though they hadn't entirely understood it.

In an hour, they'd all drift away, to their own nearby homes and lives. But these meetings in the restaurant a few evenings a week were something Luke really looked forward to.

He only wondered if they'd continue once he was married to Maria. He somehow couldn't see her breezing in here after leaving her job as a secretary, hugging his mother, tossing insults back and forth with his brothers, sidling into a booth and joining in the conversation. The Maria who'd recently told him she never wanted to eat another meatball again as long as she lived probably wouldn't.

One thing was sure—she was nothing like his family, who sometimes seemed to have tomato sauce running through their veins instead of blood. Strange, Maria's utter disdain of her heritage, since her Italian background and local roots had been what had drawn him to the woman in the first place.

"So," Joe asked, not put off by Luke's silence, "You have cold feet?"

"Sub-zero. It's a wonder they haven't fallen off from frostbite," he admitted with a rueful shake of his head.

"I hear that's not too unusual. Some guys get nervous at the thought of settling down to one woman, knowing all others are off-limits from then on."

Yeah. Luke had heard that, too. Kinda reminded him of what Rachel had said about the slimy grooms who came on to her. The thought made him stiffen because damned if he wanted to feel like one of them.

"But in your case," Joe added, "I don't think that's it. If you really loved a woman, you wouldn't think twice about whether you could be faithful to her for the rest of your life. Obviously the fidelity gene runs in our family."

Yeah. Judging by his parents' marriage, not to mention Joe and Tony's absolute devotion to their wives, maybe it did.

He didn't question his ability to be faithful. Didn't doubt for one minute that he could make love to only one woman for the rest of his life—and be happy—as long as she owned his heart. Call it his genes, his upbringing in a family where loyalty and honesty reigned supreme, or even just the basic aspects of his personality, Luke was no cheat.

Which had made his unexpected reaction to Rachel this week all the more disturbing. Because, for some crazy reason, hers was the face he saw when he pictured the woman who could own his heart.

Not his fiancée's.

Then Joe zeroed in on the question of the hour, the question of his life, really. "So if it's not marriage in general making you sweat…or freeze up…I guess you have to ask yourself…are you marrying the right woman? And, if not, what are you going to do about it?"

Luke stared at his brother, drew in a long, deep breath, and finally replied, "That is exactly what I have to figure out."

RACHEL DID a pretty good job of putting Luke Santori out of her mind for the rest of the week. The shop was busy, with many June brides coming in for their May fittings. The one bride who didn't was Maria Martinelli, which was just as well. Rachel didn't think she could look Maria in the eye without blushing over the fantasies she'd had about her fiancé.

Fantasies. Dreams. Long, hungry nights when

she'd replay that moment when Luke had so care-fully—reverently—touched the soft fabric in the dress shop. When their eyes had met and they'd both been thinking of touching other soft textures. Skin. Hair. Tongues.

"Stop it," she whispered aloud, tightening her jaw as she stood in a quiet area in the local mega book-store. What a pathetic picture. Friday night—date night—and here she was perusing the stacks, trying to find something absorbing to read to get her mind away from where it had no business going.

It wasn't easy. Getting her kicks on a Frappuccino with whipped cream and caramel couldn't compare to the way she really wanted to get them.

Well, the whipped cream and caramel might still be involved. But they'd be *licked,* rather than sipped.

"Enough," she muttered, lifting her drink to her mouth. She sipped at it, curling her lips around the straw, ordering the icy-cold coffee brew to chill her out. Then, focusing on how much she loved the smells and sights and sounds of a bookstore, she went exploring.

"No romance," she reminded herself, avoiding that section altogether.

That was all she needed, to read some steamy book to get her even more hot and bothered. Since there was no sex looming in her future for probably the next decade—or at least until she changed careers and went to work where she might meet unattached men, instead of engaged ones—she needed to avoid anything involving sex. Because as convenient as some of those cute, naughty little gadgets some of her suppliers sold for bridal showers were, Rachel had never worked up the nerve to actually take one home and try it out.

Since she couldn't go for sex and romance, she'd decided to shoot for murder and mayhem instead. Beelining for the general fiction area, she scouted out her favorite mystery writer. She'd taken another sip of the drink and begun to study the titles when the most unusual sensation washed over her. Though her drink was cold, she felt suddenly warm. Hot, in fact, in spite of the comfortably air-conditioned store. Her breaths grew shallow, and her skin taut as she suddenly went on a strange, internal alert.

Someone was watching her. Intently.

Slowly, she turned around, as if merely moving to another shelf of books. She let her gaze dart to the end of the row, almost laughing as she saw nothing but empty air. The mystery titles were obviously getting to her.

"Girl, you're imagining things."

"No, you're not," said a soft voice.

Oh, God, it was him. Luke. He'd been standing right there. Around the corner, at the end of the bookcase she'd been studying, nearly hidden and out of sight, but so *present,* she couldn't help but feel him.

She wasn't used to seeing him in anything but tailored suits and dress shirts, so the jeans and tight gray

T-shirt were a definite surprise. A breath-stealing, heart-pounding surprise.

Oh, what the man could do to a thin, worn cotton T-shirt. And a tight pair of faded, threadbare jeans that hugged his thick thighs and did sinful things to his lean hips.

"Hi," she whispered, then cleared her throat and strove for nonchalance. "This is a coincidence."

He smiled, bringing forth those dimples and that twinkle in his eyes, and suddenly Rachel forgot every single thing she'd been telling herself for days about why she needed to stay away from him.

"Do you always talk to yourself?"

"Do you always spy on people in bookstores?" she countered.

"I wasn't spying."

"What were you doing then?"

His smile faded. "Trying to work up the nerve to leave."

Oh. Wow. Damn. That said a lot, didn't it?

She played dumb. "I don't understand."

He lifted his hand, an intimate look in his eye as he raised his fingers to her mouth. She gasped, having no idea what he intended, until he brushed something off the corner of her lips. "Whipped cream mouth," he explained.

And wobbly, jelly legs, she mentally replied.

"Thanks."

He eyed her cup. "You looked like you were enjoying your drink so much, I might have to try one."

"They're sinful. The real reason I come here."

"The books are just in the way, huh?" he asked with a knowing grin. He'd obviously been watching her raptly concentrating on the shelves.

"Okay, I confess. I'm a reader, too. Hopelessly addicted to violence and mystery and sci fi and sex." She instantly stiffened, feeling her face grow hot. "I mean, uh, I like genre novels. Romance. Not sex."

"You don't like sex?"

Oh, somebody just shoot me now and put me out of my misery.

He put one hand up, palm out, and shook his head. "Forget it, don't answer that. I don't think I wanna know."

She could take his words two ways. Either he was so completely uninterested in her that he frankly didn't care if she liked sleeping alone or with ten people at once. Or else he was so interested, he wanted to steer the conversation away from such a dangerous topic.

She voted for what was behind door number two. Then she mentally kicked herself for caring. "What about you? Why are you here on a Friday night?" Swallowing hard, she added, "Where's Maria?"

He shrugged in visible resignation. "Dentist appointment."

Odd. It was eight o'clock on a Friday night. Her skepticism obviously showed.

"I know, I know. But apparently her dentist keeps evening hours for working patients."

"So her dentist has as pathetic and boring a life as I do, I guess, huh?" she asked.

"You calling *me* pathetic and boring?"

Eyes widening, she shook her head. "No. You're fiancée-less due to dentistry. There's a difference."

Oh, how she wished he was fiancée-less, period. Because she was enjoying this playful conversation with this man. And would have enjoyed nothing more than curling up on the sofa in the nearest reading area, chatting for hours with him about anything and everything. What they liked to read, to drink. The best flavors of Frappuccino. Heavy desks and big Italian families.

Whether or not she liked sex.

"So how about you tell me what flavor to order, and I'll get you a refill?" he asked, looking at her nearly empty cup. "Then we can sit down and talk more about books and gore and sci fi and other things you like to read. Or maybe we could go to the martial arts area and see whether bony knuckles really are a good substitute for karate."

The dimples flashed and she almost smiled back, liking the gentle, playful way he teased. Then she lifted her hand and fisted it, waving it threateningly at him. "You calling my knuckles bony?"

He reached out and took her hand, *oh lord, he took her hand,* and heat sparked and for a second, time stopped again.

She loosened her fist, letting him extend her fingers, so he could scrape the pad of his thumb up and down on her pinky. A simple, innocent touch—but one which sent a reaction spiraling through Rachel's whole body.

Luke's eyes grew darker and the moment stretched on. Then, finally, he said in a huskier voice, "You *do* have bony knuckles."

God, how could he make her laugh when she was so incredibly aroused? She tugged her fingers away, almost mournful at the loss of physical contact. Then she strove to return to their casual, playful interaction, as if that intense connection created by nothing more than his fingers on her own had never happened at all.

"Hmm," she said with an exaggerated frown, "maybe we should go to the self-help area so you can learn the difference between a hammer and a wrench."

He drew a hand to his chest. "Ouch. Now you're questioning my manly prowess?"

Uh, no, she would never do that. Because she had no doubt of the man's *prowess*...he merely had to touch her fingers and she was ready to leap on him. "Just your construction abilities."

"I'll have you know, I was the one who gave Joe his first K'nex construction set as a kid."

She tapped her cheek with the tip of her index finger and gave him an arched look. "Hmm...let me guess, it was because *you* got it as a gift and couldn't open the box?"

He threw his head back and looked heavenward. "What have I done to deserve such doubt?"

"Uh, nearly dropped a drill on your brother's head?"

Which he *had* the other night.

"Well, there is that," he conceded, his eyes still twinkling. "Now, what do you say, should we sit down in the coffee shop? If I'm going to be insulted, I think I should at least be allowed to do it over a cold drink."

She shouldn't. He was issuing exactly the kind of invitation she'd just been thinking so longingly about. There was nothing technically wrong about it, nothing sexual or forbidden. He was proposing exactly the kind of conversation she might have had with a girlfriend she'd run into at this same store. Or even the husband of a friend. Casual, friendly, entertaining.

It was the fact that Luke was the one offering that made her hesitate. She was already incredibly attracted to the man. Did she really want to get herself in any deeper here?

"Come on," he urged, "I want to hear what your aunt Ginny had to say about your new filing system."

"The shoe boxes are stacked on top the desk. So far, that's the new filing system," she said, not even thinking about it.

His loud bark of laughter drew the attention of a few shoppers standing in the aisle. A woman eyeing the bestsellers gave Luke a thorough once-over, which made Rachel stiffen, even though he was nothing more than a friend.

That couldn't be jealousy. She wouldn't let it be jealousy. Because she had no right to be jealous.

Oh, please, let it not be jealousy. Because that would mean she was really falling for him.

"So much for you being the most organized person on the planet," he said.

"I lied."

"I know."

She smiled. So did he. Then, with a slow nod, she said, "Okay. Caramel Frap. And make it a Venti."

CHAPTER SIX

LUKE DIDN'T SLEEP WELL Friday night, and there was no question why. He'd been much too busy replaying every minute of his evening with Rachel.

The two of them had sat in the coffee shop area of the bookstore talking for hours. They'd literally closed the place down, being ushered out by weary employees who'd have had everything cleaned up already if not for their last two lingering customers.

He still couldn't believe how in sync the two of them had been. They'd talked so easily, like they'd known each other forever and could almost finish each other's sentences. He'd even opened up to her about his mixed feelings regarding his family, and why he'd needed to move away for several years to figure out that home was really where he wanted to be. He'd never shared that with anyone before.

Somehow, even though Rachel's family background had been completely different, she'd understood. And then she'd opened up to *him*, making him smile as her southern accent grew just a bit thicker when she fondly spoke of her North Carolina upbringing. Making him ache for her when she misted up over her father's recent death.

They hadn't remained melancholy for long. They'd joked and teased and devoured more whipped cream than he'd eaten in the past five years. He now knew what she liked to read and knew what she was afraid of and knew her favorite movies and her political affiliations and her birthday.

God help him. Why didn't he know any of those things about the woman he was supposed to marry in exactly two weeks?

He mulled over the thought as he sat at a table in the restaurant Saturday, a little before noon, and allowed his mind to drift back to the last moments of the previous evening.

When everything had fallen apart.

The memory made his mouth pull into a frown even now, nearly twelve hours later. Everything had been fine until he'd walked Rachel to her car. Since it had been after midnight, he'd stayed close to her side. And it had seemed the most natural thing in the world to lace his fingers in hers, to walk close enough so their hips and legs brushed.

It had *also* seemed perfectly natural to kiss her goodnight, and he'd almost done it. Almost. He'd leaned close, brushing a strand of her hair off her temple, noting the softness of her skin against his fingertips. Inhaling her scent, he'd realized that if he didn't taste her lips soon, he was going to shrivel up and die.

Then they'd both realized what they were doing. Rachel had held her hand up, palm out, whispering, "Stop. Please stop. Don't do this to me."

He'd swallowed, hard, affected by the hurt tone in her voice. "I'm sorry. I didn't mean…"

"I know," she'd admitted. "It's nice that we can try to be friends, and you've been a gentleman. I know you have groom's cold feet, though, so let's not get carried away and think it's any more than friendship." Then she'd forced a smile. "You don't need to prove you've still 'got it' just because I'm handy and available."

Her words had stopped him cold. She thought his interest in her was simply because she was off-limits, because he was about to be tied down and wanted one last notch on his belt?

He'd opened his mouth to reply, but she wasn't finished yet. "To be honest with you, Luke, I think I'm a little more susceptible to you than I'd like to be, and I'm just not up to these games," she'd admitted, her voice shaking a little. Her whisper was so soft he almost couldn't hear it over the late night breeze. "So I think we should say goodbye, instead of goodnight." Then she'd hopped in her car and driven away before he'd had a chance to defend himself.

His first reaction had been anger that she'd accused him of playing games with her feelings, but it had quickly subsided. How could she think him any different than any of the other scumbag grooms who'd come on to her? Had he given her any *reason* to think he was much more serious about her than even he'd suspected until last night?

No, he hadn't. And it was time to remedy that. Which was why he'd called Maria and asked her to meet him here at Santori's for lunch this afternoon. It probably wasn't great to ambush her here, but he knew his mother well enough to know she'd be the perfect one to help Maria calm down if she hit the roof.

Which she might. Because the time had come to set things right. He finally knew what he wanted.

And it wasn't marriage to Maria.

"Hey, man, you okay?"

Luke looked up to see his brother Tony, standing beside the table. "Okay? Depends on your definition of okay."

He was okay in terms of knowing what he wasn't going to do—go through with the wedding. But was completely unsure of what would happen next.

Until he'd straightened out his botched engagement, he was going to respect Rachel's wishes and leave her alone. Afterward…well, that remained to be seen. But he had definite hopes about what was going to happen between him and the lovely blonde who'd occupied his every waking thought for days.

His decision to cancel the wedding was not because of Rachel. Well, not *entirely* because of Rachel. Honestly, he suspected something special would happen between them; he couldn't imagine he was alone in the intense feelings that overwhelmed him when she was around. But whether it did or not, he'd finally realized the truth: he was marrying the wrong woman for the wrong reasons.

If he couldn't even muster up enough interest in Maria to remember the color of her eyes, he knew he had to throw in the towel on this whole thing. Now. Today.

"Yeah, I'm fine," he muttered as Tony stood there, waiting for him to elaborate.

His brother raised a brow and kept silent. Tony had mastered the whole, "I'm the big brother and you can't put anything over on me," thing at a very young age. So Luke didn't try. "No, I'm not okay. But I'm going to do something about it."

Tony didn't ask stupid questions. He didn't have to. Because he really *did* have that big brother know-everything thing going on. "It'll be all right. The family will back you up."

"Ours, maybe," he muttered, bringing his coffee to his lips and sipping from it. It was too hot still. And he suddenly realized he'd lost his taste for coffee—he now much preferred Frappuccino.

"She might not take it as hard as you think," Tony said.

"What do you mean?"

Tony glanced over his shoulder, as if to be sure he wasn't being overheard. "Well, Gloria thinks she's been acting…"

Like the Bride of Frankenstein?

"Like she's not really happy about this wedding, either."

Or that.

He half suspected Gloria was right, because Maria sure wasn't playing the part of happy bride-to-be. In fact, lately she'd been behaving like someone who had something to hide. Obviously, his sister-in-law had noticed, too. But before Luke could ask Tony to elaborate, the door to the restaurant opened, and his fiancée entered.

"I'll talk to you later," Tony mumbled. As he walked away, he gave Luke a reassuring pat on the shoulder.

A pat for good luck? A reminder that his family would back him up? Or just a last touch between brothers because he was afraid the very volatile Italian bride was going to stab Luke through the throat with a bread knife when he told her he wanted to call off the wedding.

Maybe all of the above.

"God, what a morning. I hate traffic. I hate this whole city and every person in it." Her voice held a whiny edge he'd heard all too often in recent weeks.

"Good morning to you, too," he said to Maria as she took the seat across from him. Brown. Her eyes were brown. Which, of course, he knew. But he hadn't been able to call to mind the color ever since first meeting Rachel's blue-eyed stare earlier this week.

She frowned, a perpetual expression these days. "Sorry. It's been one of those days."

"One of those weeks," he said, nodding in agreement. "Everything seems to have gone crazy lately."

Her gaze shifted away, and her mouth tightened. "Yeah, more than you can imagine."

That was an opening. Her frown, her unhappiness, the slump of her shoulders. He didn't know Maria Martinelli as well as he ever should have, but he sure knew misery. This was about as close as he'd ever seen it. "Maria, tell me what's wrong."

She stiffened, but didn't meet his gaze. "Wrong?"

"Something's going on. I think it's about time both of us open up about it. Before it's too late."

She finally looked up. Her eyes grew suspiciously bright as she opened her mouth. But before she could say a word, the front door opened and his mother and sister-in-law, Gloria, came in, jabbering and chatting a mile a minute.

And the moment was lost. Whatever confession she'd been about to make was gone. Which meant Luke was going to have to do this the hard way.

He had to come right out and tell Maria Martinelli he didn't want to marry her.

RACHEL HAD BEEN ABLE to put Lucas's engagement completely out of her mind during their casual, friendly hours at the bookstore Friday night. Right up until the intense, heady moment when he'd come so close to kissing her.

She'd sensed how much he wanted to, and had longed for his kiss, which would have been absolutely perfect. Absolutely wonderful. Absolutely incredible.

If it hadn't been so absolutely wrong.

So she'd put a stop to things before they could get any worse than they already were. Thank God nothing serious had happened between them; she could console herself with that much, at least. It had been close. If he'd persisted—if he'd been less than a complete gentleman and had leaned down one more time so she could practically feel the warmth of his cheek, nearly taste the sweet, coffee flavor of his breath, she likely would have kissed the lips right off the man.

But he hadn't. And it had been too late. The moment had passed. She'd somehow found the strength of will to drive away, watching his figure get smaller and smaller in her rearview mirror.

Enough was enough. She couldn't deal with the temptation anymore. So it was time to be completely businesslike when it came to the Martinelli-Santori wedding. Starting with this: a sizeable package that had just been delivered by the mailman. The return address was a familiar Internet-based wedding favor supplier, domeafavor.com, from whom Rachel had ordered favors for several couples. The package was addressed to… "Mr. and Mrs. Luke Santori."

Something inside her clenched, bringing an almost physical pain with it at seeing the stark words, so blatant and harsh.

So much for completely business-like. She wanted to melt into a weeping puddle on the floor just thinking that the man she greatly feared she'd fallen head-over-heels in love with was about to walk down the aisle with someone else. He'd be out of reach forever.

"He's been out of reach all along, you fool," she reminded herself.

She *was* a fool for allowing that fact to slip out of her mind.

No more, however. Rachel had woken up. Gotten her head on straight and thrust all images of strong hands lingering on silk, twinkling eyes, and sexy smiles right out of her brain.

It was over. She was finished being susceptible to his wit, his humor, his charm, his laugh. Not to mention his incredible looks. "Finished," she told herself, thrusting the mental picture of him in those tight, worn jeans—and nothing else—out of her brain. "You're never going to be alone with him again."

She distracted herself by thinking instead of what was inside the carton she was about to open. She carefully cut the tape on the huge package, seeing several smaller sealed cardboard boxes inside.

To make sure she'd never again be alone with Luke Santori, she decided not to even call Maria to let her know the favors, *bomboniere*—small, imprinted boxes with colorful, candy-coated almonds inside—had arrived. With Rachel's luck, she'd send Luke to pick them up. And he'd be all hot and adorable. Maybe wearing raggedy shorts this time. And a ripped muscle shirt. And he'd be all sweaty from a workout. Glistening.

Stop it.

There was one surefire way to get heated thoughts of Luke out of her mind. She'd walk down the block to visit his family. The ones who were all excited about his upcoming wedding to someone else. She'd just bring a box of the favors down to the restaurant and let Mrs. Santori show them to her future daughter-in-law. Which was exactly what she told Maddie, the part-time seamstress, who'd come in to help out on what they expected to be a busy Saturday.

"Okay. Bring me back a small pizza, will you?"

Rachel grinned at the young woman, whose tiny frame didn't look like it could manage a single slice, much less an entire pizza. "Okay." Then she met the younger woman's eye, silently urging her to understand. "As long as you agree to handle Maria Martinelli's fitting—if she ever decides to show up for one." Lowering her voice, she said in a thick whisper, "Please, Maddie. I can't do it…for very personal reasons."

Maddie opened her mouth, obviously intending to shoot it off. But apparently Rachel's tone, not to mention the pleading look in her eyes, got the message across. She nodded. "Okay."

"Thanks."

"You're welcome," Maddie said. "And now, you owe me breadsticks, too."

Pizza and breadsticks. A small price to pay for avoiding the woman who was about to marry the man Rachel had so unwisely fallen in love with.

There were those words again. In love. *Are you crazy?*

Maybe. But that didn't make her feelings any less

real. Just her luck, she'd gone and fallen in love—
for the first time ever—with a man she couldn't have.

Unfortunately, she realized as soon as she entered
Santori's, avoiding Maria wasn't going to be so easy.
Because the woman was seated a few feet away.
Across from Lucas, in a booth near the door.

Oh, God. She instinctively began to whirl around,
then realized Mrs. Santori was watching her in avid
curiosity from behind the counter. Luke's mother
gave her a big welcome, coming out from behind the
counter, arms extended. "Rachel, you should have
told me you were coming for lunch. I woulda had
Ant'ny working on a spinach calzone for you."

Her favorite. Rachel managed a shaky nod of
hello, even though Luke had immediately looked up
at his mother's words. He appeared tense, uncomfortable even. But when his eyes met hers, his expression softened and he offered her a smile of such
unexpected tenderness, she nearly stumbled.

She wondered if Mrs. Santori kept a mop on hand
to clean up the women who physically melted under
Luke Santori's smile.

"No, thanks, Mrs. Santori, I came to drop these
off." She kept her voice low as she placed the sealed
cardboard carton on one of the empty tables. "The
favors were delivered this morning and I thought
Maria might like to see them." Casting a quick glance
toward the not-so-happy-looking bride and groom,
she added, "Maybe you could give them to her later."

Mrs. Santori said nothing for a moment, merely

giving her a long, thorough stare. Rachel willed her breathing to remain steady and her cheeks not to redden. *There's nothing to feel guilty about.*

She'd barely touched Luke, except, of course, when she'd thrown herself in his arms that first day. But only because of fat fingers Freddy. She'd certainly had no idea how much she'd *like* being in his arms until after she'd landed there, so she couldn't feel guilty about it.

Unless her innermost thoughts and wishes counted. Then, well, someone might as well call the executioner because she was guilty as hell.

"I think you should stay a little while," Mrs. Santori said. "You're very welcome here." Her voice was low, her expression caring, as if she somehow understood what Rachel was feeling.

Before Rachel could respond, she heard Maria's loud voice. "Rachel! How nice to see you."

That was about as friendly as Rachel had ever heard her, but she also noted a hint of forced gaiety in the other woman's voice. Maria's eyes were suspiciously bright as she rose from her seat and approached.

"I brought a box of your favors so you could check them out," Rachel said softly.

"Oh…those silly little almond things my father insisted on?" She gave a weary sigh. "Fine, why don't you leave them here and I'll go through them later."

Gloria Santori emerged from the kitchen and joined the conversation. "Oh, no, you're not getting out of this one. You have to open the top one right now, and end this suspense. Just how many babies are you and Luke going to have?"

Oh, God. Babies? Rachel sucked in a quick breath and clenched her fingers into fists, determined not to react in any way, though the mental picture pained her somewhere deep inside.

Maria reacted enough for all of them. "Babies? What babies? I'm not pregnant. Who told you I was pregnant?" Her voice was sharp and raised.

Luke walked over. "I don't think anyone suspects that's possible." He and Maria exchanged a telling look, both, Rachel noticed, remaining stiff and untouching. As if they weren't comfortable with one another. As if they shared no intimacy whatsoever.

Which definitely got her wondering.

"You know the custom, don't you?" Gloria asked as she reached for the box and began tearing off the packing tape. "The engaged couple opens the first little container, and however many almonds are inside determines how many children they'll have." She grinned. "Tony and I had two in ours, which means I'm off the hook for life!"

Though Rachel would rather have been anywhere else, she could think of no graceful way out. She had to stand here and watch Luke and his fiancée go through a family wedding ritual. Which she looked forward to about as much as she looked forward to her first tax audit.

Maria and Luke didn't appear very happy about this whole thing, either. Neither of them smiled, and they certainly didn't laugh intimately together at the thought of any children in their future. Meanwhile, Luke's mom just kept shifting her attention between them all, obviously sensing something was up.

Only Gloria appeared oblivious to the undercurrents as she finished tearing off the tape, then pushed the box across the table to Maria. "Go on."

The center of attention now, Maria slowly peeled up the sides of the box and peered inside. She was silent for a moment, though her face grew pale and her mouth opened.

Then she let out a scream. A loud one.

The few diners in the place dropped their forks and one woman tipped her glass over. Everyone stared in shock as Maria threw her hands over her face and began muttering something.

"What's wrong?" Luke asked.

Maria lowered her hands, displaying what looked like fear in her expression. "It's an omen. All those eyes staring at me, judging me." Staring wildly around, her gaze finally came to rest on Luke.

"What is it?" he asked, sounding much more patient than anyone else probably felt.

"I confess. I'm guilty. I'm having an affair. I'm in love with my dentist, Dr. Schwartz!"

CHAPTER SEVEN

RACHEL HADN'T stuck around for the fireworks after Maria had dropped her bomb on all of them. She'd stammered something—she couldn't even remember what—and headed for the door. Gloria had done the same thing, beelining for the kitchen. And Mrs. Santori had lowered her head and walked away.

Now, twenty-four hours later, she was still wondering what on earth had happened. Had Lucas been furious? Relieved? Forgiving? Had Maria been *asking* for forgiveness, or ending their engagement? The wedding—was it on, or off?

Was Luke free?

Heaven help her, but that question was the one that had really bounced around in her head all night Saturday night, and throughout Sunday morning. It's what had driven her so crazy, she'd had to leave her little apartment and go in to the shop, to do a few hours worth of work, even though they were closed on Sundays.

Coming to the store probably would have been fine, if it weren't just a few doors down from Santori's. Thankfully, the restaurant was closed and dark, as usual this early on a Sunday, when they only opened for dinner.

Still, even the outside of the building brought up vivid memories. She couldn't stop picturing that bizarre moment when Maria had wailed about eyes staring at her, and had made her dramatic confession.

"Lady, you are obviously out of your mind."

In more ways than one. Not for the first time, Rachel wondered what kind of pea-brained lackwit would choose some dentist over a man as amazing as Luke Santori.

Though there was work to do, she couldn't concentrate on files or receipts or bookkeeping. At the very least, she could clean off her big new desk, already covered with the shoeboxes, a sewing kit, and snippets of thread and lace. But she couldn't keep her gaze away from the mountainous stack of fabrics sitting on the carpeted platform where customers stood during fittings.

Her attention remained squarely on the lovely piece of peach-colored silk that Luke had touched so seductively the other night. Her breathing slowed and her whole body felt languorous, just remembering it.

She couldn't help it. Some wicked impulse made her rise to her feet and approach the platform. In the floor-length mirrors which surrounded it, she could see the wistful expression on her own face as she gave in to some need to connect with Luke. She was reaching for the silk before her brain could tell her she was being a fool. And even when it did, she didn't care.

"So soft," she murmured, bringing the fabric up to rub it delicately against her cheek.

She closed her eyes, breathing deeply. That same wicked impulse made her lower the silk, sliding it across her neck, her throat. To the tops of her breasts, revealed in her lightweight, scoop-necked sundress. "Would you have touched me like this?" she whispered aloud, picturing warm hands instead of cool fabric. One specific pair of hands.

"Oh, absolutely."

She froze, shocked into silence, hardly even breathing. Because that soft, husky voice had been unmistakable.

Luke.

"You're here?" she asked, still not turning to face him, though she did, finally, open her eyes.

"I'm here."

"I wondered if you'd come."

She heard him step closer. "I wanted to. But I wasn't going to walk through your door again until I was a free man."

A warm, lava-flow of happiness oozed through her veins, and she slowly turned around, letting out a tiny sigh to indicate she'd heard his softly spoken words.

"Hi," he said when she gave him her full attention.

"Hi."

He hesitated. Then said, "It's over."

Over. He and Maria were over. He was free. Here because…because… "Why are you here, Luke?"

His eyes widened in surprise and he stepped closer. "You have to know that."

Nibbling her lip, knowing she might offend him but having to know the truth, anyway, she said, "Because I'm handy and available?"

His jaw tensed, and his brow creased in anger. He ate up the few feet between them with two giant steps, grabbing her shoulders and pulling her close. "Don't you ever say that again. Don't you even think it."

She stared, waiting.

"I want *you*, Rachel Grant." He began running his hands up and down her arms, lightly, then harder, testing the softness and texture of her skin.

She couldn't deny the truth, not when it was this blatant, this strong. "I want you, too, Luke."

He kept touching her, stroking her, twining one hand through her hair and sifting its strands through his fingers. The other remained on her arm, sliding lower until he caught her hand in his.

Oh, it was rapturous. Just as she'd known being touched by him would be.

"Do you know how much I've wanted to do this? How often I've fantasized about having you in my arms this week?"

She nodded. "About as much as I fantasized the same thing."

"But I couldn't," he said thickly, continuing to play with her hair, and now, the nape of her neck. "I didn't want you to think I was one of those grooms, looking for a last fling, trying to notch my belt one last time. Because this is nothing like that."

"I know."

Rachel had suspected the way it would feel to be touched by this man, judging by the way he'd touched the silk. The reality far outweighed her fantasies until her whole body was a mass of nerve endings, anticipating each slide of his fingers across her arm, or the scrape of his hand on her throat.

But even his touch couldn't have prepared her for his kiss. He drew out the tension until she thought she'd explode then, finally, leaned down to kiss her. He lowered his mouth to hers and their breaths met and mingled for a second before their lips did. One second of anticipation.

It seemed like an eternity.

Then he kissed her, hot and sweet and hungry, until she sagged against him. Tilting her head, she urged him deeper, meeting every delicious, lazy thrust of his tongue, wanting to be as close to him as humanly possible.

His hands dropped to cup her waist and Rachel couldn't resist an age-old instinct that made her curve her hips closer. He hissed against her mouth, but she wouldn't let him pull away. Wrapping her arms around his neck, she kept kissing him, wanting more and more.

"I want you, Luke," she whimpered against his mouth as the pressure built to an unbearable level.

She didn't even have to think about it. She wanted this. Here. Now.

He didn't say a word. He simply moved back far enough to catch hold of her shoulders, and gently turned her around.

She was facing the mirrors. All those mirrors in which she was reflected over and over again, with the same heavy-lidded look of sensual desire on her face.

He stepped behind her, lowering the zipper of her dress inch by agonizing inch, when what she wanted was to rip the damn thing off and be done with it. His sultry grin told her he knew exactly what he was doing to her with his slowness and restraint. *Driving her crazy.*

Well, two could play at that game. She met his eyes in the mirror. Shrugging one shoulder, then the next, she allowed the dress to fall to the floor, giving him a smile just as sultry and inviting.

"God, you're glorious," he muttered. The desire in his stare was something she could dine on for months. It was heady, powerful, having a man so filled with hunger for her.

But the upper hand shifted yet again when he reached around her to stroke her stomach. Her legs felt quivery and she had to gasp for breath, both at the sensations caused by his touch, and the image of his dark hands on her pale skin, reflected endlessly in the mirrors. He pressed his hot mouth on the side of her neck, and she arched in delight.

Those amazing, strong hands of his teased and

taunted and built the pressure. He'd slid his finger-tips across the elastic top of her bikini panties, but no lower. Then he moved them to the lacy bottom of her bra, brushing featherlight caresses there, until she wanted to cry out for him to cup her breasts before she exploded. He never did and the urgency was making her whimper.

"I love touching you." His whisper scraped across her nape, then his teeth lightly did the same.

She moaned. "I knew I'd love the way you touch me."

But it wasn't quite enough.

Reaching around her back, she unhooked her bra. Luke's brown eyes darkened to near black as he watched every move she made. She let the straps slide down her arms, but didn't allow the bra to drop completely away, wanting to draw out the moment, to tease him. For the first time in forever, she was exceedingly glad for her curvy figure. Because the desire was practically dripping off the man in waves.

And when she did uncover herself completely, he let out a low, long groan of pleasure.

As if unable to help himself, he reached up to cup her, caressing her breasts with the same skill in his every other touch. She moaned when he toyed with her nipples, and cried out when his other hand slid lower, across her midriff and her belly, below the top of her panties.

He pushed them off, dipping lower to touch her even more intimately.

"Please, Luke…" she muttered hoarsely, needing so much more.

She didn't have to ask twice. As if in one smooth move, he pulled off his T-shirt, kicked off his shoes and pulled a condom packet out of his jeans pocket. Then he unfastened the jeans and pushed them, and his briefs, to the floor.

All the air left her lungs. She'd watched his every movement in the mirror, and the sight of him—proud and erect and throbbing—made her feel suddenly weak, yet also incredibly powerful.

Wanting to see him without the interference of the mirrors, she slowly turned around. She let her hungry gaze rove over him—his broad chest and thick arms. The flat stomach awash with rippled muscle. The lean hips. Lower.

"Oh, my," she whispered. She gasped at the thought of all that strong, male heat being inside her in a few moments.

"I didn't plan for our first time to be on the floor," he said as he looked around the crowded room. Then they both glanced at the pile of fabric on the raised platform. Wicked anticipation lit up his whole face. Rachel shook a little, picturing exactly what he was picturing.

Luke pushed the pile of material over and they watched it cascade across the carpeted platform in a rainbow of color and texture. The peach silk was on top. Of course it was.

"I pictured your skin when I first touched this,"

he said as he gently lowered her onto the cushiony, silky mound.

"I know."

Then there were no more words, there was simply soft, cool, smooth delight. She was enveloped by the material scraping deliciously against her sensitized skin. Cool silk and smooth satin and delicate lace and warm cotton. All combining in a cacophony of sensation that had her tingling from head to toe.

Luke took special delight in lifting the edges of the peach silk and rubbing it across the most sensitive parts of her body. Wherever the material touched, Luke's mouth soon followed until she was going out of her mind with the pleasure of it.

Cool and hot. Smooth and rough. Slick and damp. And finally, oh, *finally,* hard and full and deep.

Joined. In the most intimate way possible.

It was utterly amazing.

"I love you, Rachel," he said hoarsely as he drove into her body, driving out any doubt, any second-guessing.

Nothing had ever been this perfect, she realized, as she arched against him, wanting him deeper, wanting to fill herself up with him so she'd always feel like he was a part of her.

And when she finally felt the incredible climactic sensation washing over her in waves, she admitted to both of them, "I love you, too."

IN ALL HIS LIFE, Luke realized, he'd never made love to a woman. He'd had sex with plenty of them. But never, *never,* had he connected all the dots—put all the pieces of emotion, pleasure and tenderness together—to truly make love.

Until now.

After they'd shared their shattering climaxes, he'd rolled onto his back, pulling her over to rest on his chest. They lay silently for a few moments, letting hearts return to normal, breaths slow and hunger be sated. For now.

Luke began to toy with her hair, tangled amidst the fabrics, and to stroke the soft, supple skin of her hip as he contemplated how to tell her what was on his mind.

It was too soon. It was crazy. But he knew without a doubt that he loved her and wanted to spend the rest of his life with her. So he came right out with it. "Marry me."

She laughed. "Right."

"I mean it. Marry me. I want you to be my wife."

She slowly pulled away, looking into his eyes to gauge his seriousness. He hoped his feelings were as obvious to her as they were to him—to everyone, really, since his own mother had admitted this morning that she'd suspected he was in love with the beautiful shopkeeper.

"I'm serious. This isn't about cold feet or second thoughts or just how much I want you."

"You have me," she said softly, punctuating the remark by sliding her bare leg over his thighs. "And you don't have to say these things."

Rolling onto his side, he traced his fingertips over

her cheek. "Yeah. I do. I love you and I want to marry you. Whether we wait a year or a week isn't going to make a damn bit of difference."

Her gaze shifted. "Luke, have you ever heard of being on the rebound?"

He groaned and ran a frustrated hand through his tangled hair. "Yeah, I've heard of being on the rebound and I've heard of hurt pride and I've heard of grooms with cold feet going after any sexy woman nearby." Cupping her face with his hand, he added, "But this isn't any of those things. This is me realizing how damn lucky I am to have gotten out of a situation I created out of my own stupid need to carry on with tradition. I got engaged for all the wrong reasons, and not one of them included falling in love."

He kissed the corner of her mouth, then whispered, "But I did fall in love with you. And I want to marry you for all the right reasons."

She still looked unconvinced. Though it killed him, he continued. "Say it's too soon. Say you want a career for a while. Hell, say you got caught up in the moment and you don't really love me. But don't you dare try to tell me I don't know what I want."

Her blue eyes widened and grew moist with emotion. "You're serious about this?"

"Dead serious."

She still didn't say yes. But she didn't say no, either. "What will everyone think?"

"Who the hell cares? My family already loves you, and they wanted to jump for joy when they realized I wasn't marrying Maria." Then, because she didn't know everything that had happened yesterday, he explained. "And Maria eloped with her dentist to Las Vegas last night, so it's not like anybody on her side is going to have much room to criticize me."

Her mouth dropped open. He tipped it closed with his index finger.

"So she was serious? She's been having an affair? Is she out of her mind?"

He liked her vehemence, which showed her indignance on his behalf. Surely that indicated he hadn't been wrong about her feelings. "Yes, it's true. She got engaged to me for the same lame reasons I asked her. Family, traditions, all that stuff. Her father's more conservative than anyone I know and he was the one who wanted the wedding, the Italian customs, even the gown." He shook his head ruefully. "Do you know she told me she hated the dress and wanted more than anything to wear a strapless yellow sundress instead? Her father picked the final one out of a magazine and demanded that she wear it."

Rachel thought about the exquisite gown hanging on a nearby rack and rolled her eyes. "She's mental."

"Not as much as we thought yesterday when she lost it at the restaurant. Apparently there was a mix-up with the company who sent those wedding favors. Inside the box were dozens of these little round metal charms that looked like eyes. A guy eating at the restaurant—who's Greek—said they're a tradition at Greek weddings, to ward off bad spirits."

A naughty grin widened her lips. "Or bad fiancées?"

He laughed with her, hoping her light mood meant she was getting used to the idea of his proposal.

"Yeah. The packing slip inside the box said they were for another couple, with a completely unpronounceable Greek name. They just got mixed up."

"I'll have to send domeafavor.com a thank you note," she said.

He squeezed her tighter. "You're bad."

"I know. But I'm also very thankful Maria got a wake-up call. Even if she thought it was one from the Twilight Zone."

"Yeah. She saw all those eyes and the guilt was just too much. She's been involved with this guy for a couple of months, but was too scared of her father's reaction to tell the truth. Apparently he's not only non-Italian, he's also Jewish and has been divorced."

Thinking of the hell she'd put all of them through, he was angrier about Maria's silence than anything else. The thought that she'd fallen in love with someone else didn't bother him a bit—because he'd done the same thing.

Shrugging, he added, "That's why she's been such a witch to be around lately. She decided to try to get me to break the engagement by being as horrible as possible."

"She succeeded," Rachel said, her tone dry. "We started calling her the Nazi bride."

"My brothers told me last night they'd been calling her the Bride of Chuckie. Mark couldn't stand her, which was why he's kept his distance lately."

She tilted her head back and feigned innocence. "Does that make you Chuckie?"

"No, I think that makes Dr. Schwartz Chuckie. I'm *lucky*."

She rolled her eyes, even as she shook with laughter. "That was pretty lame. You're no poet." Then she added, "But you know what? We're *both* lucky."

They remained silent for a moment, absorbing everything. Their past, their future. The present, wrapped in one another's arms, naked, exposed, with their feelings laid bare.

And finally she put him out of his misery.

"The answer is yes, Luke. I will marry you."

CHAPTER EIGHT

"YOU'RE SURE it's all right with you that I'm not Catholic? And not Italian?" Rachel asked, nibbling her lip as she shared one last moment in the back of the church with Mr. Santori before the older gentleman walked her down the aisle. "I know how much that means to your family."

The elder Anthony Santori patted her hand and shook his head. "Don' you worry. My nephew, Father Frank, he's coming to the reception later to bless the union. You don' have to be married in the Catholic church to be blessed by it." Then he shrugged, his brown eyes—so much like Luke's—twinkling. "And as for not being Italian? Well…nobody's perfect."

So Rachel was walked down the aisle with laughter on her lips. Her new family all around. And a song in her heart.

The only thing that could have made these slow—but joyful—steps up the aisle better would have been if her own father could have been here escorting her. But Luke's father was a kind, loving substitute and as they neared the altar, he leaned close to whisper, "Welcome to the family, little one. Your mama and papa, they are watching and are so very proud."

She had tears in her eyes as she stepped up to stand beside her groom. He gave her a quizzical look, and she flashed him a dazzling smile telling him her tears had been happy ones.

The wedding took place at a lovely, non-denominational chapel on the grounds of a local university. Because they were getting married only two weeks to the day after Lucas had proposed to her, there had been no time for Rachel to take the required classes to be married in the Roman Catholic Church. But Luke didn't mind, and his family didn't seem to, either.

That had been a pleasant surprise. His family had been absolutely wonderful. Not with one word or a single look had anyone made her feel less than...*bridal*...during the past two weeks. If they wondered just what had gone on between her and Luke while he'd been engaged to another woman, well, they were courteous enough not to ask.

"I love you, Rachel Grant," Lucas whispered as he took her arm. "You're the most beautiful woman I've ever seen."

She *felt* like the most beautiful woman in the world, because of the love in his eyes, and the happiness of their friends and family, who filled the small chapel to overflowing.

Rachel's closest pals from North Carolina had made the trip up, and of course she had Ginny and

Maddie and some of her new friends in Chicago. And there were *lots* of Santoris.

The presence of Luke's family members from overseas had been one reason for her to agree to schedule the wedding so soon. They were all coming anyway for his, uh, *original* wedding. But she'd put her foot down on the date, and they'd compromised to have the ceremony on Sunday, rather than Saturday. Which Luke's mother said was more in keeping with Italian tradition, anyway, since Saturday weddings were originally thought to bring bad luck.

The one thing she'd allowed herself to be talked into was the dress. *The* dress. The perfect, beautiful, exquisite wedding dress that had never been seen, much less touched, by its first intended wearer.

It swished around her legs, the lace so delicate and the tiny seed pearls glowing with an effervescent light. The train trailed out behind her, its miniscule white roses swirling amid the lace, blending in and out in a pattern of vines.

"It was meant for you," Lucas whispered just before the minister began to speak, as if he could read her mind.

"Maybe it was," she replied just as softly, still amazed the dress had needed no major alterations. Just a little extra room in the bust, which Maddie had easily taken care of.

Of course, originally she'd had absolutely *no* intention of wearing it at all, even though her aunt Ginny and Maddie had tried to talk her into it. But she'd remained firm…until the day Maria Schwartz's father, Rudy, had come into the store.

He'd been an absolute charmer. Not only had he paid for the dress, as well as the bridesmaid gowns his newly married daughter had ordered, he'd also congratulated Rachel on her engagement to Lucas. And he'd told her that it would do him a great honor if she would consider wearing the gown he'd so wanted to see his daughter in. Because, of course, he was so very proud to be invited to the wedding, in spite of his daughter's actions.

It made her head spin, these traditional, old-world people who valued honor, kinship and family above all.

She liked it. She definitely liked it.

But she wasn't so sure Lottie was going to like it. Because Rudy Martinelli also informed her he and Tony Santori were talking about a match between his son and the only Santori daughter. She could only hope Luke's sister had the strength of will to follow her older brothers' examples and marry for one reason and one reason alone. True love.

"Maybe it *was* meant to be," she repeated. Maybe everything that had happened in the year since her father had died—her loneliness, the decision to move to Chicago and go into business with Ginny—perhaps it had happened for one reason.

So she could find the love of her life.

She liked to think Mr. Santori was right and her parents were watching now. Maybe they'd even been guiding her a little. With tears moistening her eyes, she sent up a little loving thank-you as the ceremony began.

Luke's strong presence by her side, and the strength of his voice when he took his vows gave her such confidence that she didn't have a moment of wedding jitters. The words love, honor and cherish came easily when spoken about this man. And when they were pronounced husband and wife, she was the one who turned and kissed him with every bit of tenderness and emotion she felt.

"Oh, wow, it's going to be a long day, Mrs. Santori," he whispered against her lips as their kiss ended and they turned to face the congregation.

"Hey, you agreed to wait after that one, umh, premarital *sampling* at the shop."

"Which I've regretted every minute of every day since." He sounded downright mournful. Rachel loved that, loved the anticipation and desire that made his brown eyes velvety with want.

Tonight was going to be an amazing night. Especially when he saw what her aunt Ginny had made for her trousseau: an utterly exquisite nightgown made from that peach-colored silk. Ginny was an artist with sewing, a da Vinci who worked with fabric instead of paint. And the gown, with a plunging neckline decorated with glittering beads, was going to make her husband lose his mind.

"What's giving you that anticipatory look?" he

asked as they walked down the aisle, past their smil-ing—or happily crying—family members.

"Thinking about tonight," she admitted, watching him out of the corner of her eye. "You're going to *die* when you see my wedding nightgown."

He stopped. Came to a dead stop in the aisle, and turned to face her. "Tell me it's the peach silk," he growled.

She gave him a nod, and a tiny, wicked grin, at which point her new groom pulled her into his arms. Ignoring everything—location and audience—he caught her mouth in a hot wet kiss that screamed of his driving need and incredible want. And his love.

By the time they pulled apart…by the time she could *think* again…she realized the entire congrega-tion had burst into a round of spontaneous applause and cheers. They were still cheering as the newly-weds left the church and dashed to the horse-drawn carriage waiting for them at the end of the walk.

As they rode together, cuddling on the velvet-cov-ered bench, Rachel had to laugh at the joy of it—the beauty of the sunny day, the profusion of flowers lin-ing the walk, and the well-wishes of everyone they passed. Chicago loved weddings. Even the drivers on the busy streets who were interrupted by the carriage didn't seem to mind so much as they clip-clopped down Taylor Avenue.

"I'm so glad we decided to have the reception at the restaurant," she murmured.

"That made my parents very happy, too," he admitted. "My father thinks French food is fit only for dogs."

Laughing, she hugged his arm close. "I love your father. I love your whole family."

"They love you too. Almost as much as I do."

They arrived at the restaurant and were greeted by well-wishers who lined the street and filled the entranceway. As they alighted from the carriage, a few of Luke's Italian relatives tossed colorful pieces of candy at them, startling her.

"More candy-covered almonds, called *confetti*," he explained. "They represent the bitter and the sweet parts of marriage and are meant to bring happiness."

As long as they didn't bring stains to her beautiful gown, or put anyone's eye out, that was fine with Rachel.

Inside, they were immediately overwhelmed by the flowers, the people, and lord, the food. Luke's parents, grandparents, aunts and uncles had all taken turns in the kitchen in the preceding days and the tables overflowed with every Italian dish imaginable. As well as a few southern ones Mrs. Santori had sneaked in, in honor of Rachel. The sight of Grandmother Santori sampling grits was one of the highlights of the afternoon.

It seemed that every time she turned around, someone else was lifting a glass, shouting, "Per cent'anni!" which, Luke had explained, blessed them for a hundred years.

A hundred years. Didn't sound long enough to live

with the incredible man who hadn't left her side all day. But it would do for a start.

In all, their wedding was a great success, in spite of the fact that Luke's great aunt Leila was a kleptomaniac who kept stealing trays full of Italian cookies and sneaking them out to her car. Mark and Nick, the twins—so tall, dark and handsome they made Rachel's girlfriends turn into flirtatious southern belles—got retrieval duty and stole back the stolen cookies.

Luke's uncle Johnny kept pinching the rear ends of all the ladies in attendance, including Rachel's aunt Ginny who, truth be told, didn't seem to mind so much.

Meg scared them all with a few false labor pains. Tony and Gloria's oldest son decided he didn't like being ring bearer if he didn't get to keep the pretty gold ring. Rudy Martinelli began to weep when he asked Rachel for a dance, then thanked her for indulging an old man's whim by wearing the dress.

They ate. They drank. They danced. Rachel kept opening her white satin bag—a "borsa" Luke's mother called it when she'd presented it as a gift last week. And people kept right on stuffing money inside.

Finally, late in the evening when she was dancing with one of Luke's great-uncles, who spoke little English, she saw her groom staring at her from across the room. His intensity and his loving expression were loud and clear, through the throngs of people, the music, the noise.

"I love you," he mouthed.

She smiled, whispering, "I love you, too."

"Che?" the uncle said.

Before she could say a word, Luke was there, answering for her. "She was talking to me, Uncle Pepi. She said she loves me."

His uncle didn't appear to understand much of what Luke had said, but he patted him on the cheek, anyway. Then he walked away, leaving the two of them alone on the dance floor.

All the noise faded away, becoming merely a dull buzz in the background. Rachel saw nothing of the other people in the room, just Luke. His face. His lips. His smile.

"Are you ready to go, wife?"

She nodded. "I'm ready."

He took her arm and led her through the crowd, who parted—nodding, smiling, laughing and crying and all, of course, wishing them many years of happiness.

"We *are* going to be very happy, aren't we, Luke." She wasn't asking a question. She was stating fact.

He nodded, his expression tender as he traced his fingertips across her cheek and pressed a soft kiss on her temple.

"We most definitely are, Mrs. Santori. Per cent'anni."

A hundred years. Yes. It was definitely a start.

EPILOGUE

FOR THE FIRST TIME IN HER LIFE, Daisy O'Reilly realized, the luck of the Irish had truly been on her side. She'd heard no screaming—no fallout—from the three engaged couples to whom she'd sent the mixed-up packages. So she obviously *hadn't* screwed up the orders.

That, unfortunately, was about the only thing she hadn't screwed up. Because since that day a few weeks ago, she'd never seen Neil again. She'd obviously scared him off with her brusque manner and standoffish attitude. Their regular delivery guy had been back on duty the next day, and Daisy had gone back to wondering what might have happened if she'd just said one word. Her name. Daisy.

Maybe it didn't matter. Because on the day she'd met him, she'd been in no frame of mind to give any good guy a fair chance. But now, having had almost a month to think about Trudy's assessment of why Daisy made the choices she did, she'd come to acknowledge her cousin's wisdom.

She'd been looking for love with losers. Because

then, when she invariably ended up alone, she'd have someone else to blame. She'd been wallowing in the belief that she'd never be able to have a meaningful relationship with a man who could love her—truly love her—for everything she was.

She'd changed, though. Somehow, since that day, she'd changed. It had taken some soul-searching, and a lot of Ben and Jerry's ice cream, but Daisy had begun to accept the fact that she *did* have something to offer. She was worthy of a nice guy, real love, maybe even a ring and some of the silly wedding favors they sold on a daily basis.

"It's not too late," she told herself one afternoon as she worked alone in the mailroom, feeling better about things than she had in a very long time.

"What's not too late?" a voice asked.

Daisy slowly turned around, almost holding her breath, not absolutely certain of the voice. But it was him. Neil. Looking at her with that same genuine friendliness—and interest—she'd seen on the day they'd met.

She smiled at him, a slow, genuine smile of pleasure. Because she had another chance. And she had the feeling something amazing was about to happen.

If she had the courage to let it.

"Not too late for what?" he asked again, his voice low and intense, as if he, too, was aware of the strange currents of certainty…Fate, almost…flowing between them.

"It's not too late to tell you my name," she said softly, praying he still wanted to know.

He apparently did. Putting his clipboard on top of her desk, he walked over to her and held out his hand. She put hers in his, feeling an instant spark, a recognition, almost. Again that sense of the inevitable.

He squeezed her fingers, lightly, tenderly. Then he said, "Hi. I'm Neil. It's nice to meet you."

She took a deep breath, then admitted, "I'm Daisy. And it's very nice to meet you, too."

They just stood there for a long moment, staring at one another, and Daisy felt as if she'd just taken the first step of a long, wonderful journey. A small step. But one that might just be the most important one of her life.

"Neil?" she finally said, still not releasing his hand. "There's something you should know about me."

"Yes?"

"I'm Irish." Then, unable to contain a low laugh of utter happiness, she added, "And I do believe in leprechauns."

Everything you love about romance…
and more!

*Please turn the page for some special
Bonus Features.*

Bonus Features:

BONUS FEATURES

WEDDING FEVER

Greek Wedding Traditions

by Tony and Lori Karayianni
aka Tori Carrington

Ah, what's not to love about weddings? A couple in love going before a priest or a pastor, a rabbi or a cleric to pledge their eternal love for each other "until death do us part." A bonding of hearts and minds and lives; a blending of families. And each religious denomination has its own special way of sanctifying this special union. Little has changed about the Greek Orthodox Church's ceremony over the years.

But we're getting ahead of ourselves. Let's begin with a few traditions connected to the entire ritual leading up to the wedding.

A couple in love exchanges engagement rings (which are actually the plain wedding bands—the diamond rings come at the actual wedding ceremony; guess that's one way to make sure the bride doesn't run off at the last minute, then pawn the ring!) in front of family and friends in a ceremony that's nearly as formal as the wedding itself. The best man and woman do the honors of placing the rings on the fingers of the bride- and groom-to-be—the left-hand ring finger. (On the day of the wedding, the rings are moved to the right hand, where the Greeks traditionally wear their bands.) It's a semiformal occasion, after which follows a nightlong party with food and dancing. This ceremony is considered as binding as the wedding.

Now, for the events leading up to the ceremony itself. As you read in our story *I Do, Don't I?*, the entire affair usually begins one week earlier. Since most Greek weddings are performed on a Sunday following the regular service, that means the week begins on the previous Sunday. Family members from out of town arrive, and celebratory dinners at both families' houses are a tradition as the blending begins.

A couple of days before the ceremony, *to krevati* (literal translation is "the bed") is held at the bride and groom's new house/apartment. It begins with the priest blessing the residence, and continues with the single relatives and friends making the marriage bed with fresh white linens and flowers. Afterward, the guests toss money and coins and sugarcoated almonds (called *koufetta*) on top as a wish of prosperity and sweetness, and either a baby or babies are rolled across the mattress to encourage fertility, or children jump on it to the same end. Afterward, food and dancing follow. (Ah, yes, Greeks love to have fun!)

On the day of the ceremony itself, the groom (*gambros*), best man (*koumbaros*) and best woman (*koumbara*) and family and guests gather outside the church, awaiting the arrival of the bride (*nifi*) in a flower-covered car. Her father hands her out and walks her to the church steps, where he presents her to the groom. The couple then walks into the church together to symbolize the beginning of their joined lives from that moment on.

Unlike traditional American ceremonies, vows aren't exchanged. No "I do's" are necessary because for all intents and purposes the couple is already married except in the eyes of the church. So the priest does all the chanting and speaking. The ceremony consists of two parts: the betrothal and the crowning. The betrothal consists of blessing the rings over the heads of the bride and groom. Then they are exchanged three times by their *koumbaros* or best man. The crowning is the main part of the ceremony, where the couple is crowned by wreaths that are wrapped in either silver or gold or even made of semiprecious stones and metals. A white ribbon signifying unity is tied between the crowns. After the ceremony, the crowns are packed in a special box and are kept by the couple for life. Some individuals are even buried with them to symbolize an eternal bond.

Charms—traditionally in the form of a small eye in a blue stone—are sometimes worn by the guests to protect the bridal party from bad luck. The bride may also put a sugar cube in her glove to signify her wish for a sweet marriage. Another amusing tradition is for the bride or the groom to step on the other's foot to indicate who'll hold the power over the union, meaning who will have the last say in arguments and the like.

As the guests leave the church, they are given *boubounieras*—sugarcoated almonds in a net or satin bag and tied off with ribbon—a gift from the couple to their guests to commemorate the event and to share the sweetness of the union.

Greek receptions are much like traditional American receptions in that the bride and groom and wedding party and parents sit at a long table apart from the other guests, toasts are made and lots of dancing is done. The difference is the dancing is Greek and plates are broken at the feet of the bride and groom for good luck. *Opa!*

Keep in mind that each area of Greece has its own customs and traditions. A wedding on the island of Santorini will be different from a wedding in ancient Olympia. We refer to those traditions that are pretty much universal. We hope you enjoyed our take on them in our novella! Please visit our Web site at www.toricarrington.com for more information on us, our books and Greek culture, including links to other interesting sites.

TOP TEN
Most Romantic Wedding Songs

One of the most romantic moments at any wedding is the happy couple's first dance as husband and wife. The song a couple chooses as their own is their personal declaration of love for each other.

So what are the songs most often chosen for this passionate purpose? This year, in celebration of love to be lived happily ever after, Harlequin asked wedding consultants to name the songs their couples are choosing most often. Here are their selections for the top ten most popular wedding songs:

1 "Unforgettable"

With 14 percent of the vote, Natalie and Nat King Cole's timeless love ballad "Unforgettable" tops the list as the most romantic song to mark this ever-so-memorable event.

2 "From This Moment On"
Country crooners Shania Twain and Bryan White vow "From This Moment On," a favorite song of 13 percent of the wedding consultants.

3 "At Last"
Etta James's passionate paean to love has been rediscovered, thanks to a popular car commercial. Ten percent of the consultants say this is the song of the moment for their couples.

4 "Because You Loved Me"
All things are possible, according to Celine Dion, in the love theme from the Robert Redford/Michelle Pfeiffer film *Up Close and Personal*. It takes fourth place, with 8 percent of the tally.

5 "Amazed"
Top wedding song number five alludes to the feeling a newlywed might express at the promise of love that just keeps getting better and better. Lonestar offers this country-rock ballad, named by 4 percent of the consultants in the Harlequin tally.

6 "All I Ask of You"
The showstopping duet from Andrew Lloyd

Webber's blockbuster musical *The Phantom of the Opera* is another perfect pledge of love for a romantic pair of newlyweds.

7 "The Way You Look Tonight"

Nothing offers a better sentiment of adoration than this classic compliment from lover to lover, first introduced to entranced young couples by the legendary Fred Astaire.

8 "It Had To Be You"

This Sinatra song in spot number eight simply says it all.

9 "Here and Now"

Luther Vandross captures many a couple's wedding fancy with his powerful ballad of love and commitment.

10 "The Wedding Song" ("There Is Love")

Nothing could be more appropriate than this Peter, Paul and Mary standard that offers the perfect sentiment for a bride and groom!

Originally published online at eHarlequin.ca

TOP TEN

Most Romantic Wedding Movies

Whether you're planning a trip down the aisle or are already blissfully wedded, nothing is more romantic than watching a movie with a happy ending. In celebration of living happily ever after, Harlequin asked 100 entertainment editors from newspapers across the U.S. to choose the top ten most romantic wedding movies.

1 Four Weddings and a Funeral
When Hugh Grant finds himself running into Andie MacDowell at wedding after wedding, the two begin to wonder if these chance meetings are just coincidence—or are they a twist of fate?

2 Father of the Bride
Whether it's the original film, starring Elizabeth Taylor and Spencer Tracy, or the modern remake with Steve Martin and Kimberly Williams, this classic tale of daddy's little girl's

trip down the aisle is certain to tug at the heartstrings of any true romantic.

3 Runaway Bride

Julia Roberts is notorious for leaving a string of husbands-to-be at the altar—until reporter Richard Gere is assigned to cover her incredible story. But much to his own surprise, Gere finds himself chasing Roberts down the aisle!

4 My Best Friend's Wedding

When Julia Roberts realizes that she's in love with her old college chum, Dermot Mulroney, she plunges into the depths of a love triangle—and she's not afraid to fight Cameron Diaz in an attempt to steal his heart.

5 The Philadelphia Story

In this romantic drama, set against the elegance of the 1940s in the elite circles of the City of Brotherly Love, Cary Grant will stop at nothing to win back his former wife, Katharine Hepburn—even if he has to sabotage her wedding to another man!

6 It Happened One Night

Forced to share a seat on a New York–bound Greyhound bus, washed-up reporter Clark Gable and heiress-in-hiding Claudette Colbert have nothing in common except a daring sense of adventure that lands them in the lap of love.

7   The Wedding Singer

The wild and wacky 1980s provide the backdrop for this romantic comedy, in which Adam Sandler, a schmaltzy wedding-reception crooner, falls for Drew Barrymore, the waitress he meets at one of his singing engagements.

8   Like Water for Chocolate

When the man she loves marries her sister, a young woman discovers that her cooking has magical powers, inspiring love and inducing heartbreak. This Mexican fable, also released under the title *Como Agua para Chocolate*, is certain to whet the appetite of any true romantic.

9   High Society

Grace Kelly, Bing Crosby and Frank Sinatra had moviegoers dancing down the aisle in this musical remake of *The Philadelphia Story*.

10   Green Card

After New York horticulturist Andie MacDowell and French musician Gerard Depardieu find themselves trapped in a marriage of convenience, they soon realize that they have been thrown into the path of true love.

Originally published online at eHarlequin.ca

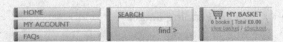

LOOK OUT...

...for this month's special product offer.
It can be found in the envelope containing
your invoice.

**Special offers are exclusively for
Reader Service™ members.**

You will benefit from:

- Free books & discounts
- Free gifts
- Free delivery to your door
- No purchase obligation – 14 day trial
- Free prize draws

THE LIST IS ENDLESS!!

*So what are you waiting for —
take a look* **NOW!**

DM/OFFER V2

Escape into...

SPECIAL EDITION™

Life, love and family.

Special Edition are emotional, compelling love stories. Enjoy innovative plots with intensely passionate heroes and heroines that make a fast-paced and emotionally powerful read.

Six new titles are available every month on subscription from the

READER SERVICE™

Escape into...

*Super*ROMANCE™

Enjoy the drama, explore the emotions,
experience the relationship.

Longer than other Silhouette® books,
Superromance offers you emotionally involving,
exciting stories, with a touch of the unexpected.

Four new titles are available every month on
subscription from the

READER SERVICE™

GEN/38/RS4 V2

Escape into...

INTRIGUE™

Breathtaking romantic suspense.

Mystery, murder, secrets, suspense and dangerous desires—solve the dual puzzles of mystery and romance.

Four new titles are available every month on subscription from the

READER SERVICE™

GEN/46/RS4 V2

Escape into...

Desire™ 2 in 1

Passionate, dramatic love stories.

Provocative and sensual love stories that capture the intensity of living, loving and family in today's world.

Six new titles are available every month on subscription from the

READER SERVICE™